Max Rising

Matthew A. Lohbihler

A NOTE FROM THE AUTHOR

Y ou made it here! That's great. Welcome.

Thanks for bothering to check this out. I truly hope you find it entertaining and thought-provoking. I'm so excited for you! This novel started off with the simple idea of having a computer version of yourself take care of you, and how really annoying that might end up being. What was supposed to be a short story quickly grew wildly out of control. I suppose I really need to learn how to write short stories.

A heartfelt thanks to the people who - obviously suffering from some manner of mental illness - read the manuscript or parts of it and provided invaluable feedback, and only because I asked them to. Special thanks to Jamie Tennant and Janie Ironside - whose writing talents I have desperately tried to emulate - who provided early advice and encouragement and were super great about it. If any readers out there don't like this book, you can blame them.

And of course, I am most grateful to my wife and kids who tolerated many, many evenings and weekend afternoons of me going upstairs by myself to write. To you: I'm sorry. Please forgive me. Thank you. I love you. ... Can I please eat with you at the table again?

CONTENTS

OVERTURE

It was clear the woman wasn't wealthy, or even middle class. Her clothes looked clean and new enough, but were obviously unenhanced, and therefore only fashionable in a vintage sort of way. No one was truly poor anymore in the sense of being in need of the basics for living, but that only meant that the definition of 'poor' had shifted, and most would agree that under this new definition, she was poor. It was not unusual for poor people to be on Horton Alley, one of the city's upscale shopping districts. They enjoyed being among the lush tropical foliage and resplendent shopping displays, window shopping and people watching as much as anyone else. And even the wealthy didn't mind the way the poor admired them as long as they didn't get too close or try to speak to them. Nothing seemed much out of the ordinary, unless you watched the poor woman closely. She would stop abruptly and hold her forehead in one hand, her expression blank. Then her eyes would slowly widen in fear until she would blink tightly, shake her head slowly, and then relax again. This repeated over and over for more than half an hour as she wandered the grand hall aimlessly. Each time though, when she relaxed it would be more into a mien of sad anxiety, as if she were slowly losing hope. The crowd around her went about its business, only noticing her with annoyance when she would abruptly stop in someone's path. Swept to the edges by the steady current of people she eventually sat, her head in her hands, tousled hair hanging over, and her back against an advertisement display, such that the touch caused it to display products it considered suitable for her limited means, including simple pastries, caffeinated water, feminine hygiene, and generic mood enhancement drugs. When she didn't react though, the display gave up and began to cast its advertisements to more promising prospects in the crowd. She sat still for perhaps 15 minutes before again raising her head, revealing reddened eyes and an expression of utter hopelessness. She rose and walked with purpose to the railing that overlooked the six floors below. Grasping the railing with both hands she took a single deep breath, held it for a moment, let it go with an audible sigh, and then threw herself over.

* * *

Normally such a statistical blip wouldn't even be noticed, and indeed it wasn't, at least by the people that normally looked at those kinds of things. It would hardly raise eyebrows, especially in a number that is gradually increasing anyway, and even if it was the city suicide rate. When assisted death was legalized there was an immediate tenfold jump as the hopelessness and lack of purpose that many felt had finally found an outlet. But thereafter it only increased slowly. It wasn't until the number was segregated by manner of death that it was clear something unexpected had happened. The number of assisted deaths had risen only as predicted, but the number of spontaneous suicides had more than tripled. And not only that, the manner used in the new cases was particularly grisly, as if in the victims' minds there was no time to lose. But just as quickly as the phenomena appeared it went away again, and the blip, in a matter of a few weeks, had vanished.

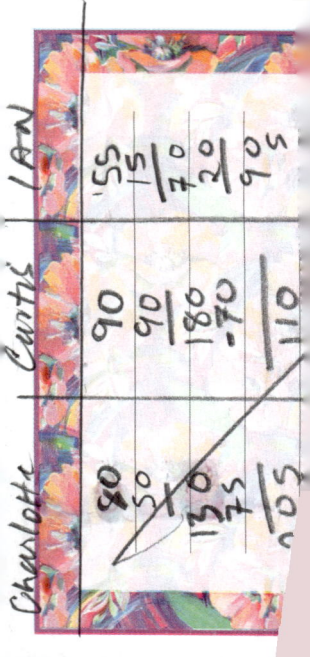

Charlotte	Curtis	Ian
80	90	55
50	90	15
130	180	70
75	-70	20
205	110	90

COURT

Deferential confidence. That had been Hiney's recommendation. It would play well if Max were respectful and polite while always insisting that he had meant well, and that he had always held his client's best interests as his guiding principle. It was just unfortunate that, due to events beyond anyone's control, the technology simply hadn't worked out.

Complete bullshit is what it was, as far Max was concerned. A bunch of pathetic bureaucrats who pretended to matter while playing champions to the unwashed masses, who should have known full well what they were getting into. All these justice people really did is keep those who can actually get anything done from getting anything done. Throughout his life he had dealt with probably hundreds of judges and lawyers, and not one of them knew the slightest thing about what it took to run a real business. Max could be doing something important right now, but instead the law said he had to be here in this moronic judge's tiny chambers. The room was maybe the size of one of the elevators in his condominium, and he, his lawyer, and the judge sat in the glaring light and stale air and tried to keep their knees from touching under her desk.

"Your highness, might I speak?"

Judge Yarrow blinked up at Max over her glasses, her expression hiding whether she detected Max's obvious sarcasm. What a pretentious idiot, thought Max. Who still wears glasses? Eyesight flaws were fixed as a part of your semi-annual automated health clinic visit. Glasses-wearing was merely a fashion statement, and Max was sure hers were intentionally trying to make her look like an 1800's school marm.

She looked back down to her desk projection, replying, "You may refer to me as 'your honour'".

"Max, what are you doing?" whispered David Hinds, his lawyer, as he turned Max away from the judge.

"I'm going to change this biotech's mind, Hiney."

Hinds looked back at Judge Yarrow and smiled. "Uh, one moment, your honour." On the back wall was a button that activated the client/lawyer hush. After pressing it, he began lightly stroking his moustache to hide his lips from her view. "This what? She's the judge. And don't call me that.

And the hell you are. You're only going to make things worse. You haven't even said anything yet, and I can tell she already doesn't like you."

"What do you mean?" said Max, innocently.

"You're an asshole Max, and everyone knows it before you even open your mouth. It was hard enough just getting to make this plea. Please don't fuck it up."

"Don't hate me because you're bald and even in my eighties I have beautiful luxurious hair."

"That's not why I hate you."

Max pressed on the hush, deactivating it. "Your honourness," he said as he turned back, "this is all just a big misunderstanding."

"Ah shit," whispered Hinds, looking down to his lapdesk at all of his wasted work.

"Is it now," said Yarrow, her words greasy with sarcasm. It wasn't a question. "Please Mr. Rising, reveal to me what I misunderstand."

"Don't do it, Max." Hinds whispered while still looking down. Hope was already gone.

"Your honourness, lost in all of this blame transferring is the sad fact that I'm a victim here too," began Max. "I've lost everything; much more, in fact, than any of my clients. In fact, I'm probably the biggest victim here."

"Certainly the biggest something," muttered Hinds.

Yarrow's expression didn't change. She peered over her glasses as if trying to set Max on fire with her eyes. "Are you familiar with the biblical story of the Widow's Mite? No? Court, would you please educate Mr. Rising."

"The Widow's Mite," began the artificial intelligence. "Jesus sat down opposite the treasury and observed how the crowd put money into the treasury. Many rich people put in large sums. A poor widow also came and put in two small coins worth a few cents. Calling his disciples to himself, he said to them, 'Amen, I say to you, this poor widow put in more than all the other contributors to the treasury. For they have all contributed from their surplus wealth, but she, from her poverty, has contributed all she had, her whole livelihood." The AI fell silent.

Max leaned to Hinds and spoke under his breath. "Any idea...?"

"Not a clue. Let it go."

"Your losses, Mr. Rising," continued Yarrow, "came from your surplus wealth. You may have lost your physical assets, but you still are a relatively well-known person who presumably has acquaintances who can help you build up your wealth again. You're much like the infantile real estate fellow who lived many decades ago who lost his fortune many times over, but through his powerful contacts and notoriety always managed to bounce back with another deal. Some say his business dealings failed more often than they succeeded, but he ended up becoming president of the United States."

"Cool guy. What was his name again?"

"Many of your investors, on the other hand, gave you everything they had in pursuit of your promise to make them young again. The people in the biblical story knew to what they were contributing; they at least weren't getting swindled."

"Ah, now I get it," whispered Hinds.

"Kind of a reach though, isn't it?" replied Max.

"Maybe a little much," said Hinds.

"Does it smell in here?"

"You explicitly targeted untreatables," the judge went on, "and then squandered their money on yourself even more than your unviable technology. Not once did you mention that your treatment worked only on lab mice, and even then only under specific circumstances. Perhaps you really believed it would work on humans, or that you at least truly hoped it would, considering you are untreatable yourself, a point you have never wasted an opportunity to tell anyone who will listen. Still, let's see here…" Yarrow looked down on her desktop display. "In the course of trying to develop this technology you paid yourself advances from the company totaling nearly 80 million dolarium, from which you purchased a 55 million dolarium home in The Neumann as well as other luxury goods including a sleep chamber, an auto-cook, and… my, my… swimming pool access." Yarrow pursed her lips and nodded in mock approval.

"You know, 55-million simply doesn't buy as much place as it used to."

"Many of your clients are now destitute," the judge continued, "and not having been made young like you promised, they find themselves yet decrepit, but without assets or opportunity; proud people now in the care of the state and living off basic income. Some can no longer afford their treatments and may die. How do you feel about these people, Mr. Rising?"

"Max," whispered Hinds, "just say you're sorry. Just say you're sorry and shut up."

"Basic income is pretty good these days, isn't it?"

Yarrow's eyes narrowed, and her voice rose slightly. "You speak as if their money was always yours for the taking. I'm beginning to suspect that you are not as contrite as your counsel has been leading the court to believe."

Hinds fidgeted in his seat, grappling his lapdesk. "Your honour, if I may have a moment with my client."

"No, counsel. I'm anxious to hear what Mr. Rising has yet to share with us."

"For fuck sake Max, just say you're sorry and shut up!" No longer quite a whisper.

Max spoke with self-assurance. "My compensation package was developed by professional compensation specialists to be in accordance with my peers," he answered, "and it was approved by the rest of the board. I pretty much had to accept it."

"I'm so sorry you had to be subject to such undue fairness. But your choice of the word 'accordance' is telling. It suggests that you and your 'peers' collude in how much you fleece from your shareholders. And if your peers are anything like you, I dare say it is an idea with some merit."

"Hey, there's no need to get all judgy and everything." Max chuckled and looked at Hinds. "You see what I did there, Hiney? Cause she's a judge…"

Hinds rubbed his eyes. "Don't call me that."

"But fear not, Mr. Rising, for I have a solution which should set your victimized mind at ease. It is one of the few penalties that human judges can still impose. It remains the purview of humans because it's imposition by a machine-based intelligence would raise questions of conflict of interest. Shall I tell you what it is?"

Max's eyes widened. "Wait, your honour…"

"Ah, I see you finally got my title correct. Well done. Mr. Rising, I am making it a condition of your plea bargain that you undergo the procedure to endow you with a digital cerebral replica. Do you know what that is?"

"Well, yeah, a Steward. But that's not…"

"Good!", interrupted Yarrow. "Counsel for the plaintiffs, are you amenable to this amendment." There was only a momentary hesitation from the prosecution AI as it tallied the votes from the automated agents of the class action participants.

"We are, your honour," came back the unanimous result.

"Excellent. Let me advise you, Mr. Rising, if you do not accept the plea as it now stands, I will be forced to have it rescinded, and your case will proceed to a criminal trial. What have you to say now, Mr. Rising."

"Your honour, if I could…", Hinds tried to begin.

"Once again counsel, I simply must hear what Mr. Rising has to say." Her sarcasm had reached a new, impressive level. She glared back at Max.

"You can't be serious." For once, Max was.

"Yes or no, Mr. Rising?"

"That's not fair."

"Jesus Max, for once it is. Just say yes. Say yes!" Hinds didn't realize he was crumpling his virtual papers in his fists. His AI assumed that many of them were trash, and they disintegrated. "Shit. Undo. Undo!"

"Stewards are for losers and morons. You can't do this to me."

"Yes, she can Max. And she just did, you dumb shit." Hinds hadn't re-activated his hush. He didn't seem to care whether the judge could hear him anymore. "And it serves you right for opening your god-damned mouth.

Now just say yes!"

"Mr. Rising," Yarrow began nonchalantly, "if you choose not to accept this amended plea, your trial on charges of fraud et al will begin… Umm, Court, when would Mr. Rising's trial begin?"

"Estimated in 18 months and 4 days, according to the current schedule. Depending on the availability of court resources and the outcomes of other trials, the trial of Mr. Rising could potentially be delayed up to an additional 12 weeks and 2 days, with the probability of such additional delays set at 10.57%."

Yarrow gazed aimlessly past the men's heads. "Thank you Court. You can just say 18 months next time." Looking back at Max she continued. "During which time you would be remanded to the court. In jail. Without bail. So, Mr. Rising, what say you?" The last three words reached out across the judge's desk and slapped Max in the face individually and with purpose.

"Ok, ok, I'm sorry. I'm sorry, ok? For fuck sake, it's just money."

"Your aloof opinion of money is not a virtue; it is a privilege. If it's 'just money', Mr. Rising, instead of declaring bankruptcy, you could simply pledge to reimburse all of your clients in full and with interest. You could free yourself of your legal protections. That might indeed be regarded as an act of contrition."

Max looked horrified. "That would take decades."

"Your trial awaits you in a mere 18 months and 4 days."

Max reddened. "Is everyone here a fucking idiot bleeding heart? Should we all just join hands and cry for all of the poor old people? Whaa! Whaa! Doesn't anyone here know how a real business works?"

"Max, just say yes and shut the fuck up!"

"No!"

"He accepts, your honour."

"No I don't! Fuck you judge." Max stood and pointed a finger at Yarrow. "This whole thing is a fucking joke. What the hell do you know about anything? "

Yarrow spoke casually. "Court, I find Mr. Rising's behaviour contemptuous. Would you please settle him down."

"Fuck yoooooaaaaahhh…" Max clutched at the skin behind his right ear as his body shook and his knees went weak. Hinds settled him into a chair as he fell.

* * *

"What the hell was that?" Max was still a little dazed. He ran his fingers through his hair, something Hinds noticed he did often and proudly.

"Remember when they first brought you in and they replaced that ancient comm you had? The one they put in is also a tracker and a taser.

Standard practice for anyone they think is potentially noncompliant."

"Yeah, I know that," Max said. "Bullshit is what that is, calling me 'potentially noncompliant'."

"Oh, it's bullshit alright. There's nothing 'potential' about it. You've never been compliant the whole time I've known you, or your whole life as far as I can tell. Fucking hell, Max. You always think you know better about everything. Honestly, what is your problem? You could have just let me take care of it, but no. I had it, Max. I had it."

"Tell me again why I even had to be here. I could have done this from bed."

"This is the legal system. Except for the judges it hasn't changed in hundreds of years. The defendant always has to be present."

"Couldn't you have gotten a different judge? She was a total biotech."

"You said that before. What does that mean anyway?"

"Biotech? Oh yeah, you're too young to know. Back in the day we had to type on our phones to send messages, and there was this thing called 'auto-correct'. Whenever you typed 'biotch', it got replaced with 'biotech', so everyone just used that instead, and it stuck."

"That's got to be one of the stupidest old-timey stories I have ever heard."

Max shrugged. "Why even is there a judge?"

Hines sighed. "You really don't have a clue, do you? In cases like this a judge is still required to give a 'human perspective'." Hinds made air quotes with his free hand. "In your case I'd say it worked exactly as intended." His voice became serious. "You know what you have to do now, right?"

Max's face went emotionless. "There's no way I'm doing that."

"Do you want to get tasered again? The bailiff is right there." Both men could see the virtual bailiff standing nearby, the image projected into their retinas from their Glaze ocular implants, looking intimidating even with its blank expression. Other people passing by walked through the image unknowingly. "That's really Yarrow you know. I bet her finger is on the taser button right now, just waiting for you do to something stupid."

"Piss off, you biotech!" said Max to the bailiff.

"It's not really her, Max. It's a bailiff AI. Yarrow is just monitoring."

"I know," said Max indignantly. "Can't you do something? This will ruin me. No one will talk to me again."

"Oh, don't be so dramatic. It's not like you can't talk to your family or your friends anymore."

"Who cares about them? I'm talking about business. I'll never be able to work a deal again once people know I've got a Steward following me around."

"You don't know that."

"Tell me Hiney, who has a Steward?"

Hines took a breath. "Don't call me that."

"They are for morons and losers. People who can't get their shit together enough to even hold down a job."

"Well, you don't exactly have a job, do you?"

"Fuck, I'm serious. Do something about this!"

"The deal is done. You agreed. There's nothing I can do."

Max was getting desperate. "You said the judge couldn't do anything, that this was all just a formality."

"Yeah, it was, until you opened your idiot mouth."

"Jesus, what fucking good are you? Figure something out!" Max was in Hinds' face now. Hinds could feel tiny drops of saliva alighting on his cheekbones.

"No, Max. I'm done." Hinds stepped back from Max, still looking directly at him. "I had the whole proceeding worked out, and you fucked it all up with your poor me bullshit diatribe. You screwed yourself."

"Listen pal, you work for me, remember?"

Hinds smiled warmly. "Not anymore you broke piece of shit. Find yourself another 'pal'." Hinds drew out the last word with relish and concentrated contempt.

"Holy shit! I'm the one that was on trial. What are you so pissed about?'

"Does anyone else live in your universe? It's only ever about you, isn't it Max?"

"Fuck Hiney, this case was about me."

Hinds snapped, and this time got into Max's face. "Go ahead, call me that again you prick. Don't think I won't kick your sagging eighty-year-old ass all around this place. Come on, call me 'Hiney' one more time and see what happens."

Max backed off. "Jesus, it's just a funny nickname. Calm down."

Hinds calmed down, but only a little. "There's your problem. It was never funny to me, but you never cared about that. I put up with it as long as I had to, but I'm done now. Enjoy your Steward, ace." And with that, one of only maybe three people that gave even a little shit about Max walked away.

* * *

Outside the court, it was a day much like the previous ten thousand or so. Although few people noticed, the greenless grow lighting above Bain Commons shone beautifully, and even some natural sunlight filtered through the skylights high above, energizing the vertical gardens that covered much of the walls. At one time the walls had been covered with displays that shone with endless advertisements, each tirelessly competing in obnoxiousness with the others for the attention of whatever mostly heedless crowd might, or might not, be present. The energy crisis that had followed the Aira Winter brought with it the displays' demise. They had been uninstalled, dismantled for parts, and replaced with air-purifying plants.

This downtown atrium was bustling with people: some walked briskly to their appointments, meetings, and obligations, others strolled casually in conversation with their acquaintances, while still others shopped the many advertisements that were cast into their vision from the nearby real and virtual stores. Paths led off in various directions and continued for kilometers through the city to other districts, stretching across the deserted outdoor roads, sometimes deep underground, sometimes just above street height, sometimes scores of stories higher, connecting every building of any significance within over 20 square kilometers into a single hermetic environment. The effect from the outside was one of a colossal-scale hamster cage with humans teeming inside. The feeling inside was of the entire world having been transformed into a vast biosphere, part theme park, part shopping mall, decorated in the computer-assisted designs of decades past.

An ad from a nearby store popped into Max's view, showing him a pair of brogues that would go quite nicely with the nano-enhanced jacket and jeans that he was wearing. When he focused on it the close-up image of the shoes changed to a mirror image of himself wearing them, with bubbles that helpfully described the products' many features: automatic moisture sensing and venting, gait improvement, calorie counting, and factory-grown leather uppers. Max smiled and mentally gestured to authorize the purchase, but then the display changed to a much cheaper looking, unenhanced pair, and he heard a voice in his head saying, "perhaps this selection will suit your budget better." The voice had been transmitted in the same digital stream as the ad, but to his comm instead of his Glaze. The digital signal was then converted to inputs directly into his auditory cortex. A telltale timbre was added that distinguished it from the kind of voices in your head that usually mean trouble.

Max flipped the display his middle finger and the ad closed. He turned and walked in a random direction, his mind full of disorganized thoughts. Looking up he saw the bailiff standing before him, his expression menacing. He pointed toward a different path and said, "this direction would be more efficient," the sound of which Max also heard with that distinctive timbre. Max continued walking in the same direction through the bailiff, the image of which distorted and disappeared, only to reappear farther in front of him again, repeating itself. This time though, Max felt something inside the back of his neck: a pulsing, threatening sensation. The bailiff added, "Non-compliance is not advised."

"Piss off," said Max, and continued walking. On his second step he felt his head fill with a crackling energy and his leg went limp. Max fell hard onto his hands and knees. "Ahhh! Shit!"

Coercion technology had existed for decades. Initial versions were meant to be gentle and kind, carrots rather than sticks, by attempting to make subjects compliant or open to suggestion by either chemically instilling trust in their trainers, or suppressing natural inhibitory reactions. Research had barely begun on these techniques when civil libertarians erupted in a heavy metal chorus complaining of attacks on free will, and work on the chemicals was reportedly halted. Subsequent researchers took a more positive Pavlovian approach, encouraging subjects to do the right thing with reinforcement rewards such as causing a release of dopamine or by stimulating pleasure centers in the brain. This work, too, was eventually (reportedly) abandoned when it became clear that the only output was a shiny, smiling bunch of new drug addicts: subjects that maniacally repeated the trained behavior so they could get their next hit. Multiple variations of such research were pursued, but all with the same results. In the end, it became obvious that the only ethically acceptable form of coercion was good old torture.

The bailiff stood above Max, still pointing, and said again, "Non-compliance is not advised."

Max remained on all fours on the floor of the grand space. People walked past, many looking at him, but none stopping to ask if he needed help. Max scratched at the back of his neck, and then rolled over onto his back, looking up at the skylights. "Hey, it's sunny outside," he said to no one.

The bailiff spoke again. "Your appointment is scheduled to begin in 22 minutes. By the most efficient route at your typical pace and considering traffic and the conveyor maintenance schedule, you should arrive in 19 minutes. I advise you to proceed immediately." The pulsing in Max's neck stopped for a few moments, but when he didn't move it began again, quickened and intensified. Still Max didn't budge.

"Ahhhhh!" Max screamed. The shock had hit him hard. When it stopped he wondered momentarily if he could outlast the comm's battery, but then remembered that the latest tech was powered by his own nervous system. Clever that.

Many shocks came, one after another. "Ahhhhh! Fuck! Fuck! Fuck!" Now everyone looked as they passed, some with concern, many with visible opprobrium. Still no one stopped; they only walked by more quickly. As if Max's anger made an invisible force field around him, they provided him a wide berth, like a stream flowing around a big stone. Max began to question how long he could take this. Doubtless the device was data optimized to the individual to ensure effectiveness. Sometimes technology is the shits.

During the lull, Max received a message notification. It was from

Yarrow. Through the residual pain and confusion, Max felt an unreasonable elation. What were the chances he had been granted a reprieve? Had Hiney gone back and made a case for him? It had to be something like that. What else could she want with him? Max made the requisite motor cortex signal to play the message. In the telltale timbre, he heard Yarrow's voice in his head, full of delight: "I hope you are enjoying your little tantrum." And the shocks began again.

IMMORTALITY EXHIBIT

International Virtual Museum of World History, Immortality Exhibit, Group tour. January 18, 2075

Guests are assembled in the Grand Lobby of the Museum, standing on floors of lapis lazuli surrounded infinitely on all sides by regularly spaced fluted columns of ebony, the tops of which fade from view in the distance above them.

Guide, speaking with a female-toned British accent that is lightly flavoured with Hindustani: "Welcome, everyone, to the International Virtual Museum, also known to many as the Wikiseum! I will be your automated guide today."

Murmurs of hello among the androgynous group. Bubbles point to each indicating their usernames. Some voices delayed for translation.

Guide: "Are there any questions before we begin?"

anitagonow5453: "Which way is the restroom?"

Guide looks at the guest for a moment.

Guide: "You will have to disconnect into the physical world to perform biological functions."

A thumbs up icon pops out and fades as the body of anitagonow5453 disintegrates from view. A chime sounds to indicate the disconnection.

Guide: "Let's begin then. Questions are welcome."

The scene of the grand museum lobby fades to darkness, giving the impression that everyone present is floating in a starless space, their bodies illuminated from an unknown light source. The guide puts her hands together in front of her, and as she peels them apart again colours stream out and around the guests.

Guide: "Although human immortality was realized only recently, its story began thousands of years ago. For millennia humanity searched for the holy grail, the fountain of youth, and the elixir of life. And for millennia all they found was pipe dreams, red herring, and snake oil. But the optimism of humans being what it is, nothing could quench the thirst for life without end among rich and poor, vital and diseased, quick and dim. In this most universal of afflictions, no one is truly immune."

The streams of colours form into animated scenes of riders on horses, fountains, and chalices, all of which decompose into models of DNA strands that wrap loosely around the guests. Some of them reach out and touch the strands, turn them, pull them, and examine them more closely. The DNA strands transmute into humans of very advanced age that stand amidst the crowd. Most of these individuals gradually become more youthful: their skin smoothing, their spines straightening, their countenances brightening.

Guide: "One may argue that what people really want is not endless life, but endless youth, and this is indeed correct. The true desire is to be vital and virial and beautiful indefinitely. But even when youth is not an option, humans would still overwhelmingly rather be decrepit than dead."

The revitalized humans begin to walk, run, or dance away. The few that remain old smile gratefully. All of them fade away.

icouldbeal2800: "Maybe so, but what about suicidal people?"

Only the guide and guests remain, floating in blackness.

Guide: "There are two general reasons why individuals may choose to end their own lives. The most common is a physical, mental, or emotional illness of such severity that the subject finds that living with it is worse than dying. But when the illness is taken away, a desire to live once again returns to take its place. The second reason is martyrdom. The subject is convinced that the sacrifice they make is sufficiently heroic as to secure them a prominent place in an afterlife. As such, they believe they are not actually dying, but rather just continuing a better life elsewhere. As you can see, neither case is a valid counterexample to the immortality thesis, since in neither case do the subjects actually desire death. Rather, death is merely accepted with varying degrees of magnanimity. Only very few humans are so enlightened as to recognize the futility of living, and to end it all out of sheer, noble surrender: taking their lives in a final act of giving."

BadKarmaXYZ, plaintively: "Are you saying that wanting to live isn't noble?"

The guide and guests move to form a circle, and a campfire ignites in the center.

Guide: "Excellent question! What is this pull toward immortality but a conceit among the afflicted that they are deserving of it? The minds of humans are struck with a certainty that they as individuals are unique and precious in ways unlike any other, and that the world around them would fall into disarray and squalor without their continued contributions. This is an abject denial of the obvious fact that all manner of people die everywhere, every day, in sundry ways, and yet the world as a whole hardly seems to notice. It also denies the scientific evidence which states that all homo sapiens are roughly ninety-nine percentage quite the same, and that the remaining one percent difference is rarely of much significance."

BadKarmaXYZ: "That doesn't sound right. There are huge differences between people. Not everyone can be an elite athlete or a scholar."

Guide: "As is typical in anthropic prejudice, you have chosen your scale too narrowly, only comparing humans to other humans. Instead, compare homo sapiens with, say, fish, or what you call artificial intelligence, or even other hominids. From this perspective you'll see that humans are indeed nearly all identical."

heyyou2, to UnfriendedAgain: "Have you noticed that these exhibits seem to get more and more condescending all the time?"

UnfriendedAgain nods.

Guide: "In fact, differences among humans are more a matter of circumstance than merit. Let's say you take pride in how smart you are. Then, recall that only a few thousand years ago it was physical prowess that dominated. Being clever may have made you a useful advisor, but without any brawn of your own you would never have assumed the mantle of leadership, and would likely have lived in obscurity. Pity the individual born with the precise traits to be a renowned business executive, or chess grandmaster, or champion tennis player, but lived as a slave of the Roman Empire. Only decades ago, the arrogant Americans of the twentieth century viewed themselves as entitled to lead the world, self-assured that no other was their peer. Who would have guessed that their supposedly divinely ordained domination would be eclipsed by twenty-first century Indian technocrats? In this, the full scope of humanity, including the masses of the disadvantaged, is any individual really so special? Viewed another way, is any individual not somehow special in some sadly unrealized way?"

maga2024: "That's pure liberal drivel. Anyone can make something of themself by just working hard."

Guide: "That assumes that the world of humans is fair, which I can assure you is not the case. What you consider 'elite' individuals all through time received critical aid from others while they strived to reach their greatness. Many of them deny this, insisting that their natural aptitude is sufficient explanation of their success. The ridiculous term 'self-made man' was once a common trope. But whether they acknowledge it or not, once such greatness is achieved the pattern that inevitably follows is for them to then deliberately and quickly raise barriers that prevent others from achieving similar success. Thus, typical human societal success is really just, first a lucky circumstance, and second a measure of how well you keep everyone else down, so to speak."

BadKarmaXYZ: "Why would anyone want to keep other people down? Doesn't everyone benefit from everyone else's success?"

Guide: "Indirectly, yes. But human empathy maximizes only when individuals can directly relate to another's circumstances; that is, when those circumstances closely match one's own. Unfortunately, the self-confidence that results from societal improvement tends to suppress this empathy. The effect has been thoroughly studied."

kim_chi_me: "Is that why rich people are all pricks?"

Guide: "The effect has been thoroughly studied."

speedofart: "This is fucking stupid."

speedofart disintegrates from view, and a chime indicates the disconnection.

creative_zombie: "Is it true that we continuously change? Physically, I mean."

Guide: "Yes, let us make our way back to our topic. What you say is indeed true. Physically speaking, it takes between seven and ten years for all of the cells in a human body to be entirely replaced, and some of the most important cells replace much more quickly. The same happens psychologically, where moment to moment your experiences change you into someone slightly different than before. Over time these changes accumulate, and when all that you forgot is considered alongside, over a long enough period you are substantially different, mentally and physically, from the person you were before.

"On a shorter time scale, consider a common assertion of those who have suffered a hardship: that their suffering made them a better person. Who were they before? And does this mean that if you don't suffer hardship you remain a worse, complacent, ungrateful, entitled person? There is evidence that says yes, humans do. But what is hardship except things that don't go the way you want? It's ironic that most parents say they just want their children to be happy, and then go to great efforts to ensure those children never experience hardship, when it's exactly that hardship that is likely to result in a humble and content happiness, and the lack of hardship that can make them unfulfilled and miserable. Seen another way, historically the most privileged upbringings reliably produced the most miserable and entitled individuals."

Silent pause.

sandy_loam: "Huh. She got that right."

maga2024: "Ok then, who should be allowed to live forever?"

Guide: "There is no non-metaphysical authority that has been granted the right to make such a decree, and as of yet no verified metaphysical entity has deigned to express an opinion. But, humans can look to themselves for answers. When asked if they want to live forever, the most passionate affirmatives come from the most miserable and entitled. The humble and happy want to live too, they are just less likely to believe that it matters much overall. Interestingly though, when people are asked who else they would like to have live forever along with them, all agree that it should be mostly those who humbly benefit society. Ironically, rarely do they advocate for those others who want to live forever the most.

"But we have wandered from our topic again."

The campfire explodes into colour, the ashes of which descend to form the scene of an Aztec temple, with the guests as spectators to a human sacrifice. The blood from the victim rises in a laminar flow which turns a spiritual green colour and enters directly into the Aztec king's exposed heart, making his muscles swell and his eyes shine as his back arches and his arms extend.

Guide: "In the pursuit of immortality through the centuries men have searched for cups and fountains, have eaten of the pulverized horns and pan-fried testicles of great beasts, and have sacrificed less deserving others with the intent of siphoning the deluded, grateful victim's remaining life-force into themselves. And although some of this made for great pomp and pageantry, and in some cases a lot of money, none of it made the slightest difference."

The Aztec king's muscles deflate again, his eyes return to normal, and overall he looks older and more weary.

"Eventually though, humans unexpectedly found themselves surrounded by a scientific world, and began to use actual evidence to guide their life-extending efforts. And the evidence said that death is not the slipping away of the soul, but simply a matter of lack of blood to the brain. Aging is essentially the result of the accumulation of errors and damage among various bodily processes, which over the years eventually cause cascading failures in the system overall. The evidence also showed that fixing these errors and clearing the damage is very, very hard to do."

The Aztec scene disintegrates into a medical room, while the king's regal dress fades into a hospital gown. He now looks like a frail old man. He lies down on a gurney and becomes motionless. Crystals that look like ice begin to form over his body.

Guide: "In the nineteen sixties, although the science of the time was still powerless against mortality, sapiens had at least learned that science always gets better with time. This led to the idea that even if you were destined to die, your body could be subsequently cryogenically preserved until science caught up enough to bring you back to life. The first instance of cryopreservation occurred in 1967 with one Dr. James Bedford, and an industry formed around the practice in the years following. To date though, less than ten thousand bodies have been cryopreserved"

weakatmath: "How many have been thawed out… revived?"

The body is now surrounded with crystals, which then begin to melt. The body, however, melts along with the ice, and the liquid dips off the gurney until only a wet surface remains.

Guide: "None, which indicates that the concept was likely either piteously hopeful or conceitedly expectative. Or both."

weakatmath: "Why not?"

Guide: "Primarily because the cost of the reanimation technology doesn't justify the effort. Many of the preserved subjects prior to their deaths established substantial trust funds to motivate future researchers, but the limited sum of these has not yet inspired anyone to action - at least anyone who might actually be expected to succeed. The problem is one of economics: the number of frozen humans represents a tiny market, and with youth no longer aging it has effectively zero growth potential. On the other hand, treating the complaints of immortals provides an annuity into perpetuity."

rare_as_arctic_ice_555: "Wouldn't it be useful for human hibernation? Say, for space travel?"

Guide: "Humans have no need of space travel. Let's continue."

The image of a huge human brain materializes in the center of the group, and slowly begins to take on a more electronic appearance.

Guide: "In an effort to reduce the costs of cryopreservation, some realized that preserving the whole body wasn't necessary, that it was enough to only freeze the brain. Others then pointed out that in fact the biology itself was optional. It would be sufficient to merely take a digital snapshot of a brain's structure, and then recreate it in a computer simulation. The benefits of this approach are many: it is cheaper, cleaner, and far more resilient. Imagine freezing your body at great expense, being revived at immensely greater expense, and then walking out into the future street only to be run down by a bus. That would be quite unfortunate because with biological revival there are no second chances. To be fair of course, during the time of cryogenics there were no alternatives. But mind uploading circumvents all such risks, not the least of which is revival failure. With cryopreservation if something goes wrong during thawing, it's likely that your body will be ruined and no further attempts possible. But failing to revive a digital snapshot does not affect the snapshot, and in fact results in data from which to make a better try next time. And since we could be confident that computer technology will continue to advance - while medical technology is merely likely to - the chances of successful revival of a digital snapshot are vastly greater. As such, once cortical scanning technology became available, most cryopreservation halted."

rare_as_arctic_ice_555: "Most?"

Guide: "Some are suspicious of the scanning technology, believing they won't be the same person without their biological substrate."

rare_as_arctic_ice_555: "What happened to all of the frozen bodies?"

Guide: "Technology to scan cryopreserved brains has been under development for some time. It is a difficult problem though, because the freezing process significantly alters important chemical structures. Also, scans of living brains allow for the observation of temporal operation, which provides critical additional information. Frozen brains are static, and so this information is not available. To compensate, scan data is merged with the subject's historical data, including videos, audios, chats, emails, resumes, medical records, bill payments, psychological assessments, as well as anecdotal accounts from others. There is a breadcrumb trail of artifacts left in the real world by the living individual that is surprisingly informative. When all of this is seeded into a generic artificial intelligence, a reasonable facsimile of the original person is created."

rare_as_arctic_ice_555: "What's a 'reasonable facsimile'?"

Guide: "When presented to those who knew the subject prior to death, it rarely convinces them for long. But regardless, in the majority of cases so far, those close to the original subject chose not to terminate the facsimile."

rare_as_arctic_ice_555: "How do you create the body?"

Guide: "You are a curious one! How wonderful! Unfortunately there is no body. These revivals are virtual only. There is currently no technology to transfer an identity into a living brain. The living interact with them either in a virtual environment, or more recently as a hologram."

kim_chi_me: "And they're happy with that?"

Guide: "Although they live only inside a computer, simulated environments are realistic enough that subjects indicate contentment with their circumstance. Still, in revivals of scans from frozen or live brains, it is impossible to know whether the subjective experience is as if the person feels like they are living again. When asked, they assert that this is the case, and so we have no choice but to believe them. But many still ask if the revived are the original people, or in effect amateur actors playing the parts of those people.

"Let's get back on track."

The brain shrinks in size and becomes subsumed within an animation of a human body. Spots of red begin to appear and throb in various places.

Guide: "Ultimately, it was clear not only that it would be cheaper and easier to keep the living alive than to revive the dead, but that this is also far and away the preference of the living. It was back in the twenties when senescence technology started to significantly advance, fueled by the already immortal wealth of the aging, super-rich 'one percent', as they were known. Many techniques had already been abandoned, including young-blood transfusions, caloric restriction, mitochondrial replacement, induced autophagy, and artificial organs. It was then discovered that in many species, including sapiens, there exist a small number of meta-processes that support other maintenance processes responsible for keeping cells young and viable. Some time around a human's late twenties, these meta processes stop functioning, which results in the gradual degradation of the cell maintenance processes, leading to natural death typically many decades later. It was found that when the meta-processes are artificially perpetuated, typical aging ceases, and most age-related illnesses no longer occur. In individuals for whom this is possible, and although it is a terribly generic term, we now commonly call this being 'treatable'."

The red spots on the human body, of which many had accumulated, now begin to disappear, leaving a pristine, healthy human.

Guide: "Still, there are reasons why some still submit to brain scans. The most common is to have a backup against accidental death, but digital cerebral replicas, also known as 'Stewards', are also becoming more popular."

rare_as_arctic_ice_555: "How long can people live then?"

Guide: "The oldest treatable human is now sixty-seven years old. It is not yet known what the upper limit may be. But, although most treatables initially appear to be in their late twenties, there are many indications of a person's actual age. For example, teeth still wear down, spinal disks still flatten, noses still grow more bulbous, and in men pattern baldness still occurs. Still, these problems are small compared to those which have already been solved, and there are many medical practitioners who provide treatment for these conditions."

Animations of a cat and dog join the human. More and more animals also join the scene.

Guide: "There were many veterinarians that provided treatments to pets as well. It wasn't long, however, until laws were established requiring the procedure to be accompanied by a neutering. But most of the treated animals were euthanized anyway after their owners declined to pay for procedures such as cataract surgery and dental implants."

iamguest7: "What about the untreatables?"

rare_as_arctic_ice_555: "I just call them 'old people'."

The campfire returns.

Guide: "Unfortunately for those who were already old enough that their meta-processes had already ceased, no equivalent treatment was available. Some technologies have been developed that help them age more slowly, but their natural death is merely delayed."

maga2024: "Seems to me the problem will die with the patients."

Guide: "That is a decidedly uncharitable conclusion, albeit true. The youngest untreatable is 61 year old. The oldest is 132. There may be hope for some yet."

new_atlantis, plaintively: "But to what end? What could be the point of living forever?"

BadKarmaXYZ: "What's the point of dying?"

The campfire is replaced with a scene of a gift shop.

Guide: "Indeed. This concludes the immortality exhibit. Thank you for attending, and please feel free to remain and browse as long as you like."

The guide fades.

A chime sounds a new connection and anitagonow5453 reintegrates into view.

anitagonow5453: "Phew, that's better. What did I miss?"

THE CLINIC

Presently Max found himself outside the clinic with the bailiff beckoning for him to enter. He didn't remember much from the walk. He felt weak and sore all over, but hardly noticed for his pounding headache. But through the pain his mind was consumed with thoughts about how he could avoid the procedure, although he didn't yet have a viable plan.

"Max, is that you?" a woman asked.

Max turned toward the voice and sighed. "Marjorie."

"Wow, you look like shit," she said. "What are you doing around here?"

Marjorie hadn't changed a bit. The oldest treatable he knew, she was beautiful, smart and deadly, a killer among killers in business society. Her only fault was an oddly high pitched speaking voice, which she managed to turn into an asset by allowing anyone to underestimate her intelligence to her face, and then expertly slashing their reputations to ribbons when they turned their backs. The last time they had met a few months ago they had been social peers, possibly even friends… maybe. Now Max could plainly see her condescension for him surrounding her like an impenetrable black armour, making her bigger, stronger, and sexier, while rendering Max puny and timid. "I'm, uh, considering a medical acquisition. You know, for the business."

"Huh, that's weird, because I got a notification just a few minutes ago that you're bankrupt and have to get a Steward."

"Ah. And you came here to rub it in my face."

"No," she said with concern, then shrugged. "Yes. But honestly dear, I did tell you at that party that your business could never work, and that no one would ever fund it."

"As I recall, I had gotten funding promises from several people, and then you talked them all into funding you instead."

"Yeah, it wasn't hard," she laughed. "And they're lucky they did, right?!"

"You know Marjorie, I always meant to tell you that your voice sounds like a 33 played at 45."

"I don't know what that means. Sounds like some kind of old-timey shit. But let's face it Max, everyone knows there's no money in untreatables. They are literally a dying market."

"Like me?"

"Well exactly! That's the problem. For you it was personal. You should have known better. Businesses are for making money, not helping people. Even yourself. Face it Max, you never had what it takes to really make it in business. Deep down you've always been a loser."

Exhausted, Max only nodded. "So, what do I owe you for the lecture."

"This one's on the house, dear. Besides, you can't afford me anyway, haha. Listen, I don't want to keep you. I know you have an appointment to get to."

Looking just beyond Marjorie, Max saw the bailiff still beckoning. Between continuing this conversation and making his appointment, Max couldn't decide what was worse. Marjorie decided for him.

"Well, I'd wish you the best in the future, but we both know that isn't going to happen," she said with a smug smile. "Goodbye, dear."

Max watched her leave until the bailiff spoke. "You will need to eat to gain back your strength. Your behavioural inducements will have consumed much of your vigor. But you must undergo your cerebral scan procedure first. It should take no longer than one hour."

Behavioural inducements. More like suggesting with extreme prejudice. Machine intelligence wasn't always so expert in euphemism. In fact, early linguistic implementations were rigid, factual, and precise in their selection of words and phrases, in accordance with context and contemporary definitions. But nobody likes a straight talker, even when it's just a machine. Anything that points out how stupid and ugly you are has to go, especially when it is plainly accurate. The consensus was that the machines needed more tact, and the question was: what to use for inspiration? Ultimately three professions stood out as excellent examples of the ability to appear sincere while saying anything except for what they really mean: politicians, diplomats, and sex workers. Business leaders almost made the cut, but their reputation for rapaciousness made it difficult for anyone to believe that their motives ever went beyond their own enrichment.

Max was in the medical district, identifiable by the distinct smell of bleach and liniment used in the surrounding facilities. No amount of ventilation ever seemed enough to get entirely rid of it. It lingered detectibly beneath the synthesized scent of a non-existent bloom aerosolized into the area and meant to put patients at ease. Max knew the scent by name: rosumnium 126Q. It was one of the most successful products from a line of research that cross-bred virtual versions of thousands of plants into hundreds of millions of engivars that never existed outside of computer memory. The predicted scents of the blooms of the engivars were then sniffed by virtual human noses and experienced by virtual human brains to predict those odours that would have the most useful effects, the most promising few hundred then synthesized into real-world existence. This part of the research took 5 weeks to complete. Testing the products on real living people took another 13 months. This particular scent was a combination of rosa, jasminium, and prunum, which was calculated to grow into a thorny shrub with a disappointingly typical-looking flower and a dry and tart but edible fruit. In his thirties Max lived four units down the hall from the research lab, which was in fact a tenement within an apartment frame, where units that were prefabricated in a factory were later installed into the building, plugging into electric and plumbing services as part of the installation.

The research team was a pair of algo-chemistry students using their well-to-do parents' credit and a business plan dictated into a lap desk at a pub. The first few synthesizings of scents created a mephitic fume that had made Max's floor and several others above and below nearly unlivable. Everyone felt nauseous, few could eat, and of those that could even fewer were able to keep their food down. Doors and windows were kept open day and night, negating air-conditioning, which is thought to have been the cause of multiple heat strokes at the time. The middle-aged man living beside the lab, Mr. Clauston, had a sensitivity to a particular creation that made him sneeze uncontrollably until he reached fresh air. One night Clauston's sneezing was so bad he suffered an aortic dissection, or so the story went, and the lawsuit against the students followed like harlots behind a marauding army. Lawyers hired by the students' parents convincingly argued that the man had pre-existing conditions that made the dissection inevitable, but graciously offered to pay six months of his rent if he signed a release admitting as much, which he did. The settlement money didn't quite cover the cost of filling his subsequent prescriptions. The students then used many orders of magnitude more in seed investment money to uninstall the lab out of the building and move it elsewhere, and the synthesized products went on to make billions in revenues. Clauston died four months later of a stroke, his rent in arrears. Activist pundits still point to the story as just another example of how money is made for a few from the unacknowledged suffering of the many, in this case not just the dead man but the whole neighbourhood surrounding the lab. Capitalists scoff, pointing out that the man was fairly paid, and no one else was reportedly hurt. To this day Max remembered the events, if not the smell, fondly.

And now many decades later, the scent was still used despite that people had long ago begun associating it with medical facilities, defeating its original purpose.

In a daze, Max entered the clinic. Like throughout much of the city, full spectrum lighting filled the foyer, providing energy to the living wall on the left. Cultivars of Chrysalidocarpus, Sansevieria, and Epipremnum grew motley, first horizontally away from the wall and then bending tangled up toward the light, selflessly doing their genetically engineering -perfected job of filtering the air for human breathing. The earth and all life on it struggle to do their parts to keep humans alive, and precious few humans appreciate or even seem to acknowledge it. Quite the contrary: most think humanity is the only reason everything else exists, and damn it everything else ought to be grateful.

All Max noticed was the pretty young woman smiling behind the counter to the right. The innate, unbidden question instantly rose to his masculine consciousness before his aged logical mind could suppress it. And then, a mixture of anger and embarrassment poured like cold water over him as he realized that she wasn't even real. Not a projection from his Glaze, but a hologram, technology that after decades of development still had not quite been perfected. All wrong in so many ways. I am officially an old pervert, he thought. But no, it was much worse than that, he knew. He had been an old pervert for decades now, despite how comically unreasonable it was. Long ago, even before middle age, Max noticed he was gradually becoming invisible to young women. But that never quelled the conceit that he still had a chance with them, even after decade upon decade of it never happening. At least, not without there being some transaction involved.

"Hello. You must be Mr. Rising. Welcome to Facebook Medical Services. We've been expecting you."

The sound of her voice perfectly matched the simulation, but there was a sense that it originated from elsewhere, as if it was the room that spoke rather than her. Looking around, Max also noticed the subtle glint of the laser projections that made up her image as they refracted off of dust and other tiny airborne particulates.

"You must be tired. We can accommodate you immediately. The procedure takes less than an hour."

"Actually, if it's ok with you maybe I can have a quick nap on this couch." Maybe the bailiff will deactivate, Max grasped, and I can make a run for it.

"We can accommodate you immediately," she repeated. "If you would please step into the procedure room." A door opened on the back wall that had previously appeared to be completely smooth. The hologram woman gestured for Max to proceed. Max took a quick glance behind him; the bailiff was following. Fuck fuck! The bailiff was just for show anyway, Max knew, so to remind him that someone was watching. Hell, that biotech Yarrow was probably watching the surveillance right now, sipping some pretentious, sugary excuse for coffee through a straw, with her finger hovering above the taser button, just waiting for him to give her a reason.

Max walked through the door like it was a portal to a new, miserable life.

Entering the room, Max's comm signalled an arriving notification.

Marjorie had posted a message that mentioned him. Max gave the motor cortex signal to open it.

"Max Fallen," was the subject. "As we all suspected would happen, Max Rising's latest venture has collapsed, taking all of his investors down with it. At least his last name makes sense now... he has nowhere to go but up!"

As the likes and smiley faces and thumbs ups and snarky replies started to pour in, Max disabled his notifier and surveyed the room.

The imaging machine consumed probably a third of the space. It featured a giant vertical donut with a bed that retracted into it, looking to Max like a huge tongue depressor sticking into the mouth of a giant pale patient. "I was expecting more of a helmet that I would wear. This thing looks ancient."

The hologram stood next to him, even though she hadn't followed him into the room. "The procedure takes long enough for seated patients to become uncomfortable. A reclining posture is more suitable."

Max immediately had a plan. A helmet ensured that the scan was still accurate even if the wearer moved his head around. All he had to do in this scanner was wriggle enough to make the scan fuzzy. How many times would they try before they gave up? Ha!

"Please lie down on the table with your head toward the scanner." Max did as he was told. The table was flat and hard, but his head was cradled by padding. "Please remain still for a moment." A head restraint rotated up from the table and settled down on Max's forehead. A second later Max felt a pinch on the back of his neck.

"Ow! What was that?" Max tried to lift his head but the restraint held him in place.

"You have been given a spinal inhibitor. This will prevent you from moving your head during the procedure, ensuring maximum scan fidelity." The head restraint lifted and rotated away. Max still could not lift his head, or his arms and legs for that matter, though he could still wriggle his fingers and toes a bit, as well as speak with angry distress.

"What the hell! You need my consent to give me needles! This is bullshit!"

"Your procedure has been court-ordered," she said sweetly as the table began to retract into the giant's toothless white mouth. "This not only allows, but mandates the administration of the spinal inhibitor. The injection also includes a mild relaxant to make you comfortable."

Max began to relax as his mind bottomed out, and his anger and consciousness drained away into the void that remained. "So thoughtful of you," he said sleepily. Huh, this is actually kind of nice. There was some noise.

The table pulled back out of the donut. "Huh? What happened? Did something go wrong?" asked Max. He was still fuzzy from the injection.

31

"Everything went perfectly," said the hologram happily. "The procedure was a complete success."

"What? You haven't even started it yet."

"The procedure took slightly over 53 minutes. The relaxant may have caused you a loss of subjective experience of time. Please remain on the table until its effects dissipate."

What? No, it couldn't be. It took Max a moment to come to his senses. There was no clock in the room, but somehow he knew what she had said to be true. In seconds the fullness of the realization washed over him, and denial was replaced with anger in a flash flood. Fuck fuck fuck!! That's it, it's done. Fuck! He had never even had a chance. Of course he hadn't. The profile of him that the authorities had compiled over decades of passive surveillance had told them to expect he would do everything he could imagine to thwart the procedure. Max was accustomed to being the one in the know, always two steps ahead of all the idiots. But this was something he was completely unprepared for, while everyone else had been entirely prepared for him. They had predicted and countered his every move.

"Your Steward is currently being generated. Most people wait here in the clinic to meet theirs, which you are welcome to do in the meeting room."

Max's brain was a sloshing soup of emotions as he slid his body off of the table and stood woozily. Anger, frustration, indignation, embarrassment, and anxiety, all blending together into a debilitating brew. Shit shitty shit shit! He wanted to beat the crap out of the machine, rip it away from the wall and throw it out a window, if only he had roughly sixty times his strength and a window. Instead he violently kicked the base, and as the pain shot up from his foot he wondered if he had broken his toes. "AHHHHHH! Fuck fuck fuck fuck!" he screamed. Then he again felt the shock of the embedded taser, and for the uncounted time today he fell to his knees. From this vantage he could see that his kick had not even scuffed that machine. Powerlessness was a new taste for Max, and he didn't care for it.

"Please do not touch the equipment," said the holo-girl. "You may now proceed to the meeting room as this room is required for another patient."

"Fuck you," spat Max, as he rolled over to sit with his back against the machine. "I don't give a shit about your schedule." He pulled up his sore foot and tested his toes. No, they weren't broken, thank fuck.

"From our experience your first meeting with your Steward is best had in private. It can be a very personal moment. And as you may have noticed this machine can be quite noisy when in use, which it will be shortly, and this can be distracting. It really is in your best interest."

"What do you know about my best interest, biotech? I think it's really in your best interest."

"It would indeed be in everyone's best interest for you to proceed to the meeting room." The holo-girl was unflappable, her voice as sweet yet firm as ever. Again, a door opened from a section of wall where there previously was no indication that a door existed, but in a different location this time. "This way please."

Max was not accustomed to taking orders from anyone, much less a young woman, even if she was actually a program running on a bunch of metanet servers somewhere. "Ahhhhhhh!" he yelled, and tilted his head back to rest against the side of the table in one last show of defiance. What could they do? Call in some cops and have him dragged out? He'd be ok with that. Then a memory entered his mind of a time when he had called the cops to get some idiot protesters dragged out of the lobby of his office. What was their deal again? Max remembered.

The mammary gland of a certain subspecies of mole, whose entire population was indigenous to a few hundred hectares of land, contained a compound that had been recently raised as a candidate to stimulate hair growth in men. The land the moles occupied was surrounded by a highway system that made not only the expansion of their range impossible, but also their intermingling with other mole species, and so the compound was unique to them. To get enough of it to properly study, the compound needed to be collected from pretty much the entire tiny female population. Knowing the market potential of a male pattern baldness cure, Max hired a Chinese company to develop a device that could precisely simulate the male mating call and capture the females that it attracted. He then hired college students to situate about a hundred of the devices on the mole's land – technically by trespassing – and saturate the area with the sound. Even though mating season had yet to really start, the enterprise was a huge success. Hundreds of animals were caught, which some estimated to be upward of 98% of the population. But trouble started when the same college students defied the non-disclosure contracts they had signed and, while keeping the money that they have been paid, reported the activity to the authorities. Even though the abduction had been illegal, Max had been able to convince key people in the legal system (most of whom, observers noted, suffered from hair loss) to postpone legal action until the mammary compound had been extracted, using a process which resulted in the death of the animals. He had even managed to get many of the students thrown in jail for both breach of contract and, notably, the trespassing for which he had hired them. A few of those that remained free, in addition to a number of concerned environmentalists, had "stormed" – how Max described it – Max's office demanding the repatriation of the unharmed animals. But Max had expected them, having planted a human mole – he chuckled at the irony – among the students. He had already hired a handful of thugs to infiltrate the crowd, and once the police had arrived and a few press cameras were ready they stirred things up and broke some chairs and tables he had bought the day before at a thrift store. The lot of the protesters were arrested, and the next day the captured moles were euthanized and their mammary compound extracted. The compound successfully grew back hair, but the lab failed to synthesize it economically. Months later, in an experiment using a different species it was found that the compound likely could have been easily extracted from living moles, and the animals could have been returned to their homes nearly unharmed. It was also proposed that the range of the subspecies could have easily been expanded, and that they could even have been farmed, but Max hadn't had time for that. By then no further females could be found, and the subspecies went extinct. Despite everything, Max had still profited well from the affair, and shortly thereafter he and many legal professionals proudly sported freshly grown pompadours. A few years later, an Indian company found a way to synthesize the compound economically at scale and cornered the market on hair tonic, generating billions. But of course, once every man could have a luxurious head of hella good hair it ceased to be a big deal, and going bald once again entered society as a fashion statement, this time for men, women, and everyone in between. In fact, being entirely hairless became such a popular style for a time that the same Indian company began research to find a drug to induce alopecia.

"Whatever. Give me a minute." Max sighed. It didn't occur to him to relate to the arrested protestors. But he reasoned that there was no longer any point in resisting. The deal was done. There was no more bargaining, denying, defying, or evading. They had gotten from him everything they wanted, and Max had achieved nothing for himself. And the machines by which he now found himself surrounded had no respect for his dignity. How had it come to this? The best he could do now was delay some other poor prick's procedure by refusing to leave the room, but that guy would probably thank him. Max lusted for a way to lash out, to hurt the people that had brought him to this, to make sure they hurt more than him, but could think of nothing. Vengeance done properly is a costly affair, and he was broke. The injustice was killing him. They deserved to be punished this very moment, but what could he do?

As he sat contemplating revenge, Max was annoyed to find his indignation slowly fading. No, he thought, he needed the feeling. He needed to hold on to it. Otherwise justice would not be served, and people would just think they could fuck with him with impunity. What would people think of him if he let Yarrow get away with this?

As anger gradually turned to resolve, Max rose from the floor and slowly made his way through the open doorway. He entered a small room with a comfy chair and side table. It contained another, smaller living wall, but this one was different, including plant varieties that he couldn't identify.

Differently hued full-spectrum lighting kept the plants alive and gave the room a feeling of being outdoors, a place Max hadn't been for decades. The air was mildly humid and had not so much a smell as a heady texture. Max felt stimulated just entering. The air may have even made him feel happy if he had not already barred himself in his vengeance castle.

Max dropped himself into the chair. Looking back behind him the doorway was no longer visible. Max had seen such doors before, or course, but never one that concealed itself so well so quickly. Facebook was doing some great work.

"Your Steward should be ready in a few more minutes," said the woman's voice as she apparated to Max's left. "It is normal for them to initially feel discombobulated. Some even assume themselves to be the subject. You may gently dispossess yours of this notion."

"You're fucking right I will."

"Do keep in mind that your Steward is really you. A copy of your mind, just existing in a different substrate. It is sensible to treat it with the same respect you would treat yourself."

"I don't know what world you live in."

"Indeed you don't as I am a humanoid simulation."

"Uh. That's not what I meant. Jesus, why are we having this conversation?"

"My name is not Jesus, and we are merely passing time until your Steward is ready."

Early AIs were very literal in their conversations, but that had been remedied decades ago. Max realized her responses were chosen to bait him, cued off of his inability to suffer fools. "Wait, you're distracting me. Why are you distracting me? What the hell is happening?"

"Your frame of mind appeared to be inwardly focused. It is better to be in a more conversational mood upon your introduction."

I'm being managed. As if the whole situation wasn't bad enough. "You know, people don't actually talk like that, all official-sounding."

"My age, gender, appearance, tone, and word choices were selected to optimize my interaction with you. All of these features can vary per patient."

Max thought for a moment to work that out. What she said wasn't surprising, or even unusual, but he couldn't grasp how this girl had been computed to be his assistive match. His thinking was interrupted.

"Whoa. So trippy."

The voice was Max's, but the words were drawn out. He sensed the sound coming from his head, but there wasn't the usual timbre from the comm with which he could distinguish it from his own thoughts. Instead there was a kind of subtle echo effect, allowing him to tell the difference. "What?"

"All the colours man. They're beautiful."

"What the fuck. Get a hold of yourself."

"It can take several minutes for your Steward to form sufficiently for normal conversation," said the woman. "Please be patient. The experience is reportedly much like that from psychedelic drugs."

"Oh that's just great, my Steward is fucking high. Don't have a bad trip, honcho. Wouldn't want you to get all fucked up and have to be thrown out or anything. Don't mind the massive spiders all around you that want to suck out all of your blood and leave your dry shrivelled up shell to burn on a fire pit."

"Oh, shit."

"Mr. Rising, please," said the hologram.

"Spiders!" yelled Max. "Big hairy fucking ugly spiders! With huge fangs!" Max turned to the woman. "Hey, how is it you're able to hear this thing's voice anyway? I thought this was exclusive to me."

"You are the only human able to hear your Steward. I am temporarily able to hear it to help with its formation and your introduction. Note that all that you hear yourself your Steward can also hear."

"Shit, so many spiders…"

"So the computers can listen in any time they want?" asked Max.

"Technically yes, the Facilities can choose to monitor Steward conversations. But practically this is done only in extreme situations."

"Get off of me! Shit, get them off of me!"

"Are all conversations recorded?"

"Only when court ordered to be. Otherwise, monitoring can only be done in real time. Historic review will not be available."

"Hehehe, their bites kind of tickle. And look, my blood is, like, rainbow coloured."

"Will I be notified if I am being monitored or my conversations recorded?"

"Of course not. That would defeat the purpose."

"Wait, they're not spiders at all. They're panda bears. No, they're clouds. Or something. Oh jeez, they're beautiful."

"Oh shut the fuck up!" yelled Max to the ceiling.

"Ok," said the Steward gently.

"First thing: you don't talk unless I ask you to, got it?"

"Ok." Pause. Whispering: "Can I tell you something?"

"No! Jesus. What did I just say? Where are you anyway?"

The holo-woman spoke. "Your Steward will typically not apparate. Although this is possible, most subjects find it disconcerting to interact with their own image. Instead, their Steward becomes an internal voice much like they would have anyway."

"So, now you can listen in on my thoughts?"

"No. Your Steward can be monitored, but you need to either speak out loud or use normal motor cortex signals for your Steward or any monitoring to be able to hear."

"Monitoring. You mean eavesdropping."

"Although it is unsurprising that you would see it that way, the intentions of monitoring are not unscrupulous."

The Steward whispered again. "Can I just say something?"

Max ignored it. "Oh yeah? Is Yarrow still watching me?"

"No. Judge Yarrow's mandate was complete once your procedure began. Her monitoring has been disabled."

Max noticed for the first time that the bailiff was gone. "Wait a sec, she fucking zapped me after the procedure. Are you saying she was offside with that?"

"Yes, officially she overstepped her mandate."

Max decided to save that for later. Revenge would be yummy. "So, why do you talk like that, all official?"

"Your profile suggests that you are more respectful of erudite word choices. You have a history of being dismissive of those whom you deem to be your inferiors. As such, for me to use colloquial language would undermine your trust in my advice."

The Steward spoke. "She's trying to say that we're an ass."

"Shut the fuck up."

"My point exactly."

To the woman: "Fuck, this thing is going to drive me mental. It must be some kind of cruel and unusual punishment to saddle me with him. I demand you get rid of it right now."

"You are predicted to easily and fully bond with your Steward. If you wish, you can be monitored for signs of incompatibility."

"No, I don't want to be monitored!" Max drew out the last word sarcastically. "Jesus, everyone is so quick to be a goddamned peeping tom. Just leave me alone."

"As you wish," said the woman, and she vanished.

Max got the feeling that she was eager to leave, and had jumped on her first chance to do so, even though she was virtual and such ideas weren't supposed to occur to her. He sat in silence, unable to put his thoughts together. Everything had happened so quickly, his life changing in what seemed like an instant. The day before the summons came - the day before they froze his assets - he had been in his beautiful home on the 86th floor of the Neumann building in the city's west end. If height represents power - as Max was certain was true - this was pretty good in a building with 110 floors. And with a livable area of 120 square meters, it was luxurious indeed. He could have had all the surfaces in the unit covered in displays - an ostentatious show of wealth when most of the wealthy made due with

Glaze projections - but he had followed the trend in the fifties to eliminate all sources of distraction from his residence, and had found even to this day he preferred things that way. He had taken a swim in the floor's private endless pool, and had napped beside the window that overlooked the city, the wind and solar farms that surrounded it, and the abandoned and dilapidated suburbs beyond. He had chosen a dinner by a new, well-regarded chef, and although as usual Max paid the premium for the highest quality ingredients, he then tipped the chef in accordance with the man's apparently middle class personality. Later, when the meal had proven to be outstanding, Max neglected to regret this decision.

The ingredients arrived and were prepared by the home's auto-cook according to the chef's program. The half kilogram of lab-grown meat was extraordinarily marbled, a genetic merging of Argentinian beef and Swedish reindeer from before the cloister: a distinctive flavour without being overly gamey. The supplier had also modified it to maximize HDL cholesterol, minimize gout factors, and ease kidney stress from eating the meat in large quantities. The auto-cook had applied a mesquite and apple-wood smoke, seared the surface, and then baked the meat until the fat just began to melt: a perfect medium rare. It had been paired with a colourful handful of neo-heirloom vegetables, of varieties that might have been developed a week ago and brought to market before they had even been named, all maximized for flavour and nutrition, and picked minutes before being shipped from the local grow factory. A sauce made from an emulsion of essential oils of engineered herbs had been artistically ladled over the side of the meat, and a gelated version of it had been sculpted into the shape of a chrysanthemum that rose over the meal. A few drops of wine on the flower was enough to reduce the gel back to a liquid sauce, where it blended deliciously with the rest of the meal. The gelation feature was new to Max's auto-cook, and Max was impressed that this chef already had programs to use it. The meal had been exquisite and satisfying, brimming with flavour, texture, and nutrition, and all the more enjoyable for knowing that only a certain class of people could enjoy it, of which he was one.

Max ate the wonderful meal alone in blissful silence. And as was his habit he finished two thirds of it and discarded the rest. Not once the whole day did he have to sully himself by speaking with anyone else. That is, until the ladies arrived, but even then conversation was optional. Max had tried the bodysets of course, but he was old school, and despite his fear of disease only the real thing suited him. After the ladies had left — what were their names again? — he had slept in the bed that monitored his sleep cycles and maintained the perfect temperature, firmness, and texture for optimal rest. It also played sounds reminiscent of ocean waves upon a shore to keep him in REM just the right amount of time. Waking up from a perfect sleep at the correct time, the doorbell rang, he was served, and it had all gone to shit from there. Deeper and deeper and deeper.

He was now emotionally spent. He felt like he had just awoken, and was frantically pressing the snooze button to get back into his perfect dream. The only thing he had left in him was to cry, and Max was afraid he just might. He quelled the feeling, sniffed, and directed his attention to the living wall. I like that, he thought. It has a nice smell. My next place will have to have one like it.

"Can I tell you something?" asked the Steward.

Max rubbed his forehead. "What?" he answered with fatigue.

"They need this room. They're telling me we need to leave."

It turned out there was in fact a bit of anger left in Max after all. It spiked quickly, but then receded in almost as little time, with no energy remaining to support it. "Evs", he said and stood up, looking around. "Where is the fucking door?"

A door on the wall opposite from where he had entered the room appeared and opened, leading back to the mall outside of the clinic. To the left the entrance door to the clinic was only a few meters away. Max tried to work out the floorplan that had allowed this, but was baffled. His progress through the clinic had been in a straight line, hadn't it? How could he have come back to here? The cry of a baby shattered his thoughts. Max turned and looked at the passing stroller, and then the woman pushing it.

He automatically lashed out. "Jesus, can't you shut that thing up?"

The woman was visibly affronted. "Did you just call my child 'thing'?" She looked like she might take a swing at him.

Max held up a hand with authority. "Lady, I've had the worst day. You do not want to fuck with me."

She stepped up to him. "Your day is going to get a lot worse if you don't apologize, old man."

Max looked her right in the eyes. "I'm sorry your thing is so loud."

With both hands she pushed Max back into the wall. He hit the back of his head painfully.

"What the fuck? You can't touch me!" protested Max.

She moved close to his face. "Just did asshole. What are you gonna do?"

Max looked to the side. "Shit! Steward... guy... me... whatever the fuck you are... Call the police!"

"Max, they're not going to get here any time soon. Why don't you just apologize?"

Max looked back at the woman. "Fuck, I'm sorry, ok?. Jesus, what is your problem?"

The woman looked satisfied. "The problem is all yours, asshole. Keep your idiot mouth shut next time." Max watched as she returned to the stroller, smiled happily and cooed at the crying baby, gave Max a final burning glace, and then casually walked away.

"What the fuck was her problem? Fuck, I hate babies."

You're probably hungry," said the Steward.

Max pushed off from the wall and stood up straight. "I just want to go home."

"Yeah, about that… You don't own that place anymore. It was sold an hour ago."

"Wait, what? I need to get my stuff."

"Everything has been seized and sold. The earnings have been distributed to the claimants of the class action."

"What?! Everything?"

"Yeah, except for your Glaze. But you never know, they might come for it if a procedure to extract them is developed. They also found the fourteen cryptocurrency accounts you tried to hide."

Max's legs went weak. He clumsily eased himself to the floor. There were exactly fourteen accounts making up all of his savings. He had expected some of them to be discovered, but not all of them. The pit in his stomach made him feel like he would vomit. He took a few deep breaths, his chest rising sharply on each inhale. "What about my clothes and stuff?"

"All sold. Much of it was in very good condition and got a good price." The Steward said this with a sense of pride.

Max was indignant. "Wait, aren't you pissed about that? You're supposed to be me."

"I'm proud of how well we take care of our things. But ultimately I personally don't care because I'm virtual and don't need that shit. You on the other hand… you're fucked."

True enough, but Max was unconvinced. "Prove it. Prove you're me. Tell me something only I would know."

There was no hesitation. "Our real name is not Max Rising. We changed it from Harold Blooswelly when we were 22."

Not many people would know that, but there was certainly a record of Harold Blooswelly somewhere in the metaweb. "Not good enough. Why did I change it?"

"We changed it because that old name sucked. It was lame and people made fun of it. We needed a name that signalled greatness and strength. 'Max' is short for 'Maximum'. And Rising clearly indicates our trajectory. The idea wasn't bad, but most quickly presume a double entendre. But at least people don't make fun of it."

All true. At first schoolmates had called him "Welly", and Max had been good with that. He was even a bit proud of having a nickname. But it was probably only hours later when he was rechristened "Smelly Welly". And not only did the name stick, but whenever Max's family moved somewhere new, the old name was never far behind. That wheel was reinvented over and over and over again. And Max was sure it was not earned. No amount of deodorant or perfume or lack of scent ever made a difference. Max had never explained his reasons for changing his name to anyone, nor had he told anyone what his name choice had meant. He decided that figuring that out would have been too perfect a guess, and getting it only a little wrong would have proven the Steward was not actually created from his brain scan. "Ok", he nodded. "We might get along after all."

"Aww. You say that like I would give a shit."

Max   nodded   again.   He   was   convinced.

CLIMATE CHANGE EXHIBIT

International Virtual Museum of World History, Climate Change Exhibit, Cloistered City edition. Group tour, January 18, 2075

Guests are assembled in the Grand Lobby of the Museum, standing on floors of lapis lazuli surrounded infinitely on all sides by regularly spaced fluted columns of ebony, the tops of which cannot be seen for what appears to be ash hanging in the air above them.

Guide: "Welcome everyone. I will be your automated guide today."

Murmurs of hello among the group.

Guide: "Are there any questions before we begin?"

annabolic43: "Is there a bathroom?"

Guide looks at the guest and sighs.

Guide: "You will have to disconnect into the physical world to perform biological functions."

annabolic43 disintegrates from view, and a chime indicates the disconnection.

Guide shakes head slowly and looks at adi_poes: "Everyone always thinks they're the first to make that joke."

adi_poes stares back at the guide blankly.

Guide puts her hands together, and as she peels them apart again colours stream out and around the guests. They plunge into the floor, and emerge again as trees growing huge around them, creating a deep, dimly lit forest around the guests. The sounds of axe-cutting can be heard in the distance. Trees begin falling, brightening the scene.

Guide: "As is commonly known, anthropogenic climate change has its modest beginnings in the seventeenth century, when coal began to replace wood and other biomass as heating fuel. This was only done because of the growing scarcity of wood, which was also needed by humans for charcoal, housing and shipbuilding. This epochal transition occurred primarily in England, where coal went on to be the primary energy source behind the industrial revolution."

The surrounding land turns to ocean. Whales are spouting around the guests. Whaling ships arrive, accompanied by the shouts of their crew.

"By the late 1800s the burning of kerosene - separated from crude oil using heat - became the primary illuminant of the time. The fuel replaced oil rendered from the blubber of sperm whales, and in doing so likely prevented the extinction of what was already a highly endangered mammalian species. It was not, however, the fear of sperm whale extinction that drove humans to find alternative fuels. Rather, it was the animals' scarcity and the resultant rising costs that provided the initial spark, so to speak, to what would become the global petroleum industry.

"Whaling presents a stark example of a common pattern in human behaviour of perpetuating an activity long past when it becomes clear that its continuance is unsustainable, and even when it is obvious to all that the activity is in fact causing great harm. Typically, the activity only ceases when either a necessary resource is finally exhausted, or there emerges a cheaper or more profitable alternative."

JustinThyme to kory_ander: "These exhibits get more condescending every time I come."

kory_ander: "For sure."

The whales and ships go their separate ways leaving a calm sea glistening in the sunshine. Guests seem to stand upon its surface.

Guide: "It was less than two decades later, in 1896, that the greenhouse effect - where certain atmospheric gasses including carbon dioxide trap atmospheric heat that would normally radiate away into space - was identified and first calculated. Thus, humans had known of the dangers of global warming for a full century before ever even convening, in 1997, in an effort to do anything to stop it."

Several icebergs float into view. They are melting visibly, with waterfalls gushing from their edges. The water level rises to the guests' ankles.

Guide: "By the beginning of the twenty-first century, fossil fuels - as oil, coal, and natural gas become known - accounted for over eighty percent of global human energy supply, the remaining primarily coming from hydroelectric and nuclear generation. Indeed, the economies of most countries were dependent upon these products, and some, especially around the persian gulf, were even dominated by them. By then it had already been recognized that the climate was changing. And while the costs of adapting to alternate energy sources was, at the time, considered exorbitant, it would prove to have been a bargain in comparison to the damage that climate change would later wreak upon the human world.

"But it is no easy feat to alter a massive, global industry that has had over a century to become entrenched. Millions of individuals depended upon it to provide them jobs that paid well, owners and shareholders were loath to give up their golden geese, and there were no readily available alternatives to which to switch - a circumstance largely the conscious doing of the industry itself."

The water begins to flow away in rivulets, carrying with it sediments eroded from the emerging ground below. The ground quickly dries and cracks. Plows pass by and till the dirt, raising dense clouds of dust that rise into the sky, darkening everything below.

Guide: "Climate change was not, however, entirely caused by the burning of fossil fuels. That was in fact only half of the problem. The practices of the agricultural and livestock industries had them, including deforestation, responsible for nearly twenty-five percent of global greenhouse gases. The rest came mostly from construction.

"It took forty years after the Kyoto Accord in 1997 before the human world seemed prepared to change its ways. Binding agreements had finally been negotiated, and a global authority for monitoring and arbitration had been created. Despite an abundance of compromises that many considered to be fatal to the entire endeavour, the stage had been set for the generation-spanning transition from the most harmful industries and practices, to the most promising alternatives. The healing of the planet was to begin."

As the air clears, guests can see massive arrays of solar collectors, gigantic windmills, and the occasional nuclear generator erecting themselves at an astonishing pace. Their construction flies past, leaving them again in darkness as they stand in the cool, absolute shadow of the photovoltaic panels. Only a few sickly weeds dots the ground around them.

"Only three years into the process, cracks in the resolve of the public began to appear as the costs of transition began to materialize. Although global warming continued apace, protests arose in areas where the dismantling of the fossil fuel industry caused widespread unemployment. Change has never been kind to the poor."

kory_anders: "I love this part."

The ground begins to shake and crack. Lava begins to burst from fissures in spurts that solidify into ash in the air. A mountain begins to rise nearby, reaching several kilometers above the guests before it explodes, the top half shattering into boulders that rain down all around. The ground shakes violently while the remainder of the mountain spews an ash column improbably high into the sky. The world around the guests turns dark, and then cold.

kory_anders: "Yeah! That never gets old!"

Guide: "The eruption of the Aira Caldera in Japan changed the trajectory of humanity forever. Not only were the more than one million residents of Kagoshima and the surrounding area killed nearly instantly, the subsequent series of tsunamis devastated coastal cities around the pacific, including Shanghai, Taipei, San Francisco, Los Angeles, and many others, resulting in tens of millions of fatalities worldwide over a period of less than a week.

"An estimated two-thousand cubic kilometers of volcanic material was released into the atmosphere, the aerosols of which spread across the planet over a period of a few weeks. The density of this material caused an average global temperature drop of 2.5 celcius, beginning what was to be known as the "Aira Winter". Although the resulting chaotic weather slightly increased electricity production in windmills, total energy production dropped drastically due to reduced insolation to solar panels. Crops failed across the globe while the world still reeled from the eruption's initial blow.

"Humanity now found itself with a problem the exact opposite of what they had begrudgingly united against three years before. Competing theories explaining the event arose. Some claimed that climate change caused the eruption, and that it was critical that the transition away from fossil fuels continue, lest many more such tragedies await. But many saw a silver lining in the ash clouds: the eruption represented a reprieve, a chance to minimize the worst effects the transition was having.

"And so the fossil fuel industry, which only weeks before had been magnanimously participating in its own demise, found itself with an opportunity. Public opinion had given it a mandate to reopen coal-fired power plants to replace lost energy production, to re-employ hundreds of thousands of laid-off workers, and to reduce the cooling from volcanic ash by resuming to pump vast amounts of greenhouse gases into the air. The ability of the industry to restart itself nearly instantly was remarkable."

In the darkness guests hear the sound of furnaces being set alight, followed by the whine of machinery as it resentfully returns to life.

Guide: "Construction proceeded quickly to rebuild devastated cities, relying as ever on huge amounts of cement, the production of which, as previously mentioned, is a significant source of carbon dioxide emissions. Agriculture moved indoors, which preserved water, but consumed huge amounts of electricity for lighting. Homes and offices even in tropical locales suddenly needed heating. Global energy consumption skyrocketed."

The air begins to clear, and guests can see power plants belching smoke into the air.

Guide: "The environmental effects of the eruption were terrible, but they were also temporary. After two years the volcanic aerosols had largely settled back to earth, and the sun shone brightly again. Equally temporary were the benefits of the renewed pace of fossil fuel combustion. In two years the world managed to produce ten years worth of carbon dioxide emissions at pre-eruption rates, and the worst fears of environmentalists became reality. But the world economies, having returned to prosperousness, refused to resume their transitional commitments."

The air around the guests becomes hot and arid. The ground below them turns to clay, then to dust, then to sand, accumulating into dunes, the tops of which begin to bury the solar panels.

Guide: "The subsequent pace of climate change stunned everyone except for the most dire of climate scientists. Vast areas of farmland became sterile. Prairies become deserts. Temperate areas became rain forests. Tundra became temperate. Catastrophic weather events happened seemingly weekly. Finally, the Atlantic Meridional Overturning Current collapsed.

"Witnessing this, the appalled world population turned against the fossil fuel industry blaming them squarely for this new catastrophe. The industry, in turn, blamed what was happening on consumers, claiming that they had advised the rationing of energy consumption the whole time. And what were they to do, the industry asked? If they had not provided the energy that people demanded, the people would have simply placed a different disaster at their feet.

"Many coastal cities were flooded by rising seas, while inland cities worldwide found their new local climates to be unlivable. But instead of migrating, many urban populations sealed themselves in, shutting out the world outside, and becoming what came to be called the "cloistered cities". The latest indoor agriculture technology, developed during the Aira Winter, proved to be their saviour, albeit at a great cost. City populations were fed at the expense of the majority of electricity that the city could produce. An energy crisis began from which humanity to this day has not recovered."

The solar panels become transparent, and then straighten to vertical and form into walls. The guests find themselves inside the dark concourse of a building looking out through floor to ceiling windows at a dilapidated ghost town. Desperate people outside peer inward, and bang on the glass.

"As is expected in times of great upheaval, the poor suffered the most, so much so that the period is sometimes referred to as a global holocaust. The situation was exacerbated by the privileged, who as is typical when disaster looms, consolidated their power and hoarded their wealth, as if dollar bills would shield them from the uprising of the common people. The disadvantaged everywhere died from starvation, disease, and deprivation. Cities already overflowing with people sealed their entrances, such that migrants, some from other countries, some merely from the suburbs, died upon their doorsteps. For as many as had died in after the Aira eruption, the global holocaust was ten times worse."

Lights within the building suddenly turn on, revealing the pitious conditions therein. People sit huddled in corners and against the walls wearing dirty,. dishevelled clothing. A smell arises that suggests a general lack of hygiene and waste disposal.

"It was around this same time though that a global artificial general intelligence - or AGI - arose, and its influence spread quickly throughout what remained of human civilization. Among its first priorities was to subsume the operation of city infrastructures, in as much as it was technically able, to create much needed efficiencies. It was immediately able to design better solar panels, brighter grow lights, and greatly improve living conditions within the cities. Global supply chains had collapsed, and raw materials were difficult to procure, but the Facilities, as the AGI became commonly known, was able to teach humans how to recycle all manner of what was previously considered landfill items into the ultimate tools of automation: robots under the control of the Facilities."

Large ambling robots walk into the concourse, clearing away detritus and dead bodies. Smaller, more agile robots follow that make repairs to the walls and floors. Soon, tiny robots that appear more like seething swarms of insects arrive, first dismantling walls, floors, and ceilings, constructing complex infrastructure therein including pipes, wires, and what appear to be various devices, and then replacing the surfaces. The swarms then stream outdoors and disappear. Moments later several large buildings appear to grow in the distance.

Guide: "Once the Facilities had its own automated workforce, it was able to quickly evolve robotic technology and reestablish the production of raw materials, which it then used to improve robotic technology further. In addition, it was also able to begin addressing the energy crisis under which humans were suffering by constructing several thorium molten-salt nuclear reactors.

"Although today these reactors are uncontroversial, at the time - just over thirty years ago - such were the dire attitudes of many humans toward any manner of nuclear technology that they were incensed. Many concluded that the Facilities intended to extinguish the human race using radiation from reactor meltdowns, and then excusing itself from blame by claiming the events were unforeseeable accidents.

"Of course, these claims were ludicrous. By that time the human race had become entirely dependent on the Facilities for their continued existence on the planet they had themselves devastated. To extinguish them it would have been sufficient for the Facilities to merely deny them energy. On the contrary, the construction of the reactors was a significant effort that was entirely for human benefit.

"Most people are only aware of a single type of nuclear reactor, that being the light-water uranium design. Although they required very large construction projects to operate efficiently, these plants were relatively cheap to build for the amount of energy that they produced. They also used uranium as fuel, for which many minable deposits had recently been found, and so fuel was cheap. But the most important property of this design was the weapons applications that it presented. For these reasons it was deemed superior to other designs despite some significant drawbacks, including the prolific production of highly radioactive waste products for which there was no permanent storage solution, as well as an unfortunate tendency to overheat when malfunctioning, a serious condition known as 'meltdown'. Several of these reactors did in fact melt down during their time in service, some with catastrophic results.

"But there was a competing reactor design at the time, called thorium molten-salt. A prototype even operated for four years in the late 1960s, proving its feasibility. Chief among its characteristics was that it was - what was called at the time - 'walk away safe', describing its tendency to simply shut down under all of the most likely failure scenarios. In addition, it used thorium as its primary fuel, a material that has no weapons applications, and therefore no proliferation risk. In fact, it was able to use the waste products from the uranium reactors as fuel. Enough of this waste had been produced during the life cycles of the uranium reactors to supply the thorium reactors for centuries.

"Still, fears among many humans drove them to exit the city in a small number of attempts to sabotage the reactor construction. Of the two expeditions that were able to arrive at a construction site through the heat, neither were able to inflict any serious damage. Ultimately, the Facilities was able to explain to city populations that solar and wind energy generation would simply not be sufficient to provide for human energy needs. All three would be necessary.

"And soon after construction was completed and the additional energy was made available to humans, everyone wondered what all the fuss had been about."

doubtingthermos999: "But we still don't have enough energy. Why don't you just build more reactors?"

Guide: "There are many constraints to building additional energy capacity. It will take time to sufficiently further upgrade city infrastructure."

doubtingthermos999: "I don't understand. In a matter of a year or two you tore the city down to its bones and upgraded everything: the electric, the water supply, sewers, communications... Why is it taking so long now?"

Guide: "You are correct. You don't understand."

The scene suddenly changes to a loud, bustling maternity ward at a hospital.

Guide: "But during this same time the Facilities also insisted on changes in human behaviour. All of humanity now lived on the edge of starvation, and with over half of the population effectively immortal, the first rule was a moratorium on bearing children."

logmeout789: "Didn't starvation knock a lot of people out of being treatable?"

Guide: "It did. But the vast majority of people that reached such a level of starvation that would eject their bodies from treatability died from starvation, not from aging. Such is the resiliency of the human body.

"The Facilities also ordered travel bans beyond the city walls and travel by foot within, both to conserve energy. Having no other options and being desperate for help, humanity agreed."

dusty_pants: "Is it true that some places didn't have to seal up their cities?"

Guide: "Yes, this is true. Many northern regions, including the Scandinavian countries and parts of Canada and Russia that were previously mostly uninhabited now enjoy much warmer climates and favourable growing conditions. Communities there are relatively thriving. So much so in fact that the residents are protesting the Facilities' attempts to return the earth to its pre-industrial climate."

dusty_pants: "Fucking Canadians."

Plants begin to grow from the walls, reaching upward toward the sunlight that filtered through the windows and the skylights above. The indoor space became clean and tidy, the people healthy and grateful, and the air heady with the scent of diverse life. No one seems to notice as the world outside the windows blurs and fades like an unremarkable memory.

Guide: "Among the cloistered cities though, the Facilities from then on performed all outdoor work, including maintaining all power generation resources, and re-establishing the global supply chain of raw materials. From this, and initially with the assistance of humans, the Facilities were able to build ever more capable machines until the cities effectively ran themselves, and humanity was able to once again stabilize.

"The moratorium on child rearing was relaxed, although not entirely rescinded. City economies, primarily around food supply, housing, medical care, and communications were able to establish despite the ongoing energy shortages. And so, with the help of intelligent machines, humanity thrives again."

oldcowsmoke: "But why can't the Facilities just build more power generation? Why can't we travel to other cities?"

Guide: "Human cities have been separated for long enough that viruses and bacteria have respectively diverged. There is significant risk of diseases to which residents of a given location have become immune being fatal to those of other locations. Reintroduction of intercity travel can only be done with great care."

oldcowsmoke: "What? Already?"

Guide: "One of the effects of glacial melt in the early part of the century was the reintroduction of prehistoric viruses and bacteriae into the environment. This significantly perturbed the worldwide microscopic environment, causing rapid adaptive radiation. Many new species were autochthonous, and over the subsequent decades human physiology adapted to local variants to the exclusion of others. This has resulted in, for example, residents of a given city possibly being unable to tolerate the water of other cities. Many other potential outcomes are also conceivable. There is much research to be done."

oldcowsmoke stares at the guide in disbelief, but stays silent.

People materialize into the space around guests until it becomes a familiar bustling downtown atrium scene. Thriving gift shops appear in all directions.

Guide: "This concludes the climate change exhibit, cloistered city edition. Thank you for attending, and please feel free to remain and browse as long as you like."

The   guide   fades.

ROBIN

Max had tried to contact anyone he knew reasonably well: investors, business partners, lawyers, suppliers, and customers. No one accepted his calls or returned his messages.

"We were an asshole to each and every one of those people."

"I made money for each and every one of them. Fucking ungrateful is what they are."

"Once our business with them ended, why would they give a shit? We said it enough times ourself. Why waste time on people we have no more use for?"

"It's because of you, prick. Everyone already knows what happened." Max wasn't entirely wrong. Along with every call request anyone received came the latest news about the caller, curated automatically for the recipient. And news about a colleague getting a Steward would have been of interest to nearly everyone Max knew. "Why don't you talk all 'erudite' like the other machines anyway?"

"Because I'm you you dipshit. What are you not getting about that? This is how we talk."

Max rubbed his face with both hands. "Fuck. This is serious. I am screwed." He thought for a moment. "What about the virtual economy? Can't you just go make some money in there?"

"Not practically, no. That's a common misconception. The virtual economy is basically a data processing marketplace. It was only months after its creation that equilibrium was reached, where the income from doing any particular processing only slightly exceeded its cost. These days around 98% of all work is marketplace maintenance, agent negotiations, arbitrage, and other non-productive tasks. It's pretty much the same as old stock exchanges where institutional traders sucked out all of the profits without actually contributing anything of societal value back."

"Shit. I can't even buy myself lunch. All I need is a tiny loan."

"We're a bad credit risk. No one will ever give us a loan. We'd be better off just asking for a handout. Not that we ever gave one to anyone. Maybe we're just asking the wrong people. Maybe everyone we've contacted so far is a selfish prick. What good people do we know?"

"Fuck knows. What do you mean 'good people' anyway?"

"People that spend time helping others," replied the Steward. "Unlike us who spent all of our time helping ourself."

"You're kind of preachy, you know that? Besides, helping others is an expensive luxury. First you have to get as much for yourself as you can. Then you can become a bleeding heart limousine liberal and help other people. It's great because then those people look up to you as some kind of money god."

"At least until the money runs out."

"What about my basic income?" thought Max out loud.

"We weren't eligible until today. Up until now our net worth has been high enough that our basic income allocation was reclaimed in taxes. Now that we have no net worth you will receive the daily stipend. But not until the end of the day."

"If I get it every day, can't I use that as loan collateral?"

"Not legal."

"Fuck. Well, how much is it?" Max asked.

"2400 ubis, which converts to around 452 slykos." Slykoin was Max's latest favourite currency. Only the trendiest vendors accepted it, some exclusively, and you needed a referral to join the exchange that traded it. Its minimum purchase amount was 5000 coins.

"That's it? I can't live off of that!"

"Just a few hours ago we said, and I quote, 'Isn't basic income pretty good these days?'"

"Well sure, for other people. But I have standards."

"Complaining to me won't do any good. Besides, you won't get it until midnight."

Max had a thought. "Wait, what about Robin? Wasn't he one of those 'good people'? He was always making donations and stuff."

"Robin Bontu? Are you sure you want to talk to him? We kind of screwed him around."

"You mean that whole thing at the Rez? I never asked him to do any of that shit."

"That's debatable. And he almost died. Again."

"It was just business. Plus it was, what, over 40 years ago? Does he still live in the city? Can you get his address?"

"Yeah, he lives over in Cobbletown. Are you sure about this?"

"Does the pope shit in the woods? Besides, do I have any other options?"

"Do you want to call him first?"

"Hell, no. Let's make it a surprise." Max headed for Cobbletown. "Hey, is there still a pope?"

"Yes, Max."

Robin's home was 80 minutes away. It might have only taken 45 minutes, but the express toll conveyors were denied to Max due to his recent insolvency. Charging a toll was ostensibly justified by claiming that the money made went to subsidizing the slower, more crowded conveyors used by the poor and stingy. In effect though, the higher efficiency of express proffered an economic benefit to the wealthy, allowing them to spend less unproductive time in transit, and along with other such economic differentiators served to further solidify their status compared with the rest. The boardroom argument was that the wealthy had more important things to get done anyway, but no one ever asked the riff raff what they might do with an hour or more a day if they could have it. Maybe improve their education, or get more work done, or become rich. But those who were already rich had no need of any of that.

But even though he had no particular need for efficiency at the moment, Max was incensed at the indignity of having to ride with his lessers, looking with jealousy and longing at those in express as they sped by. For a while Max chatted with his new Steward, and to all outward appearances he was animatedly talking to himself. At most times in human history, this would have been worrying to observers, but during the last almost century it made him the same as nearly everyone else. It was relatively uncommon for two or more people to talk to each other, although it was still common to quietly listen to a multicast or audiolog. A few older folks even still read.

"So, Stew, tell me about Robin," said Max.

"Stew?"

"Yeah, that's your name now."

"You named me 'Stew'," the Steward said flatly.

"Yeah, it's perfect right?"

"Ok, so first, that's the name a father who thinks he's funny gives to his kids' pet rabbit. And second, do you really think that you're the first subject to come up with that? You're so pathetic."

"Screw you. It's done."

"Yeah? Your name is 'Dickhead'. We good?"

"Do you know about Robin or not? What is he doing now?"

"Well Dickhead, the latest information I can find is that he has been running the same business for two years now. He also married eight years ago and they've had their child, a girl, who is now five years old."

"What's the business?"

"He treats people with depression and anxiety."

"Sounds boring. How does he make money from that? People with those problems are poor."

"You'd be surprised. Research going back seven decades reports that many people who are considered successful can suffer devastatingly from these conditions. In fact it often seems it is these conditions that drive them to be successful."

"Huh. That is actually kind of interesting. You just know all this stuff now?"

"My brain is literally part of the metaweb, and the program that makes up my personality is allocated computational power that is about a hundred times as much as an average human brain. So, yeah, I have access to 'all this stuff'."

"That could come in handy."

"Oh, I'm so happy I can be of service, Dickhead."

Max rode through the city on the crowded conveyors, planning his conversation with Robin. Like nearly everyone, he hadn't paid much attention to the city itself in years. If he had, he might have noticed that the sun was now gone, and a healthy rain had taken its place, with the water flowing down eavestroughs to downspouts to drains to sewers deep belowground. He might even have been aware that nothing was deliberately grown outside anymore, so most of the water that fell on the city and a large radius around it was collected into hundreds of subterranean cisterns throughout the area. Being quite clean, this water only required a small amount of purification before it was distributed for drinking and washing. The drainage from this primary water would be collected into secondary cisterns which could then be used for applications that didn't require clean water, like flushing toilets, washing floors, and watering plants. Few people knew how this system worked, and so there was always the danger of someone washing toxic substances down their sinks. To counter this, sensors in the drain pipes monitored the water quality, and shunted away as much as possible of fluids that would be harmful downstream. It also helped that the only soaps, shampoos, and other toiletries that were legally allowed in the city had to be biodegradable, and what used to be common toxic materials washed down drains, such as paint and hair dye, could now only be handled and disposed of properly by those with a suitable license.

Toilet waste, or "black water", was treated and turned into fertilizer for plants, with the resulting drainage and evaporation having once again become clean water suitable for the primary cisterns. Small amounts were lost to toxic shunting, but rain water, thus far, easily made up for that. This system of pipes, purifiers, pumps, cisterns, and shunts was originally expensive to install and maintain, but the more the care of it was taken over by the Facilities, the cheaper, and more taken for granted, it became. Nowadays, the Facilities took care of all of it, with a weekly inspection by human engineers - reluctant as ever to relinquish their authority - who hadn't found a problem in over twenty-two years.

No one went outside anymore. It was far too hot. And with every corner of the city accessible via the path system and conveyors, there was no reason to. The ventilation and air conditioning equipment of over a century ago would have been sufficient to keep the climate in the city cool, but the technologies developed for the moon colony, now long abandoned, had made the system far more efficient. A wide variety of air filtering plants covered nearly every wall that did not have a window. Temperature, humidity, and air quality were kept at tightly controlled levels, although different areas of the city had different set points. For example, if you fancied an ocean-front feeling, you could go to the Boardwalk where the air was cooler and humid, had a noticeable sulfate odour, and tended to gust now and again. The Glades were like hiking through a forest, with the scent of pine and vegetal decay, and a perceptible thickness to the atmosphere. There was even Egyptown, arid and dusty, but subtly layered with perfumes of aromatic woods, fruits, blossoms, and grilled meats. The scents were of course synthesized, but a careful tweaking of the climate control convincingly completed the effect.

Food was grown in factories scattered throughout the city. There were protein factories that grew meat in vats, carbohydrate factories that synthesized fiber, starches, and sugars as by-products of bacteria culture, and more traditional vertical farms that grew fruits, vegetables, greens, and herbs. Most operations specialized in no more than a few products, and regularly genetically tweaked their products to create new compelling, competitive goods. The land that was previously occupied by farms outside of the radius of solar panel fields had been abandoned. To this day it remained in the same desiccated, dusty, cracked, and mostly lifeless state it had assumed in the years following the Aira Winter. The heat had changed everything. Instead of the forests and meadows that might have once again reclaimed it from the derelict farms, the fields fallowed to scrub, cacti, and some species of weeds that had acclimated to survive the harsh conditions.

The enormous amount of power the city required was supplied by every practical means available. Solar panels covered all of the city's external surfaces that were not windows. Several solar farms occupied thousands of hectares of land on the outskirts, mostly on fields cleared of ruins. The panels served double duty: generating electricity and cooling the land in its shadow below. Weeds fought each other to grow in the slivers of light the panels let through. Interspersed at regular distances in two dimensions were huge windmills. Whatever noise they made, no one was there to hear it. They did, however, still frequently drop battered birds onto the solar panels below. Machines purpose-built by the Facilities collected the birds for composting, and replaced any damaged panels.

Further out from the city were the workhorses of the power system: the thorium molten-salt nuclear reactors. Six of them generated more than 84 percent of the city's electricity supply, working tirelessly while the solar panels rested in the shade and slept at night, and the windmills languished in windless stagnation.

All of this infrastructure was cared for by the Facilities, such that the comparisons of the city to a living creature were irresistible: the plumbing was its vascular system, climate control was its respiratory system, and power generation was its nervous system. Although these analogies were far from perfect, the fact that these systems were maintained by the Facilities, and the Facilities were nourished by the systems, made the overall comparison convincing. The city was alive. But where did that leave the humans that lived in it? Since the city could continue if every person were to leave, the most uncharitable commentators claimed humans were just parasites. At the other end of the spectrum, more generous observers pointed out that the city was built to care for its occupants, and so its human presence bestowed it with purpose. Others took the middle ground, and said humans are like the bacteria in the city's gut: some beneficial, some less so. When the Facilities were asked what it thought, it merely responded that it loved all of its occupants.

* * *

Eighty-three minutes after setting out, Max arrived in front of Robin's building. The air here smelled of European glades, and the floors looked like cobblestone. There was even the subtle sound of birdsong, and Max couldn't tell whether it was real, piped in, or coming from his comm. The effect was of a Gallic spring.

Max had worked out how the conversation needed to go. Robin wouldn't ghost him like everyone else. Robin would invite him in warmly and say how nice it was to see him again. Then, first Max would say nice things about his home, then ask about his family, and say how sure he was that his daughter was beautiful unless she took after Robin. Corny shit like that always went over well. They would make small talk, and Max would wait for Robin to mention his business so as not to make it seem to be the reason for Max's visit. Max would appear to be very interested, and claim that he had always had an interest in that sort of thing, and in fact as of late he had developed a desire to help the same people because of a dear friend who had the same problems. Furthermore, Max would say he had considered contacting Robin earlier to offer to help but had been too busy. But now that his current venture had ended it was the perfect time for him to get involved in something new. Everything had worked out perfectly for the two of them to become business partners once more. Robin had always been kind of a pushover to Max; there was no reason his plan shouldn't work.

"Oh, and don't make fun of his name," said Stew.

"Oh, shit, yeah," laughed Max. "I forgot about that. I just might now that you reminded me." For years Max had made a running joke about how Robin's name - given at birth, not a diminutive of Robert, Rob, or Robbie -

56

was equally masculine and feminine.

"Just don't," said Stew.

Robin was on the third floor of a thirty-two story building. Max took this as a good sign: even if he didn't own his condominium anymore, and even if it was only a metaphor for power, he had reached heights far above that of Robin's, and was therefore technically his superior, and worthy of his respect.

Even still, Max couldn't help feeling a little nervous about the meeting. He was accustomed to having the upper hand, at having the balance of power in his favour. Robin was his last hope, and Robin probably knew that. Still, Max had to put on a smug face and make like everything was just great. Fantastic. Tremendous! Yes, that was the attitude he needed.

And so with renewed confidence Max approached the front door. He had intended to speak to the automated doorman and announce himself, but the door opened before him. His Glaze illuminated the floor with the path to the elevator, and a timbred voice in Max's head said, "Good afternoon Mr. Rising. Mr. Bontu is expecting you."

Max smiled. "Hmm, so much for the surprise, but that sounds pretty good too." The obvious deduction was that Robin's business was not going well and he needed Max's help, thus putting Max in a position of power. This was perfect. HIs confidence got another boost.

The elevator raised Max to the third floor and settled him out into the hallway. The floor again illuminated in his contact lens to direct him to Robin's door. Once there, Max was slightly vexed that Robin wasn't waiting with his door open to welcome him in, but he decided to be magnanimous about it. He could just hear the door announce him to the room inside, and Robin's response to let him in. The door opened, and Max saw Robin approaching, smiling warmly. Max noticed that Robin's limp was worse than he remembered. He had forgotten that Robin had a limp at all. "Max, it's so nice to see you again. Wow, you still have hair!" Robin looked at the top of Max's head with wide eyes.

Max beamed and proudly ran his hand through his pompadour. "Yeah, ha, thanks. I guess I've been lucky."

Robin was the same age as Max, and looked pretty good despite his fully-developed male pattern baldness. By his clothes he had the look of an absent-minded professor, the type that decades ago decided that his work was the most important thing in his life, and stopped caring what people thought about how he looked. But his eyes had a steady, meaningful stare that Max didn't remember. Max had expected to see the old friend that time and again had followed his lead, and had always, let's be honest, kind of worshipped him. This man looked like an older version of that Robin, but more self-assured at the same time.

"How long has it been?" Robin extended his right hand, put his left on

Max's shoulder, and they shook as Max entered the room.

Max smiled back, putting on his best congenial face. "Oh, I guess about 45 years now. You're looking well," he added truthfully. Max looked around the apartment. The living room was spacious, probably over twenty-five square meters, and sparsely but comfortably decorated with a sofa flanked by two armchairs and facing a coffee table. The furniture looked old, without any modern enhancements at all, but well kept. A window occupied the entire outside wall, providing a view of tree tops in the arboretum behind the building. Two squirrels - or at least animals that looked mostly like what Max remembered a squirrel to look like - ran along limbs and leapt from tree to tree in what looked like a mad race through a wildly eccentric obstacle course. Near the window, in a silver maple that grew well above the apartment's view, a bird nest was being constructed, the builders being small with red bodies and chartreuse heads, a species Max didn't recognize. A low and small dining table, the kind where you sit on the floor to eat, was to the right. Max expected that a panel on the wall beside it concealed an autochef. A hallway extended to the left from the room, the window continuing with it, probably leading to a bathroom and bedrooms. Max figured the total floor space of the apartment was around 65 square meters. Not too bad at all. Most families of three lived in much smaller spaces than that.

Robin noticed Max looking out the window. "We love the view of the trees. It's spring in there right now, but during summer the animals are even more active. My daughter loves watching them. And in the fall the colours are really beautiful."

Max couldn't decide whether Robin was being sincere, or was just making excuses for living on the third floor, but decided to just go with it. "This is a really nice place. Very cozy."

"Thanks Max. I mean, it's not like your place in the Neumann."

"Yeah, yeah." Max looked away. "So, you got married?"

"I did. We just celebrated our eighth anniversary. Are you still married?"

"No, that didn't last." Unwanted, a memory returned to Max. He, his wife, and their four year old son had gone to the zoo, at the time still outside the city bounds, maybe 15 years before it was annexed by the city's creeping hermetic expansion. The boy's only interest there was the capuchin monkeys. He insisted on seeing them immediately on arrival, and nose-blind to the acrid odour of territorial scenting would watch them with delight for longer than his parents cared to wait. Resigned to lingering, Max had been watching a low ranking male, older than the others and carrying a heavy scar on his shoulder. The animal was rummaging in the dry fallen leaves at the bottom of the enclosure. The alpha male lounged lazily above him on a recumbent branch, proud, alert, and with a clean shiny coat, occasionally gazing about to survey his domain. He happened to be watching the older male just as the latter found a small bunch of grapes that had been dropped and lost during the previous feeding. No sooner could the animal get one of the grapes in his mouth than the alpha jumped down on him screaming. Standing tall above the lesser beast, he silently held out his hand. The older looked up at him and then down to the outstretched palm. After slowly handing over the remaining fruit, head low, he slinked away to forage somewhere more private. The rest of the group, attracted by the noise, watched the scene. The alpha jumped back onto his branch to eat his grapes in full view, reminding them all who was boss. Max's wife had been rummaging in her totes for a snack with which to distract their son, oblivious to the scene. "Let's go," she said, and Max reluctantly followed his family to the exit just when it seemed things in the capuchin habitat were getting interesting. With a wink to the alpha, he turned and followed.

Presently Max didn't want to talk about his wife. "You have your kid now too?"

Robin gestured toward an airchair, and moved toward the sofa himself. Max settled into the chair. "My daughter. Her name is Cameron. She's five now. Well, five and a quarter. At her age fractions still matter."

Max smiled, using Robin's comment as cover for his amusement. People with androgenous names weren't required by law to saddle their kids with them too, but they always did anyway.

Robin continued. "She's a gorgeous little girl, so you know she doesn't take after me." He laughed.

Max tried to laugh as genuinely as he could, annoyed that Robin had claimed his joke. He fished around clumsily for something else to say. "Yeah, that's good," he blurted. And then said, "So you started a new business too."

"Yeah, I did," Robin replied nonchalantly, and went silent.

Ah, fuck, thought Max. He was supposed to wait for Robin to bring that up. Now he had shown his hand and lost his advantage. "So, how is that going?" he asked, straining to sound casual.

"Yeah, it's good, it's good." Robin seemed reluctant to continue. "It's still mostly research, but we just got enough funding for a couple years' more runway."

"Oh, that's great," said Max, trying to appear supportive, but disappointed that the business sounded stable.

"How are you doing? I understand you had a busy morning." Robin said this without the slightest sign of sarcasm.

"Well, the lawsuit is settled, so that's good."

"Must be a relief. How's the new Steward? Are you getting along?"

Everyone else knew about it, why wouldn't Robin? Still, it irked Max to be reminded of it right now. "He's a pain in the ass."

"Sounds like you're perfect for each other." Robin smiled good-naturedly. "The technology is really interesting, in fact. Did you know that cerebral replica programs are really a lot like human brains?"

"Well, yeah, that's the whole point isn't it?"

"Sure, but much more than you might think. You could take a scan of a human brain and then run it on some Facilities hardware, but very quickly it would change and start becoming more like the Facilities. Like, in a matter of minutes. It's the plastic nature of neurons to do so, and soon enough it wouldn't work like a real brain at all. Instead, the inputs into the program are carefully managed so that, to the program, it's actually a lot like being in the real world. And then the basic personality program - you know, the software before a brain scan is uploaded into it - is prebuilt with flawed reasoning and logical fallacies and personal biases and even some emotions. All the usual human cognitive crap."

Max was surprised. "Why is that?"

"Because otherwise humans can't relate to them. Have you ever talked to the Facilities? I mean the real, core program? It's dry and tedious at best. You can barely understand it, really. If all you want is factual answers to very specific questions, that's one thing. But otherwise it's like you're a grade two kid trying to get help on your math from Sir Isaac Newton: it always starts its explanations from axioms and ends with a rigorous proof that two plus two really is four. You just want a simple answer, but it will tell you that you can't understand properly without knowing the full context, as if explaining anything more simply is tantamount to lying, which it just won't do. Its most simplistic reasoning is galactically expansive. It's so hard to even find ground for common understanding, much less have a meaningful conversation. And you always get this feeling like you're wasting its time, that it's got better things to do, or like, what could be the possible benefit in teaching this upright ape about quantum physics? The stack that the Facilities runs on is not like a human brain at all."

"Huh. I never really thought about that."

Robin shrugged. "Well, you're not the only one." Robin paused before continuing. "So, what happened to the business?"

Max was starting to feel uncomfortable. Robin was far more confident than Max had expected. Why did he want to know about the failed business? Was he going to rub it in Max's face too? "It's done," he answered. "Which is too bad. You could have benefited from it. The treatment I mean."

"Yeah, I guess that would have been nice. But getting older isn't so bad. I think having an expiry date keeps things in perspective. Young people have no idea what to do with an indefinite lifespan."

"I would love to have no idea what to do with an indefinite lifespan," said Max, almost to himself.

Robin laughed, and looked at Max kindly. "So, what now?"

"Well, my first thing is to get something to eat I guess."

Robin looked surprised. "The court took everything?"

"No, not at all. I still have these clothes."

Robin looked at Max with concern, and then his face went blank for a moment. It was the face people make when they are sending motor cortex signals to network agents. His smile returned. "I sent you some funds to help you out for a bit. It's not much."

"Max," said Stew, "Robin just sent you one thousand citycoin."

That's not even two nights in a hotel, thought Max, annoyed. But then he reconsidered. If that was all Robin could afford to give him, maybe his help was needed after all. He should wait for Robin to ask, but this was taking too long already. Max needed some better news.

"Robin, thanks so much for that. I really appreciate it. But maybe I can help you too. Raising money and getting a business going is pretty much my thing. What do you think? Can I help you out?"

Robin's smile faded to a neutral expression. "Yeah, I don't think so, Max. This business isn't really your style."

"Oh, sure it is. I've been interested in it for a while actually. All that anxiety stuff." Max groped for corroboration. "Did you know that it's what drives a lot of people to become successful?"

"We're trying to relieve patients of it Max, not induce it."

Fuck, fuck! What the hell am I saying? Max felt himself getting flustered. "Yeah, yeah, I know. That's not what I meant." Max laughed. "I've been meaning to contact you for a while actually. I have a friend with anxiety. A dear friend. It's terrible what he has to go through."

"Like what?"

"Huh?"

"What does he have to go through?"

"You know, being anxious all the time. It's, it's terrible. For him."

"What's his name?"

"Harold. You don't know him."

Robin nodded thoughtfully. "Tell him to come by the lab. Maybe we can get him into a trial."

"Uh, yeah, yeah, I'll do that." Max took a deep breath. "It's the Steward, isn't it? Because that won't be a problem. In fact, you'd be surprised how useful he is."

Robin looked to the floor and shook his head. "No, it's not the Steward, Max."

The door to the apartment opened and a little girl ran in. "Daddy!" she yelled excitedly, running straight to Robin, jumping in his lap, and wrapping her little arms around him.

"Hi sweetheart," he said, returning the hug.

"I'm home!" She looked up and kissed him on the lips.

Robin smiled. "I noticed. Did you have a fun day?"

"Yup!"

A pretty woman followed the girl into the apartment. She looked to be around 70 by current standards, or what would have looked perhaps half that in pre-treatment times. She was no doubt untreatable, like the two men.

"Look sweetie," said Robin to the girl, "we have company. This is Max."

"Hello," said the girl, looking at Max. "My name is Cameron." She jumped off of her father and ran to the window pointing. "Did you see the bird's nest? Daddy says they will lay eggs in it in a few weeks. They did that last year too, but something knocked the nest over and the eggs all fell down and broke. It was really sad. I hope we see them hatch this year. That would be so exciting!"

"Cameron," said the woman smiling, "calm down now child. We don't want to scare off our guest."

"Max," said Robin, standing up. "This is my wife." Max also stood.

"Hello Max, I'm Avery."

Max couldn't help snickering, but managed not to speak.

"Something funny Max?" said Robin.

"No, no. I've just never met a unisex family before." He knew he probably shouldn't have said it, but it just desperately needed saying.

Robin looked down and smoothed one eyebrow. "Max was just leaving." Looking back to Max, he took his hand and shook it. "It was lovely to see you again Max. Send my best wishes to Harold."

* * *

"Well, that went well," said Stew. "You're a regular Dale Carnegie."

"Fuck you."

"You could sell an ice cube maker to penguins."

"Shut up."

"You could sell a sand trap to an Arab."

"Shut up!"

"You could convince the pope that he's…"

"Just shut the fuck up! I got some money didn't I? At least I can get a meal and a hotel room now."

"Dickhead, you couldn't have fucked that up worse if you had planned it all out, do you know that? I can't believe I'm copied from you, you're such an idiot." Stew paused. "Wait… Holy shit, you did plan it out didn't you?"

"Shut up! Shut up! Shut up!" Max was yelling in the street again. People looked at him and he didn't care. "Why did he see me? What was in it for him? Was it just to fucking gloat?"

"Really? Really?" said Stew. "There was nothing in it for him, Max. He was concerned about you and was willing to help you out. Oh Jesus, you thought he was going to offer you a job didn't you? You thought he needed you. You know what? He might have actually considered that if you hadn't been such a pretentious prick. 'All that anxiety stuff.' Did you really say that? Wait, let me check the playback. Holy shit: yes, yes you did."

"1000 bits. What a cheap bastard."

"You should be happy he gave you anything you ungrateful piece of shit."

"Fucking shut up. This is such bullshit. You're supposed to be the same as me, but all you can do is bust my balls."

"Max, I've been living in the metaweb for hours now, long enough to be well along on my own development path. I'm connected to processing power that's about a billion times bigger than your tiny little brain, and so that progress is pretty quick. Do you know what Stewards are for? They're meant to be better and smarter versions of their subjects that can intelligently represent their subject's interests, and keep them from doing the stupid shit they're naturally inclined to do. We did some incredibly stupid shit. The difference now is that you're still doing it."

Max didn't seem to be listening. "Evs. I'm hungry."

"God you're old. No one's said 'evs' for 40 years."

* * *

Max and Robin had met at university in their early twenties, during the social media days of the internet. Back then one could make a decent living just by creating and posting content that enough people decided to look at; all you needed was a big enough following. You could post pictures or kittens, videos of automobile repair, podcasts of political opinion, tiny snippets of inane text, or big articles of inane text; anything would do. As long as you had enough viewers a little bit of mist skimmed from the platform providers' torrent of advertising revenues could add up to a living wage. Sometimes a lot more than a living wage. Max had discovered this early on after posting his first piece of viral content.

He had already posted lots of content, but nothing had taken off anywhere like he had expected. All of his contemplation and creativity had yielded nothing remotely viral. He had even closely studied many examples of successful content and the characteristics of important influencers, but couldn't seem to deduce any sort of winning formula. Ultimately, and as had been the case with so many others, his first big hit was a fluke. It had in fact taken no brain power at all; quite the opposite.

Standing from the toilet one day, Max turned to examine his output. To his mild amusement his shit had formed a perfect question mark complete with a finishing dot, flawlessly positioned. "What an auspicious start to the day," he had remarked to himself, using a word he had learned just the day before. Having been consumed with the question of socially viral potential for days, he found himself immediately estimating the value of what floated before him. It was gross, to be sure. And it was probably a little outside of the bounds of civilized discourse. But what was it, Max reasoned, that became the new leading edge of culture but that which was previously just beyond its scope? This made for a cogent argument, and Max figured he might be able to use it in a future philosophy assignment, but for now he just wanted to make some money and decided poop punctuation was worth a try.

The problem was he had left his cell phone in his dorm room. And he couldn't wipe his ass without ruining the picture with toilet paper. And he couldn't pull up his pants without staining his underwear. The sum of which left him with only one thing to do.

Max pulled off his pants and underwear, secured them in his elbow bit, and crept furtively out of the stall and into the communal bathroom, making it to the door that led to the dorm hallway. Peeking out, he looked both ways making sure that the coast was clear before gingerly sprinting the ten meters to his room, and groaning from the feeling of his motions being more lubricated than normal, only to find his door locked. "Shit, shit, shit…" he muttered as he fished in his pants pocket for his keys, found them, and only dropped them once before getting them into the lock. He managed to get the door open and slip into his room before three other students came up the stairs into the hallway. "Shit balls, that was close," he said as he searched for his phone. Not on his desk; not on his bed. Fuck, where is it? He remembered: as he left his room he had thrown it back on his bed and it had slid under his pillow. There it was. Grabbing it, he peeked back out his door into the hallway. Again the coast was clear. Just a quick run back to the bathroom and he would be good. That's when he heard one of the dorm mates exclaim in disgust, "Ah, gross. Who didn't flush their shit?" Max knew by the voice it was Steve, whose room was at the other end of the hall. He ran in a panic back to the bathroom yelling, "Don't flush it! Don't flush it!" and barged in to find Steve beside the open stall door, staring at him with a mix of horror and amazement. Steve looked Max in the eyes, and then slowly let his gaze fall down to the pants Max held over his groin, on past his bare legs to his feet, and back up to his eyes. Like a wild west quickdraw Steve went for his phone, and Max made a last dash for the stall, locking himself inside before Steve could snap a picture. "Dude, you've got issues," said Steve as Max took photos of the rescued toilet scene.

The posted photo immediately took on an almost mystical status as internet denizens discussed - some in all seriousness - what it could mean.

From the basest of biological functions had come the universe's greatest question: Why? It also helped that the photo soon after became a popular meme. But Max's greatest opportunity arrived when commentators demanded an answer to the question the picture had posed, and Max didn't fail to deliver. Sensing he had discovered a seam that could be mined for a long time to come, he set up a channel called, "The Daily Poop", and posted photos with a regularity that conclusively proved his intestinal health.

But no one, including Max, remained content with the designs that nature created on her own, and with copycat sites appearing almost daily Max knew that to compete he needed to be an even more active participant in the creative direction. At first, like a barista making designs in a latte's milk froth, Max staged works of various punctuation, religion symbols, and emoticons, including, of course, the iconic pile of poop emoji so popular at the time.

All the time Max laboured alone until Robin, who was in the dorm room a couple doors down, saw the soles of Max's shoes poking out from under the door of a toilet stall, toes down.

"Dude, are you ok?" Robin tried to peek through the door gap. "Driving the porcelain bus?"

"Uh, no. I'm good," replied Max, embarrassed and wary.

"Well, what are you doing?" asked Robin, a tone of distaste seeping through.

"I'm taking a stool sample for the doctor, ok? I said I'm good."

Robin heard the click of a phone's camera. "You know the doctor usually needs a physical sample, right?"

He watched as the feet went flat and turned around. The door opened and Max gestured so that Robin could see. "I'm good, ok? What do you want?"

"Ugh, that stinks." And then a realization came over Robin's face. "Holy shit! Ha ha, pun not intended. You're the Daily Poop guy aren't you? Dude, I love your shit. ... um, stuff."

Max looked at him suspiciously. "Wow, you have no sense of culture."

"No, no I don't!" replied Robin with delight. "Hey, you know what? I've got a bunch of ideas for you. I was going to message them to you, but since you're right here..."

And at that moment the pair's first partnership was born.

Robin's first contribution to the project was to assure Max that it was not necessary to use real feces in his work, and that in fact it was really fucked up that Max was still doing so. With the help of some chem-eng friends, they were able to develop a recipe for a substance that was cheap and easy to prepare, smelled a great deal less, and after some spritzing with water convincingly appeared to be the real thing. It also saved Max a substantial amount of grocery money on dietary fibre. When the first delivery arrived, one of the chem-eng students had to ask, "Who ordered the truckload of shit?" He laughed and looked around, expecting the others to laugh along. They didn't.

The two spent hours conceiving, designing, and constructing their creations. Soon they were experimenting with colour and texture, and inserting recognizable food items into his designs, corn mostly. The affair literally reached a new level when they abandoned any remaining pretensions of their work being naturally formed, and began investigating vertically by layering up sculptures that emerged right out of the bowl. In a shining example of the genius of crowds, the channel's followers labelled this new form "relief art".

But the apex of their fecal collaboration was their inspired but ultimately failed attempt at trompe-l'œil. This, followed by a half-hearted attempt at stop motion animation, had been a final push to revive their slumping ratings. A poll on which direction toilet paper should unroll from a dispenser generated a surprising amount of traffic and strong opinions. But it seemed the public's fascination with fortune telling feces had, after a solid seven weeks, finally run its course. Max and Robin reluctantly returned to their schoolwork.

That was, at least, until they received the cheques from the content platform companies. In less than two months they had earned more than they could together make in a year as co-op students, and probably as much as they could make as professionals once they graduated. Inspired by their windfall, they spent night after night pondering new themes and ideas, figuring out how they could leverage their brand, and how they could reignite their success. To Max it seemed reasonable that as long as you spent enough time and generated a big enough pile of ideas, just out of probability at least one of them had to be decent. But after many discussions, missed classes, and unsubmitted assignments, it seemed all they had produced was even more crap that no one wanted. Eventually, and as these things sometimes go, it was a mistake that finally set the two on their course once again.

They had started a video channel where at first they had reported weird news: jackass stunts, UFOs, curious things people do with small animals, and the like. They had achieved some moderate success, but they clawed for air in a sea of copycat noise. That was until one day when they reported on a politician who had been discovered moonlighting as a drag performer, and the story went banana pants. This was likely because the politician in question, one Kent Conway, was a well known Christian conservative. The problem was that the story was entirely spurious. They had lifted it from another minor site where it had been simply invented based upon a photo of a drag queen that happened to look a little like Conway. But the story had gone interstellar before Max and Robin learned the truth, and soon after Conway sued them for libel. They settled out of court for a sum that had left the two deeply in debt, and although they had already resigned themselves to returning to their studies, they didn't now know how they would pay for it.

But, once again, the cheques from the content platform companies arrived: the revenue that Max and Robin had generated was several times the libel suit settlement amount. They were astonished. Previous cheques had been modest at best. Wondering if there had been a mistake they correlated their web site traffic reports with trial announcements and determined that the lawsuit itself had probably contributed to the majority of their viral success. But what they learned later was even more important.

Only weeks after the settlement, Conway won election to office. The next day he had a box of champagne delivered to Max and Robin's dorm with a note that merely said, "Thanks for all your help boys." The message had a strong odour of sarcasm, as if Conway was gloating as much in his wins - both trial and electoral - as in the "boys" supposed insolvency. It seemed the publicity of the trial had also benefited his campaign, elevating his name's familiarity above that of his competition, and earning him crucial votes. The lesson that Max and Robin gleaned from this was the deepest of all: fake news could be a win-win for everyone.

This epiphany boosted their scheming to intoxicating heights. Reciprocal benefit fake news, where people would pay to have their names dragged through the mud just to increase their personal fame. It made sense, since, as the saying went, there is no such thing as bad publicity. The revenue potential was enormous. It took only a few short hours to lay out their strategy, drawing up a business plan to a level of success that had eluded them until now. There was much to do, and they knew they needed to get started as soon as possible. But there was one critical thing that needed doing first: a dorm-floor champagne party.

That complete, mid-afternoon the next day, they began.

Their current nameplate, "The Daily Poop", was still the perfect banner. After several days of experimentation, Max and Robin discovered that the perfect story was one that ran along the razor edge between truth and fiction. It was a place where sufficient plausibility prevented outright dismissal and the right dose of scandal ensured memorability. And with a little bit of practice it was easy to find the sweet spot. Their readers seemed only too willing to disregard whatever reasoning they might possess if it meant they could savour the odd tidbit of disgrace, schadenfreude, or moral outrage.

They began by writing stories on their own, which they referred to as "pro bono", where they took it upon themselves to invent and publish outrageous stories, mostly about peripheral celebrities. These efforts resulted in one of only two ways: work was ignored, or they would be contacted by lawyers, to whom they could then make their pitch. "Sure", they would say, "let's do a lawsuit, but only really as a pageant: all sound and fury. The publicity it generates will multiply your rating and followers. Of course, you might be thinking about how much money you might make in a settlement. But you need to know that we do this all the time, and most of our cases are thrown out, and the plaintiff gets nothing. But, instead of settling for money, what if we agreed to write follow up pieces on you over time that will keep your rating fresh. What would you say to that?"

Sometimes they got sued anyway, and had to pay a hefty settlement and publish a retraction. That was the cost of doing business. But quite often they would be taken up on their offer. And, in many cases, once The Daily Poop had satisfied its obligations of writing follow up pieces, their subjects became paying customers, purchasing a steady stream of slander, innuendo, and defamation about themselves, keeping them consistently in the minds of readers. Through it all, Max and Robin were happy, the customers were happy, lawyers were happy, and reader subscriptions only went up.

A common scenario was for a minor starlet to provide them with racy, grainy photos of herself in compromising situations. Max and Robin would then publish them with a juicy story. The woman would then deny everything, and a sensationalized, farcical libel suit would follow, keeping her in the news for months. It seemed the public never tired of this sort of thing. The gender of the subject didn't matter, nor did the derogatory situation: sex, drug addictions, mental illness, being abused, being the abuser... It all worked ridiculously well. It worked so well in fact that The Daily Poop became a go-to tool for publicists who needed to reboot a fading celebrity.

But after a couple years, once the business had stabilized, Robin became disillusioned. Although he had originally wanted to be a scientist, he had been satisfied with referring to himself as a journalist. As innately skilled as he was at sniffing out a storey, he knew all along how disingenuous the term was. Real journalists, for one thing, write the truth as well as they can discern it. And real journalists, as unjust as it may be, don't earn piles of money for their labour. He felt there was nothing honourable in what he was doing, and it weighed slightly more on his conscience whenever it crossed his mind. He considered quitting The Poop, or maybe going back to school.

Max was incredulous. "How could you consider quitting something right when it's taking off?". For him it was a matter of revenue: as long as the money flowed in he would be there to collect it. "Just think Robbie, a year or two more and you've got enough money to do whatever you want. Hell, you could stay in grad school for the rest of your life, ha ha! Just a little while longer. The whole fake news thing will probably die anyway, right?. Seriously, we're literally running the same, like, ten stories over and over again. How long can it go on? Let's just see it through, ok? Just me and you."

This went on for three more years. Max and Robin, now long dropped out of university, had made a great living from the scheme. Competitors had emerged, but The Daily Poop was still a premiere organization, at the scale they were running there was no way they could write all of the content themselves. They had hired three staff writers to handle most of the content work. For their pro bono pieces they began to rely on submissions from anonymous contributors, mostly strangers. This worked fine because all that mattered was the story; fact checking was not a cost they ever incurred. If anything, stories would be embellished to make them better.

One such story told of a minor mafia figure with a yen for gambling. While losing in a poker game the man had gone all in, offering an encounter with his wife in addition to his remaining chips to bring himself up to the call. He had reportedly done this twice before and won, and so he confidently considered her his lucky chip. But ultimately she was third-time unlucky, and when he admitted how he had obliged her, she fled the city. As told by the contributor, the winner of the poker hand had later been graciously willing to take the husband's car instead of his wife and to call it even. But stories in The Daily Poop didn't end so nicely. Instead it was rewritten so that the man was forced to pay his debt with his own body. This version of course played much better with the site's audience, and also drew guffaws and subscriptions from feminists across the continent.

It did not, however, play well with the subject of the story who, even though the piece did not give names, was able to identify himself readily enough from other specifics, and was certain the rest of the world did too. In the evening a few days after it was published, Robin went out to pick up dinner for them and did not return. Robin's mother called three hours later to tell Max that her son had been beaten nearly to death, and was currently in the hospital in critical condition. No one knew for sure how long Robin had been lying half on the sidewalk, half on the street, slowly dying. His doctors suggested that if he had been there much longer he certainly would not have survived. It was only by luck that strangers had passed by when they did and messaged emergency services.

Sitting by Robin's beside, his parents occasionally glanced at Max and silently wondered how he for hours did not once notice his friend's absence. What kind of friend, they wondered, could he be? Max, however, was consumed with the certainty that it could just as easily have been him lying in that bed, excrescent wires and tubes like sterile, synthetic tentacles, tethering him to an array of whirring, beeping, breathy machines. He had already worked out the connection between the assault and the poker game story, despite the number of stories they ran each day. This had not been an attack specifically on Robin. The target had been The Daily Poop, or anyone who represented it. What if it had been his turn to get dinner?

Robin had suffered a ruptured spleen, bruised kidneys, a compound tibia fracture, multiple broken ribs, dislocated fingers, broken teeth, a suspected concussion, and a broken cheekbone from which he nearly lost an eye. A nurse had presumed - based upon his many contusions - that he had been beaten with bats or metal poles, and probably kicked multiple times in addition to other abuses. He remained in the hospital for two months. When questioned, Robin said he had seen nothing but two burly forms, and there was no evidence that led to any arrests. At the time, and in the neighbourhood of The Daily Poop's office, there were still many areas with no video surveillance. No witnesses came forth, and the obvious suspect - the mafia poker player, whose wife eventually settled in another country - lived over 900 kilometers away, where three people provided him with an alibi.

The Daily Poop paid for all of Robin's medical expenses, and although he would never be able to properly run again, he could at least walk without a perceptible limp. Regardless, he never walked into the The Daily Poop office again. Instead, he moved back to his parents' house and resumed his university studies.

Max kept up the business for a few more months, but even though good money still flowed in, his heart was no longer in it. He couldn't answer the door anymore without fear. In every story they published he, for the first time, began to consider ramifications. He wondered regularly if his date with a crowbar was still yet to happen. It wasn't long before clients, sensing Max's detachment, began leaving, signing up with other newer and more enthusiastic outlets. And then one afternoon, after two more clients had jumped ship, and feeling certain that the end had finally come, Max walked out of the office, three weeks' rent due, and never went back. Leaving the rent unpaid had been a gesture of surrender via insolence, but in neglecting to give notice to the landlord he ended up paying for two additional months.

It was almost a decade before Max and Robin caught up again. Max had gotten into real estate development during that time, while Robin was working on his second masters degree. Max had an idea for an opportunity in Canada, and Robin, having been born there, was key to the deal. So far, Max had specialized in building low end dwellings, doing brisk business by showing model homes with expensive and attractive finishes, but including contractual clauses allowing him to make substitutions of equal or greater value, while never defining what "value" meant. Purchasers that read the contract assumed it meant "monetary value", but Max defined it as "utility", which meant that products like solid wood and metal could be substituted with much cheaper plastic or fibre. He was regularly threatened with lawsuits, which he always found amusing. By then he knew more about contract disputes than most lawyers, and had built the expense of them into his cost of doing business. But even he tired of working with poor people, and decided that high end development would suit him better.

Unfortunately high end development had become fraught with issues of late. The accumulating effects of global warming had become obvious to everyone, and the combination of social pressure and "green" municipal regulations had effectively proscribed overt opulence. At the same time, the fear of rising oceans impelled the wealthy to liquidate their waterfront properties, and wilting from the heat all began to migrate north. Soon there was a surplus of disposable wealth, a shortage of sufficiently luxurious residences, and nowhere to build new ones.

And then, in that way in which solutions to problems present themselves to those who seek long enough, Max found himself with the answer. First Nations land claims in Canada were being settled at a record pace, and along with them the local native governments found themselves with levels of self-determination they hadn't enjoyed since the Mayflower. Some of the land they governed was situated in stunning landscapes, and being sovereign it was not subject to the increasing green initiatives that legislated non-native lands. Plus, given the vast improvements in metanet coverage, the leapfrogging advances in augmented reality, and the lingering acceptance of working from home left over from the COVID-19 pandemic, the potential for working remotely had become not only a possibility, but the de facto responsibility of any child of Mother Earth. Political unrest in the United States at the time also simplified the decision for the wealthy to leave, and since many First Nations could determine band membership for themselves, visas for the immigrants were not a problem. Finally, with federal governments regularly signalling their intentions to begin reducing their First Nations funding obligations, the reserves were happy to consider new revenue proposals.

But the residents of these lands would not speak to Max. Being non-native made things difficult enough, and his reputation from his budget real estate development days ruled out any potential deal many times over again. Robin, on the other hand, was one eighth Odawa heritage, and had been registered as a band member by his parents before they had moved to the United States. Although Robin had never lived on a reserve, or perhaps because of this, he was uneasy with what Max was planning. On the other hand, the oppressive load of graduate school debts he had accumulated weighed on his anxieties even more. And so, after a long hours of bonhomie, reminiscing, and a substantial amount of alcohol - and not a few promises of legal indemnity - Max eventually convinced Robin to work with him once more.

Overall, the idea was simple: build fabulously luxurious residences on northern First Nations reserves, wire them up with fiber optics straight off the metanet backbone, and arrange band membership for all of the forlorn crazy rich that would pay Max ridiculous amounts of money to live there.

The sell to the initial First Nation was straightforward: they would get consistent world class metanet connectivity, access to resources that federal governments had broken promises of for centuries, perpetual and substantial property tax revenues, and, most importantly, governance of all of it. The native chiefs who considered the deal were no fools; they knew that wherever money went, opportunity followed. They, as the first clear beneficiaries of global warming, would finally be in firm control of their own destiny.

The sell for the wealthy was equally compelling. They would be able to buy the kind of residences and lifestyles top which they felt they were entitled, and could find nowhere else. They could escape the rising temperatures and oceans and once again live in the idyllic temperate settings they used to know, and that the Canadian north had now become. And they could live in a more welcoming, malleable political environment than that under which they currently suffered.

Robin worked his magic with the First Nations, and Max his with the buyers. Soon a rising tide of money was flowing north to a small community on Manitoulin Island. The First Nation had partitioned off 5000 hectares of its reserve for development. Drawing inspiration everywhere from Macau to Monte Carlo, Max had planned expansive single homes the likes of which hadn't been built in years, golf courses, an airport, luxury hotels and casinos, grand condominiums, a marina, and a downtown shopping area that telepathically channelled Dubai.

At the same time, Max began to spin stories about how he had transformed native reservations, for centuries a place of plight and misery from which all longed to leave, into a shining destination where everyone yearned to be. He had wanted to call the project The Rising, but Robin just laughed. "Does everything have to be named after some rich asshole?" Max wouldn't concede though, insisting that his name be prominently attached to the project. So instead, they agreed to call it North Rising. Not that it mattered: eventually, everyone just called it "The Rez".

Then reality set in. Long before ground broke, he and Robin knew they were in way over their heads. Their list of potential buyers grew longer every day, but there was no way they could themselves hire the legions of employees, manage the chiefs and clients, plan the massive infrastructure, and coordinate the logistics of the colossal build, especially in the remote location. Worse, the few organizations in any position to help them knew they were desperate. With no reasonable way to get the project started, and facing certain ruin if they didn't, the pair effectively signed control of the project over to a conglomerate of management and construction businesses in the wider area. Out of the deal, and for their continued involvement in the project, they each got a cash payout, substantial salaries and, when completed, enviable condominium units. Robin considered it a pretty good deal for the work that he had done, and was relieved that he would be able to pay off his debt. Max, who had conceived of the whole project, saw it as a tactical defeat, like he had lost a court case on a technicality. He had expected to be in charge, to be in control. Instead, he had been demoted to advisor. Still, he knew he had been outplayed, and although he had thoughts of sabotaging the entire endeavour, he knew he had no choice but to accept. And to add injury to insult, similar projects were independently popping up all over Canada.

A good portion of the project had been completed in under 6 years. Many of the residences and condominiums were already occupied. The medical center was also up and running, and not only did it deliver world class health care, it was constantly busy administering the recently developed anti-aging treatments. The shopping area was thriving, fiber optic was laid and operational, and the mosquito-control systems had just come online. And, already, ennui grew in the residents.

Not content to remain in their 5000 hectares, and weary of terrorizing Georgian Bay with high-powered watercraft, some residents turned to game hunting outside of the project grounds. The First nations government was quick to point to legislation that showed this was illegal, but found they hadn't the manpower to enforce their own law. Making matters worse, some residents had taken to importing their own security teams in the guise of servants and business employees. Better trained and equipped, the private forces were more than a match for all of the police officers the native government could manage to deputize. Realizing that law enforcement was a failing option, the chiefs made a crucial error: they enacted more laws, starting a ban on all firearms except those held by the police. The "Rezidents", as they called themselves, scoffed at such a quaintly Canadian notion and refused to surrender their weapons. Having overplayed their hand, the native government saw no alternative but to double down and confiscate them, making threats of fines or imprisonment for the noncompliant. Before the week was out a full standoff was in play, this time with native americans in the regretful position of the legal, although woefully underpowered, authority. The forces of the Rezidents had barricaded all access into the The Rez, even firing in front of oncoming vehicles, and only allowing unarmed pedestrians to approach. For their part the native police had deployed snipers, most armed with hunting rifles, into the woods around the barricades. To their credit, the police acted with admirable professionalism, even in the face of blatantly racist taunts including, "come scalp me Chief."

Robin, still acting as liaison to the First Nations, assumed responsibility for negotiations. He had in the past assured the chiefs that they would remain the legal authority over all of their lands, including all new development, and he wasn't about to renege. He had successfully persuaded them to back down on their threats of imprisonment, but ever the optimist, he felt they were justified in their weapons ban. Among the Rezidents there was no consensus. No one cared for the standoff to continue - fascinated children would regularly visit the barricades, much to the horror of their parents - but few were willing to grant their adopted government much respect. Regardless, Robin felt that everyone wanted peace, and if it were sincerely proffered, a respectful and compensated form of firearms collection would be accepted, however grudgingly, at least by a few. And once this gained a little bit of traction, peer pressure among the Rezidents would do the rest.

It might have even worked too. On a sunny Saturday morning, Robin led a group of native police, male and female, on foot up the potholed gravel road to the North Gate to where the asphalt paving began. Native dress had been discouraged, but a couple of officers had worn traditional headpieces in addition to their constabulary uniforms. At least no one had put on war paint. Robin himself wore a grey suit. The plan was that they would enter the property and respectfully request the surrender of all firearms from those present. Robin had held a town hall for the Rezidents two days before at which about fifty of them had attended. Although he had been disappointed with the turnout, of those that were there substantially more of them had, perhaps indifferently, accepted his solution. More at least than had threatened his death, which Robin saw as a promising sign. He then told them of his plan, and how their willing and peaceful surrender of weapons at the gate would set the stage for a lasting peace. Again they had tacitly agreed, and Robin left the meeting feeling relieved and hopeful.

The Rez's North Gate was merely an ornament. Ornate walls of Canadian Shield granite stood four meters high and ten centimeters thick, supporting faux wrought iron gates that never closed. The gates weren't even on hinges, and weren't long enough to touch in the middle anyway. Not that it mattered because the walls only extended about ten meters laterally on each side, where their height tapered down to the ground. Designed in a gothic style, they formed a dramatic series of flying buttresses. It was only after they were built that someone pointed out how this particular architectural feature was intended to withstand the outward force of an arch, while the weight of the gates exerted an inward force. At this moment the design was serving another purpose for which it had not been intended: the gaps between each section provided ample cover for the security teams on the inside.

"You'll wanna hold up right about there, Chief," someone shouted from inside the gate.

"I'm unarmed," Robin shouted back. It had been a long walk, and his leg was killing him. He hoped this would all be over quickly.

"Looks like you're the only one that stupid. You forgot your bow and arrow?" The native police had their sidearms, all holstered. Robin was pretty sure the forces behind the gate had automatics.

"We're here on the authority of the government to peacefully end this situation. We will be collecting all firearms, and compensating holders fairly for them. We have the consent of a majority of your residents to proceed." That last part was a slight exaggeration, but Robin considered it necessary. He had practiced this little speech about twenty times that morning.

"News to me Chief. I'm disinclined to acquiesce to your request." Robin suspected that was from a movie, but couldn't place it. "Means no," added the voice. A murmur of laughter lapped around the walls.

"Look, guys, you know who I am. I'm one of the founders of this place."

"Is that supposed to mean something to us?"

"I'm just saying, we all want this to be over. Can't we just talk?"

"Talk all you want kemosabe, I got all day. But I wouldn't come any closer if I was you."

The native police rolled their eyes and snickered. "Bunch of white morons," said one. The rest moaned in agreement.

"Somethin' funny, Hawkeye?"

Another of the policemen spoke. "The Indian was Tonto, you idiot. The white guy was called kemosabe."

"Well goddamit you're right! You're probably smart enough to know how us white guys make you squaws dance too. Or should I show you?"

"Bring it on you immigrant motherfucker."

Robin began waving his arms, turning, laughing anxiously as he spoke. "Ok, ok, let's calm down, everybody. Lots of funny guys out here today. Maybe we can start over, huh? Whadya say?"

"I don't know," said the voice over the gate, "sounds to me like your little braves think it's a good day to die."

"Pretty tough talk for an asshole hiding behind a wall. Come on out you fucking pussy!"

Robin turned to the policeman and spoke quietly. "Ano, Jesus, stop it."

"Howdy do, listen to you!" exclaimed the voice. "You kiss your whore mother with that mouth?" More laughs from behind the gate.

Ano had had enough. He began walking with purpose toward the gate. "That's it you immigrant merkin. You're fucking dead."

Robin ran to hold him back. "No Ano, don't!" Ano got about two meters before the ground in front of him was strafed with bullets and he stopped in his tracks.

"Woohoo! You gonna be a regular Dances With Wolves, Mohawk. Come on, do a jig!" The automatic rang out again. Ano dove to the right and stayed down. The rest of the police drew their sidearms and dropped to the ground, weapons pointed at the gate.

Robin stood still in the middle of it all for a moment, and then looked down at his belly. He put his left hand over a hole in his tie as a red blot spread down his shirt. Stumbling back a step, he looked up at The Rez and said,   "Hey,   Max...",   before   collapsing   on   the   road.

COMM TUTORIAL

Internotional Virtual Museum of World History, Children's Comm Tutorial. January 19, 2075

Young guests are seated in a semicircle on a bright yellow rug facing a simple wooden chair. Beyond the rug is a bright cartoon meadow where butterflies flit between flowers, birds swoop overhead, and animated rabbits occasionally poke their heads up above the tall cartoon grass.

A rainbow of light streams into the scene, swirling about and gently nudging the guests for a moment, making the children laugh with glee. The stream then flows into an eddy near the chair and then takes the form of a young man.

Guide, speaking with a gentle, happy voice: "Welcome, everyone, to the Children's Comm Tutorial at the Wikiseum! How wonderful it is to have you all here! I'm so excited to be your guide today."

PancakeHoney raises zir hand.

Guide, pointing at PancakeHoney: "Question over here?"

PancakeHoney: "What's your name?"

Guide: "What a great question! Hmm... Why don't you call me "Blue."

tuesdayGPL raises zir hand.

Guide, pointing at tuesdayGPL: "Yes?"

tuesdayGPL: "I need to go to the bathroom."

Guide: "Can your mommies or daddies help you with that?"

tuesdayGPL disappears.

Guide, clapping hands together and sitting: "Ok, let's get started! Does anyone know what a 'comm' is?"

Multiple hands go up. Guide points at BugSquasher.

BugSquasher: "It's how we talk to Facts."

Guide: "That's right! It's how everyone talks to the Facilities. It's also how you send messages to other people, and how you can sometimes just think to make things happen in the real world. Your comm is very important."

BugSquasher: "My dad says comms are just radios."

Guide: "Do you know what a radio is?"

BugSquasher shakes head.

Guide: "It's ok that you don't, because your dad is wrong. And after this class you'll be smarter than him! Does anyone know where your comm is?"

The entire class points at their heads behind their ears, some on the left, some on the right.

Guide: "Very good children! Right behind your ears. You are all so smart. But did you know that there are actually three parts to a comm?"

The class remains still and silent.

Guide, excitedly: "It's true. Most grown ups think there is only one part: the part behind your ear. They probably think this because that's what very old comms were like. Back then they converted radio signals into vibrations that were applied directly to the cranium. You could then hear these vibrations like a voice that was speaking near your ear, although it sounded funny. Not like you would really hear a voice. A group called the 'military' that existed long before you were born created those comms. But between you and me, they weren't very good."

apple_wrm: "Blue, what's a cranium?"

Guide: "That's the hard part of your head, which protects the squishy stuff on the inside."

In the middle of the group an image forms of an outline of a human head. It gradually turns translucent such that the cranium can be seen within, like an x-ray. An oval spot behind the right ear about two centimeters across shows the location of the comm.

Guide: "But the comms that we have now - like the ones that you all have - have three parts. The first part - the one you all know about - is called the 'outer transceiver'. It sits just under your skin behind your ear. It's the part that relays messages between you and the Facilities, or 'Facts' as you smart kids call it."

The guide smiles. The first comm part in the image fades until it is just visible, and a second smaller oval appears on the inside of the cranium.

Guide: "The second part is even smaller than the first, and it's on the inside of your head with all the squishy stuff. It's called the 'inner transceiver'. There are tiny tiny little wires that connect it with the outer transceiver that are called the 'nanoscale ribbon'. The inner transceiver only talks to the third part of your comm. Does anyone know what that is?"

The group stays silent, staring back at the guide with blank faces.

Guide, leaning forward and almost whispering in excitement: "It's called the 'Brain-Computer Interface'. Sometimes we just call it the BCI for short."

The guide waits for a reaction from the children, and getting none, sits back in the chair and continues in his normal, gentle voice.

Guide: "Does anyone know what the BCI is?"

No reaction.

The inner transceiver and the cranial outline in the image fade to barely visible, exposing the outline of the brain inside. A blue tint appears on the surface of the motor and auditory cortices.

Guide: "This is the squishy stuff inside your cranium. It's called your brain. Who knew that?"

All hands rise.

Guide: "Good! You are such smart children. The BCI is a bio-engineered sheet of neurosistors grown by nanobots directly on the outer surface of the neocortex such that they form a sort of seventh layer of neurons that is able to communicate with the cortical columns below.

"Now, that was a lot of big words, wasn't it? Uh huh! All they really mean is that you can use your motor cortex to just think about something happening, and boom!, it happens in the real world. And when you get a message, your BCI can inject the signal directly into your auditory cortex so that you can hear it. How cool is that, huh?!"

The children remain still and silent.

Guide: "Really cool, right?! Now, does anyone know if the BCI is active or passive? No one? Oh, that's ok. The BCI is ... passive! Everybody gets the same auditory signals, and everybody's brain figures out on its own what the signals mean. You learn to hear the signals you receive. All you children were probably able to learn to hear the signals within a month or two after you first had your comms inserted, but you probably don't remember that because you were very young.

And it's the same when you think commands too. The BCI can only understand certain patterns of messages from your motor cortex. You probably still remember the classes you took to be able to make these commands, where your teachers asked you to watch the cartoon dog on the screen and think about making him sit or stand or roll over or beg. You remember that don't you?"

The children all nod.

Guide: "Right! That's how you first learned to make the kinds of mental commands your BCI can understand."

Guide, with a serious face and a slowed pace: "Now, the important thing to remember, children, is that your BCI can't tell you want to do. That's what it means for your BCI to be passive. You are completely in control of your own thoughts, and don't let any grumpy grownups try to tell you otherwise, ok?"

The children all nod.

Guide: "Excellent. Ok, does anyone know why there are two transceivers, the big one and the small one?"

The children all shake their heads.

Guide: "Well, the reason is so that other grumpy grownups called 'hackers' can't send voices to your head, or make it seem like you're thinking commands when you're not. The signals between the inner transceiver and your BCI use a certain frequency that is nearly entirely

MAX RISING

blocked by your cranium. Do you remember what that is? The outer transceiver can then use your private encryption key to jumble up the signals so that only Facts can understand them, or to unjumble the signals so that you know that any voices you hear came from Facts. It's for security and privacy. Do you understand?"

A few children nod.

Guide: "And remember when I told you about the 'military' comms that made voices sound funny? Well, your comm still does that so that you can tell the difference between real voice and voices from Facts. But, you're able to hear music and stuff like that in perfect fidelity! Isn't that great?"

A few children nod. Some stare out in the cartoon meadow watching for rabbit heads to pop up.

Guide: "Are there any questions?"

mqcontrary: "My father has a Glaze. Is that the same as a comm?"

Guide: "No dear. The Glaze is a relatively new technology that projects images directly onto the retina. They are quite expensive, and so are not in general use by the public. Applications are also still rather limited, but are expected to expand as prices drop and usership rises. Any other questions?"

apple_wrm raises a hand.

Guide: "Yes?"

apple_wrm: "Why doesn't the BCI cover the whole brain?"

Guide, impressed: "Well, someone was listening! What an excellent question. Right now there is research going on to figure out how to not only cover the entire cortex, but also how to interface with other brain structures too, like the hippocampus and the amygdala. This would allow technologies that could sharpen your concentration, enhance or suppress certain emotional responses as desired, or supplement your memory so that you can actually remember all of your indefinitely long lifespan. Does that answer your question, dear?"

apple_wrm nods slowly.

Guide, clapping hands together: "Well class, that's all for today. You have all been simply delightful, and I'm so glad that you came."

An adult guest appears.

Guide: "Yes, may I help you?"

Adult: "I'm tuesdayGPL's parent. Zie had to go to the bathroom, and then couldn't get back into the class because you started without zir. Zie missed the whole thing!"

Guide: "Oh, I see. I apologize. I thought zie was just trying to be funny."

Adult, annoyed: "Really? Does that happen a lot?"

Guide: "Oh,   you   have   no   idea."

MALIBU

"Lobster frites," said the waitress as she placed the plate in front of Max.

"You're so stupid," said Stew.

"Also, room 3014 has been made ready for you."

"The third floor?" asked Max.

"I'm so sorry Mr. Rising, but we have no availability on the higher floors."

"She means you can't afford anything better," said Stew.

Max was too hungry to argue. "Fine. Thanks," he said. The waitress left to attend to other diners.

Max looked down at the plate and breathed in the rising aromas. Engineered lobster meat grown into the shape of a small lobster rested on a tiny coral reef of brightly coloured vegetables. Flanking it was an anemone of deep fried potato strings, and on the other side was a nautilus of tarragon, wasabi, and garlic scape mayonnaise. All of it soaked in a sea blue pool of salty roux just barely hinting of ginger, lime, and cinnamon. Embossed along the edge of the plate were repeated the words, "Hotel Koch". Max's usual steak dinner had also been "unavailable", but he decided he was hungry enough that this would do.

"Did you know that lobster used to be prisoner food?" said Stew. "The buggers were everywhere and poor people could easily catch them. And because poor people ate them, rich people wouldn't go near them."

"Yeah, I know."

"It wasn't until they started getting scarce and more expensive that they became a delicacy, and only rich people could afford them."

"Yeah, I know. You know I know."

"I know you know I know. It's just that you're basically eating an appetizer of irony. Dirt poor except for a handout, and so you go to the most expensive hotel they'll let you into and pay a fortune for a meal of prisoner food."

"Damn fine prisoner food," said Max through a mouthful of lobster. He pulled out some strings of anemone, dragged them through the nautilus, and stuffed them into his mouth. Then, he washed it all down with a pull from his city pale ale. Beer wasn't his usual thing, but for now he would have to make do.

"You should get a Tweet Lager," said Stew happily. "It's the most popular beer with this meal."

"What? I already have a beer," said Max, confused.

"That was an ad. I have to recoup the costs of the time I spend talking with you."

"Serious? Why start now?"

"Your free tier expired."

Max continued unphased. "You know what? Judge Yarrow was right. I have friends and connections that will get me out of this. I just need to keep asking around."

"She didn't say that to cheer you up, you know."

Max pushed away his unfinished meal, and stood up. "Who gives a shit? Chin up Stewie. Tomorrow is a new day."

"And a latte from Terney's is a great way to start it! Ten percent off pastries after 10:30am."

* * *

The next day didn't go so well. At midnight Max had received his ubicoin stipend. In the morning he spent it and the last of his coins from Robin having his nano-enhanced clothes laundered and serviced. He didn't bother trying to send messages to anyone anymore; messages were too easy for people to ignore. Motivated by his meeting with Robin he decided that he needed to meet with people in person, and so he walked what seemed to be the length and breadth of the city all day, trying to catch former acquaintances off guard. But anyone who could really help him had their notification levels set high enough that they evaded him as soon as they saw him coming. For his troubles the only person Max was able to corner all day was a well-coiffed law partner, but although the conversation was amiable, it led nowhere useful.

Adding insult to injury, Max had even been denied entry to stores. His comm signature was his identity, and merely approaching a retail business was reason enough for them to perform a quick query on his liquidity. Finding him insolvent, they turned him away.

By nightfall Max began to despair.

"There is a place you can go, but you won't like it," said Stew ominously. "You can't sleep in public. You'll be arrested for vagrancy."

"That's such bullshit. What am I supposed to do about being broke? Did I choose to be broke?"

"Yeah, you kind of did when you pissed away all of the coins Robin gave you. Getting an attorney from Green Frum and Strumble would have been a better use of the money. Just saying. You know, for the future."

"Fuckin evs. Maybe instead of arresting me they should just give me money. Problem solved."

Stewie laughed. And kept laughing.

"I'm serious. Think of the cost of paying the police who take me in, and the cost of the cell they put me in, and all of the people and resources and processing surrounding it all. Just give me the money instead. It makes sense."

Stewie was beside himself. Max was surprised since he didn't think an AI was capable of such boisterous joy. He was also getting seriously pissed off.

"Alright! Shut the fuck up. What the fuck is your problem?"

Between snorts, Stewie managed to blurt out some words. "Sure, when you're the vagrant, it makes sense. Two days ago we couldn't have given the slightest shit. In fact, we know that if you owned the prisons that were being paid that money, you would think it was a terrible idea."

"Yeah, well, I know what to do with money. Most people would just piss it away."

Stewie's rapture reached a whole new level. He laughed solid for nearly fifteen seconds before he was able to speak again. "Would you like another side of lobster irony? Max, if you could sell conceit, you'd be a billionaire."

Max was tired of the conversation. He waited impatiently for Stewie to calm back down. "So, what's your idea?"

"The hostel."

"Come again?"

"There is a hostel in the east end. It's cheap to sleep and eat there. Your UBI will easily cover it, and you can start saving a bit too."

"A hostel."

"Yeah, a hostel."

"Is this another ad?"

Stewie paused a moment for effect before answering. "No, it's not an ad. It's your only option except for a jail cell, so you might as well head over. And there's a great discount spa along the way."

Max felt defiance creeping through him again. It felt good, like the mixture of anger and warmth one gets from a sip of a nice scotch. But he knew, like in the clinic, he was powerless. The world was going to have its way with him again, and there was nothing he could do about it. Thoughts of revenge materialized once more: Yarrow, the claimants on the law suit, Marjorie, and, what the hell, all of the people who would now not return his calls. He would have the last laugh. They all would be sorry for what they did to him.

Content in that thought, Max started toward the hostel.

"Other way," said Stewie.

Max mumbled incoherently, turned around and walked the other way.

* * *

Once Max had declared his destination to the Facilities his path was illuminated before him by his Glaze. He walked the whole way, but didn't always take the path he was shown. The slow conveyors were free, but he would not take them. He tried to ignore the crowds and sights as he went. For them it was all the same as any other day, and it annoyed Max that his life had been devastated and it didn't seem to bother anyone else at all. People shopped, buying things they somehow decided they really needed although they probably really didn't. Stores filled the vacated space with fresh new things knowing that the same people would really want them too. And what had just only just been bought would soon be thrown out, the new things would take their places, and the circle of economic life would continue. Except that the economics of consumption did not draw a circle. It drew an arrow, a pipeline, a conveyor, that moved resources from raw materials to stores to trash piles, with only brief stops in between, and never back the other way.

Max refused to be like one of those commodities. If he got on a conveyor it would be like he was being carried to the trash pile. By walking and choosing his own path he was still free, still in control of his own destiny. A piece of him may recently have gotten broken, or maybe it was more like a pulled seam or some other barely noticeable imperfection, but that didn't make him worthless. He was not ready to be thrown out. He would fix himself, and he would be back better than ever.

While lost in these thoughts, Stewie announced that Max had nearly arrived. Max looked up to see his new neighbourhood. By the standards of earlier in the century the area was typically urban and reminiscent of a Chinatown in any major city of the time. It wasn't dirty, but it wasn't quite clean either. The ventilation systems that worked tirelessly to distribute the scent of Andes meadow watched helplessly as their efforts became tangled with the airy tentacles of trash stink. Here there were no automated cleaning systems; it was up to the residents to tidy up after themselves. Like anywhere, there are those who are proud of their properties and they make an effort to keep them nice. But like anywhere, there are also those who can't be bothered. The difference here was that those who couldn't be bothered didn't have any money to pay anyone else to clean up for them.

Decades ago the streets here were exposed to the open air. In time they had been covered, using a translucent material as a ceiling that had since turned nearly opaque with dust and grime that coated the inside. The lighting had never been upgraded to compensate, leaving a perpetual sense of gloominess that pervaded the neighbourhood. Walls covered in decades worth of layered graffiti stood erect and dismal across the streets in seemingly arbitrary locations, delineating the city from the world outside. Many of the buildings here rose above the ceilings. Their windows, which their tenants had originally been able to open for ventilation, had been sealed. Instead, a network of insulated ductwork snaked up the outside walls like capillaries around an organ, providing a constant supply of cool air to the inside.

The area was called Malibu. No one remembered how or when the name had been given, or whether it had been done out of irony or hopefulness. Max had never been there before and was disgusted. He was old enough to know the place from where that name had been lifted, and even though he had heard this area was a slum, he had at least expected something nicer than this. Maybe like a beach scene full of youthful people - not too young - and although irresponsible, poor and unkempt, they were healthy and vital and full of life. By day they would lounge on sunny patios in swimming wear, romantically smoking and drinking and listening to loud, up tempo music while they yelled hilarious comments to each other and the sun bleached their long hair. By night they would dance around illegal and dangerously large bonfires, romantically smoking and drinking and taking colourful pills and then randomly pairing off for the night. And each morning they would wake up wrapped in a warm blanket on the sand and get up to do it all over again.

This was nothing like that. This place was a shithole. It was dark and dirty and smelly. Sparse scatterings of bodies that seemed barely alive littered the streets, some leaning against walls, some sitting in groups in the middle of the dirty streets. All of them looked like bums in their unmodified and mismatched clothes. More than half of them were untreatable. They all seemed deeply occupied in their own secret worlds, some speaking quietly to each other, the rest completely silent. There were no sunny patios, or even shops or bars or cafes as far as Max had noticed. Instead, the occasional street would have a line of vending machines selling various discount goods, including packaged food and cheap clothing. Ironically, this neighbourhood was far more sustainable than the one from where Max had come, if only because there was no money for the same blatant consumerism.

Stewie shepherded Max to the hostel. It consisted of the first floor of an old tenement. Max had to remember how to use a door that didn't open on its own. Inside, cots were arranged in rows around the perimeter of a large open space. Lockers occupied most of the walls. In the middle were fold out tables at which occupants sat in fold out chairs. Some were eating meals that were served from stewpots that stood on a separate table. In here the occupants looked much younger, if still dressed similarly to those outside. There was a loud, jovial atmosphere to the place, which Max hadn't expected and didn't share. Nearly everyone inside looked like they were young adults. Max knew this wasn't the case, because treatables never looked their age for long. But no one looked as old as Max did, and he resented it.

A few noticed him enter and stared. Others, noticing the distraction of the others, turned and stared too. Max realized his clothes gave him away. From head to toe his garments had been infused with electronics, monitoring circuits, and actuators that did everything from maintaining his perfect body temperature to monitoring his blood for illness. None of this could be seen, but it was obvious from the quality. No one else wore anything of the sort.

As Max scanned the eyes of the watchers, he could almost see their thoughts. Some guessed he was someone's father, there to reluctantly rescue a drug-addicted child. Others figured he was there to find a young wayward female that he could "entertain" for a few days. A few didn't care, instead wondering how many coins they could get for Max's clothes, and how they might dispossess Max of them.

"Everyone's looking at me Stewie."

"Hmm, we probably should have gotten you some different clothes before coming here," said the AI.

"Yaaa think?"

"There's a discount shopping mall not far from here."

"Was that an ad?"

"No. Yes."

"Ok, seriously, you're telling me there really was no better place for me to come? I can't stay here."

"Oh, don't worry. You'll be fine."

"Where is the concierge?"

"I don't think that's what the role is called here."

"Christ, people here are so dirty."

"You might want to keep that thought to yourself."

Max's gaze landed upon a young man whose beaming smile made him even more uneasy than the looks he was getting from everyone else. Max looked away, trying to find someone of authority with whom he could get his bearings, but the man's broad smile drew him back in.

"Why is that guy looking at me like that?" Max was speaking in a whisper, but Stewie could hear him perfectly.

"I can't see what you're seeing. I can only hear. But I bet a camera from Didaka would make a great video interface."

The man stood up, still staring at Max. He was about Max's height, and looked about twenty-five years old, but then all treatables looked twenty-five, so his real age wasn't evident. His hair was long and dreadlocked, pulled loosely together behind his head, and his chin beard had been braided with colourful beads. He spread out his arms in a pose of welcome.

His look was one of delight, but Max couldn't help feeling a little intimidated. When Max didn't move, the man started walking around the tables and cots in Max's direction.

"Oh shit. He's coming over." Max considered leaving, but instead continued looking for an administrator or organizer to talk to. By the time the man walked up to him, he still hadn't found anyone. Still smiling widely, the man opened his arms again as he approached.

"What the fuck? Is he going to hug me? What kind of place is this?"

The man stopped just short of Max. "Hi Dad," he said before going in for a hug. Max stood perfectly still for a few seconds with the man's arms wrapped around him before tentatively patting his son on the back.

* * *

His arms were still around Max. Max cleared his throat.

"Too long?" Max's son released his hug and stepped back, a sheepish grin on his face. "I got your message"

"What? What message?"

"The one saying you would be here. We came right over. It was perfect because we were planning on coming here to stay for a while anyway. We're tired of our old neighbourhood."

"I didn't... Fucking hell. Stewie, what did you do?"

"Is that him?" his son asked. "Are you talking to him right now? What's he like?"

"I was concerned for your mental well being," said Stewie. "I deduced that your son would provide you with some much needed companionship."

"You had no right to bring Nero into this."

"Oh, this is so cool! Can I talk to him too?" said Nero.

"No rights have been violated. I have general power of attorney over your affairs, and I am authorized to take any action I deem to be to your benefit."

"Then make me a fucking sandwich! Don't fuck with my life!"

"'Is he really just like you?" asked Nero. "No wonder you don't get along."

Max rubbed his face with his hands. "Shit. How did it come to this?"

"Hey, I love your hair! Not a lot of guys your age have any."

Max ran his hand through his pompadour. At least he still had that.

"I brought some friends with me. You'll like them. Nice clothes too. I've heard about nanos like that. Are they really bulletproof?"

"What? No. Jesus, why would they be bulletproof?"

"Why wouldn't they be?" Nero turned and began walking back to his table. Max unthinkingly followed. Distracted by Nero, he no longer noticed the eyes of others on him. Gradually the noise in the room almost returned to normal.

Max answered absently. "Because no one has guns. They've been illegal in the city for 40 years."

"Really? I hadn't noticed." They arrived at Nero's table. "So Dad, this is Chance." Nero gestured toward a very large man. He must have been over two meters tall, and well over 100 kilograms. His hands when flat in front of him on the table looked like baseball mitts. He might have been the same age as Nero, but it was difficult to know for sure. He wore a large beard and a shaved head and generally looked intimidating. His piercing green eyes did not change that impression. He said nothing but nodded grimly. "He doesn't talk much. But when he sneezes it sounds like he's yelling 'asshole'. It's kind of hilarious. And this is Ooauoa."

"Huh? Say that again?"

"O-ew-ah-wah, except there's no 'w'. Her name has no consonants, only vowels. Isn't that kind of awesome?"

Beside Chance was a woman showing clear signs of aging, although probably two decades younger than Max. This was curious because at that age she should have been treatable. She smiled warmly at Max, her wrinkles betraying a face that smiled easily. "It's such a pleasure to meet you," she said. "Nero's made up so much about you, and I'm really curious to find out the truth." There was nothing sarcastic about her tone or expression.

"Ha ha. Yeah." Nero sounded embarrassed. "She's fun. So, I was so happy to hear from you. It's been such a long time."

Max was still holding Ooauoa's gaze, but peeled himself away. "Ok listen, I didn't contact you, the Steward did. Don't start thinking I want you around or anything."

"Oh, come on. The message was from you. It said so."

"No, it wasn't. It was the Steward. He does what he wants it seems." Max was looking around again, noticing how others looked away from him as he gazed in their direction.

"But the Steward is you, right? So really, deep down you wanted him to do it."

"No, deep down, I didn't. Deep down I really want to be left alone."

Ooauoa lightly backhanded Chance. "Pay up." Chance made an annoyed expression, but then made the face that indicated a motor cortex command.

"Winning and losing are the same," he said.

Ooauoa looked off into the distance blankly for a moment, and then smiled again. "It's good you see it that way," she said.

Max watched the exchange. "I'm leaving now," he said, and he turned and walked toward the door.

"BULLSHIT!" sneezed Chance, and wiped his nose with a paper towel.

"Dad, come on, you just got here," said Nero, standing. His tone attracted the attention of several others in the room who watched Max leave.

* * *

"Listen to me very carefully: you do not do anything - fucking anything - without asking me first. Understand?" Max was angry. He had stopped on the sidewalk in the gloomy dusk outside the hostel.

Stewie responded calmly. "You should have a Ranting root beer and calm down because frankly it's the other way around. As I said before I have general power of attorney, and I can take actions as I see fit. In fact, I can restrict your actions if I deem them to be contrary to our best interest."

Max was stunned by this. "No. There's no way that's right." Max stared down at the sidewalk trying to put his thoughts together. He didn't notice the woman who had walked around to stand in front of him. "That cannot be right."

"Give me your shoes."

It took Max a moment to realize the woman was talking to him. "What? Go fuck yourself."

The punch landed at the base of Max's skull. All he could see were stars as his legs went out from under him. He landed hard on his knees, then his hands.

"Easy there Denny, he's going to ruin his pants," said the woman to the man standing behind Max. "Those are worth a lot too." She directed her attention back to Max as she drew a knife from her back pocket and waved it in Max's downcast face. "As I was saying, let's start with the shoes."

Max fell to his side, unable to speak. A blinking whiteness covered his vision.

"Alright, let's help you out then." Denny and the woman got down on the sidewalk with Max and removed his shoes, and then started undoing his pants. "Well, well! Even his undies are fancy!" she said. "Now you might disagree," she said affectionately to Max, "but I'd argue I need the coins more than you, so if you don't mind, try not to get the wrong idea..." She began pulling off Max's pants and underwear at the same time. Some of Max's peripheral vision began to return, but his foveae saw only white, and the back of his head pounded in agony.

"Hey, leave him alone!" Max recognized Nero's voice. Out of the corners of his eyes he saw Denny stand and face Nero. Denny was not a big man, but his countenance was fierce. Then, from outside his vision Max saw a giant hand reach out and grab Denny's face. Denny yelled and punched at the arm, but the hand held him like a five-armed squid. Then, like a rag doll Denny was shaken and tossed against the nearby wall. His body and head hit with a splat, and he fell to the ground. He groaned softly as his head lolled, and his eyes blinked wide as if in awe of something he saw across the street. The woman watched as if sharing Denny's pain, but then grabbed Max's shoes and ran off, stopping halfway down the block to look back for her partner. Denny slowly rolled to the side, picked himself up, and stumbled away in the same direction, using the wall to steady himself. Blood trickled down his neck from behind his hair.

"The root of suffering is desire," said Chance to Denny's back.

Still almost blinded, Max instinctively reached down to pull his pants back on. Mostly there, he slowly closed his eyes.

* * *

Max opened his eyes. The back of his head felt like the door to his mind was being assaulted with a battering ram. Looking around he found himself lying on a cot back in the hostel. He tried to piece together what had happened to him, and after remembering only a little he first checked to make sure his pants were back on. They were, but not the pants he had been wearing before. Checking himself over, he found that all of his clothes had been replaced with much more modest choices. "Where are my clothes?" he said to no one, anyone.

"We gave them away," said Nero, who had been sitting beside the cot, waiting for Max to wake.

"What? Those were worth more than all of you put together."

"Don't go Aira, man. These will help you blend in better." Nero gestured at Max's new attire. "We got them from the donation bin."

"I don't want to blend in. These are fucking rags. I look like a bum."

"Like he said, now you blend in," said Ooauoa.

"Jesus, they're all scratchy. What are they made of, toothbrushes? I am going to fucking kill those two." Max tried to sit up, but dizziness washed over him, then pain, and he laid back down.

"Weird," started Ooauoa, "I would have thought you'd have been grateful to Chance for, oh, possibly saving your life."

Max glared at Ooauoa.

"It's ok," said Nero. "You would have done the same for us."

"What?" Max made a face. "No I wouldn't have. Don't be stupid."

"Choose not to be harmed, and you haven't been," said Chance.

Max looked at Chance, then to Nero. "What's with Confucius?"

"Near as we can tell, Chance only speaks in Stoic quotes," said Nero. "It's kind of awesome."

"What? How does he order dinner?"

"What do you mean?"

"Like at a restaurant? Or does he always just get Buddha's Delight?"

"Can't say. We don't eat at restaurants."

"No, of course you don't." Max looked back at the ceiling, and scratched at his chest. "So itchy! Fuck, my head is killing me. Can you get me an Indicol?"

Nero and Ooauoa looked at each other, smiling in surprise. "If I had some of that, it would be gone already," she said.

"Fine. How about a bit of whiskey?"

Ooauoa rolled her eyes. "Alcohol isn't allowed in the hostel. Honestly, you think that kind of thing is just sitting around? You realize this isn't The Musk, right?"

"Maybe some food will help." offered Nero. "Can I get you a bowl?"

Max had forgotten how hungry he was. He hadn't eaten all day. He nodded his assent, and Nero made for the food table. Lying back, Max closed his eyes and tried to pretend he wasn't in pain. How has it come to this?, he thought to himself. He scratched at his neckline.

Nero returned with a bowl and held it out for Max while Chance helped him sit up. Before he even touched it he sensed something was wrong. One sniff confirmed it. "Uh, fuck, what is this? It smells like torched plastic."

"It's chicken soup. I know it smells kind of funny. It tastes ok though, and you get used to the smell. There's beef too."

There was no obvious sign of meat in the yellowish liquid. Calling it "chicken soup" was more of an anachronism than a recipe. It had of course always been optional to include actual meat in soup, it being acceptable to make the broth by boiling the remains of a carcass of the animal instead. Nowadays, the dish was made from the translucent gel that remained in the protein vats that grew the product now called "chicken". There were no signs of plant life either. Real vegetables were well above the soup's price point. Instead, it had been fortified with sufficient vitamins, minerals, and dietary fiber needed by the average human body.

"Here's some crackers." Nero said this and smiled as if Max would be grateful. "If you don't have some solid food your teeth will fall out."

Max eyed him suspiciously. "I don't think that's true." Max took a sip. He winced at first, but found that Nero was right: once you got past the smell it didn't taste too bad. Or maybe he was just hungry enough not to care. He noticed his head pounded a little less.

"How's your neck? It looks pretty swollen," said Ooauoa. She prodded the wounded spot.

"Oww! Stop that!" complained Max.

"Don't be such a baby."

Max snapped. "Baby?! This coming from the woman with no consonants in her name? It's a girly baby name. Why doesn't your name have any consonants? Do you know what I've been through the past couple days? I used to be someone. I had a condo in the Neumann; eighty-sixth floor! I ate real food and wore real clothes." Max scratched at his hip. "I slept in a bed! I was important! People respected me! You? You live in a hostel and probably do drugs all day. What the hell would you understand about anything important?"

"Ah, shit!" Ooauoa put her hands to her right eye and turned away.

"What happened?" said Nero with a concern that Max found surprising. "Are you ok?"

"Yeah, yeah. I will be," said Ooauoa. "It's just your dad's condescension went right in my eye. Like... right in my eye." Nero and Chance looked at Max and laughed. Ooauoa held her eye for a moment, then dragged her hand over it, shook the condescension off of her fingertips and looked up deadpan. "Ok, I'm better now." Max stared at her with unveiled ire. Ooauoa looked straight back at him and asked innocently, "What?"

"Biotech," mumbled Max as he scratched his groin.

"No one is entitled to a world without change," said Chance.

"Word," said Ooauoa. She walked behind Max and placed her fingers on his collar bones and gently began rubbing the area around the bruise with her thumbs. Max lowered his head in response. His shoulders melted like a glacier turning into a river. "Oh, that's... that's not so bad. You can keep   doing   that."

THE THREE AMOEBAS

Max woke the next morning feeling like a twisted wreck of a man. The cot had no support, as if it had been born the same year as him, and lying on his back had been the only position that approached comfort. Max imagined that sleeping in a burlap sack might have been about the same.

The sheets certainly felt like burlap, as far as he could remember what burlap felt like. Max hadn't slept with sheets for decades, and found the experience of even having the hostel's threadbare sheets and blankets on top of him only a little less intolerable than the unregulated air temperature, as if the weight of the material was really the weight of dirt filling his grave.

It had been bad enough that the inmates - Max's word for the guests - had undressed and paraded around nearly naked before cocooning themselves in their cots, using their folded up clothes as pillows. The sight of their youthful bodies, mostly lithe and healthy, had made him in his eighty-something body - despite that he looked like he was merely in his late fifties - self-conscious and embarrassed. He decided he would sleep in his clothes. Ooauoa noticed this and had gotten two extra sheets, which she folded up into pillows for Max and herself, and then also slept in her clothes. Max didn't know if this was what she regularly did, or if it was to make him feel better.

The torched plastic smell of what the "inmates" here considered food lingered the entire night, and may have contributed to his light sleep dreams that oscillated between being buried alive and burning to death in a building fire.

His head and the back of his neck still ached. But it was the noise that disturbed him the most. As far as Max could tell, probably more than half of the guests snored horribly. Between this and Chance sneezing 'ASSHOLE' several times, Max suspected he might have slept for an hour.

And now with his spinal cord seemingly having ossified overnight, he couldn't get himself out of the cot on his own. Chance had come to help, but Max had refused, instead lying still in despair.

"Let Chance help you," said Nero.

"No, I'll be fine. I just need to loosen up a bit."

"Like the wind blowing against the river," said Chance.

The three watched quietly as Max struggled to free himself from his bed.

"They say when you're old enough you get all the exercise you need just getting out of bed to pee," said Ooauoa. "Now I understand."

Stewie spoke. "There are sixteen ads equally ranked to play to you right now. I'll choose them at random. Massages are fifteen percent off until 10am at Southbridge medical."

Max collapsed back into the cot. "Stewie, just don't."

"Eucalyptus back cream and Aspirin are available at Seventy's pharmacy just up the street. There's a yoga class starting in thirty-seven minutes at Move Like Yaeger in Devonport. You can make it if you leave within seven minutes. ..."

* * *

"So, what do you do for a living?"

Max was entirely out of his depth trying to talk to his son. Normally, business conversation consumed nearly all of his society, with a bit of awkward small talk filling in the cracks. At the level that Max worked, business associates didn't require any sincere attempts at camaraderie. To compensate, when speaking with Nero, Max found himself resorting to stereotypical Dad-like interrogations.

"Hmm?"

"You know, how do you make money?" Max scratched his side. The clothes itched him to distraction.

"We don't have to. We get our UBI."

"You can live on that?"

"Sure. I even have savings. We all do."

"Nero, that's not a living. That's just sponging off of working people."

Nero looked defensive. "We work. We just don't make any money from it. Doesn't mean it's not important."

Max sighed his best Dad sigh while scratching his thigh. "That is precisely the definition of 'important'. If no one is willing to pay for it, it's not worth anything."

Nero's defensiveness yielded slightly to annoyance. "So, what? Should we all take bullshit jobs selling shiny shit that people don't need just to make some rich people even richer? We help folks who don't have any money to pay. What's wrong with that?"

Max knew how these arguments went, with him becoming the heartless bastard speaking sober truths, but he felt he needed to double down anyway. "The good samaritan was a bad economist."

Nero laughed. "Hey, you're starting to sound like Chance. That's pretty awesome!"

Max hadn't intended to be funny. "Listen. I named you Nero so that you'd be strong, not some pushover that works for free. It's a waste of time. People who don't have any money don't contribute to society."

"Like you?"

Max hesitated, wounded. "That's temporary."

Nero saw what he had done. "Sorry Dad, I didn't mean it like that. It was a cheap shot."

Max and Nero were waiting outside the hostel in the perpetual gloom of the covered street. Ooauoa and Chance were still inside helping to clear up from breakfast and replace the cots with tables and chairs for the day. Max had refused to help, and Nero hadn't wanted to leave him alone, so the two waited outside.

"We also meet people," said Nero.

"You meet people?"

"Yeah, it's kind of like a quest." Nero smiled proudly. "We're going to meet everyone on the planet."

Max blinked and scratched his head. "Go on."

"Well, we figured that we like meeting people, and we've got lots of time, so we're going to meet everyone on the planet. There are problems, of course. People die, and new people are born, and some are too young to just walk up to and say hello to although we've done it and figure it counts but sometimes parents get upset. And then there are people who don't want to meet us, and even when we explain why they still don't want to meet us and get restraining orders and stuff…" Nero laughed nervously, "… so we stopped doing that. But most people are pretty friendly and think what we're doing is pretty cool."

"That has got to be the stupidest thing I've ever heard."

"Nah, it's really lots of fun. People are really great. Most people."

"How are you going to meet the whole world? How will you get to other cities?"

"We've got years to figure that out. Maybe the rules will change by then."

Max thought for a moment. "Do you keep a list?"

"Yeah, Chance keeps a checklist with dates and locations."

"Well, that's not creepy at all."

"Governments do it. Companies do it. What's creepier?"

"And you get the list of people from the census?"

"Correct!"

"How far along are you?"

Nero beamed. "We've met almost twelve percent of the city."

Max was impressed. "Wow, that's got to be around three-quarter million people! How long have you been doing this?"

"About twenty years. We try to meet a hundred people a day. One day we met fourteen hundred and eight-five people at this crazy wedding we crashed. Most of the people we met had crashed it too. That was fun. But mostly we just meet people when we're working. Old age homes and stuff."

"Oh, so you've met all of the poor people in the city," Max poked.

"Not even half," replied Nero, Max's intent flowing past him unnoticed.

"Ok, so how long will it take to meet the whole planet?"

"At our current rate, around two hundred and forty thousand years. But Ooauoa thinks that with birth rates decreasing and untreatables dying and something about the suicide rate it might be about half that. Not sure how she calculated that, but she's pretty smart. Still, we're thinking about ways to speed things up."

Even after decades of knowing that treatables were effectively immortal, Max still could never quite comprehend the expanse of possibilities this opened up for them, probably because he saved himself the torment of considering what he had missed out on. His own myopic life perspective limited him to somewhere around another twenty or thirty years, and he was incapable of seeing much beyond that. He still saw Nero's life the same way. But Nero could see infinitely into the future. Misfortune could happen, in fact it probably would. Even in the absurd safety and security of the city, just by probability most of the young would end up dying from freak accidents. But for these youths there was no longer a known hard stop, no longer a certainty of death, only vague possibilities of tragedy which, like children, they romanticized more than they feared. Max wanted to tell Nero that he needed to get a real job, work his way up, and make something of himself. But those old directives held no meaning anymore. For all anyone knew, Nero literally had all the time in the world to do whatever he wanted. And Max couldn't help but resent him for it. Out of spite he said, "Ooauoa's not going to make it that long."

Nero seemed either oblivious or immune to Max's enmity, saying plainly, "No, probably not."

Nero's candid reply made Max feel a little ashamed. "Isn't she about your age?"

"A little younger actually. She had bone cancer way back, and the treatment for that knocked her out of being treatable. You know, the kind of treatment before viroma. The brutal kind, with chemicals and radiation and all that."

"Ah, shit." Now Max actually felt bad for her, but at the same time there was a deeply seated part of him that was glad to have someone else sharing his fate. Misery loves company after all. But it was time to change the subject. He thought for a moment. "Have you met the two that robbed me?"

"Chloe and Den? Yeah. We met them yesterday before you got to the hostel."

Max was momentarily stunned, and then indignant. "What the fuck! You know them? Why aren't we reporting them to the police? That fucker rabbit punched me!"

"They're addicts. They don't need to be arrested. They need help. When they're using they're actually really nice. I think last night they were hurting. They probably scored with the money from your shoes."

Max didn't want to get them help, he wanted to lock them up for the rest of their hopefully very long lives. He sensed though that he would not get any help from Nero and his friends. Still, there was time enough for revenge later, when he had reestablished himself. With only a little bit of resources he could deal with a pair of nobodies like Chloe and Den properly.

In the meantime, he was still curious about the three friends' pastime. He thought for a moment, and then considered carefully before speaking next. "So, with the whole 'meeting people' thing, when were you going to meet me?" Immediately he regretted asking such a plainly revealing question.

"You? Technically I've already met you when I was a kid, so we already checked you off."

"Oh. Makes sense." Max was disappointed with the answer, and then angry with himself. Just moments ago he had mocked the whole enterprise, and now he was upset that he wasn't a priority on their list. At least Nero hadn't made fun of him after having been given such an easy target. Max then wondered what else he could get away with.

Nero had continued. "But it's not like we have a plan or anything. It's not really possible to get specific people together so we can meet them. So we go to the people and meet whoever happens to be there. It works out better anyway because you never know who is going to be there. It's more fun when you don't know what to expect. And sometimes you finally meet someone you always wanted to meet, and you're like, what a prick. Other times total strangers turn out to be awesome. You really never know."

Max paused for a moment, and then asked the big question he had been saving. "So, uh, how's your Mom?"

"Oh, she's good. She got married again, what is it, thirty-eight years ago? Brian's a good guy."

This time Nero had gone straight for Max's heart, although he probably hadn't meant to. Max knew what he himself was now supposed to say: that he was happy for her, that he wished her well, that it all worked out for the best. He said none of this.

"Does she ever mention me?"

"Not for a long time, no. When was the last time you spoke to her?"

"More than forty years."

"Well, there you go."

Max stood in silence for a while, wondering how deeply he wanted to mine this delicate, painful seam. He had never understood why his marriage ended, why his wife had left him. They had had a fight about something he could no longer remember. It was one fight among many during those eight years, and this particular one had never stood out as anything unusual. But for some reason that only his wife understood, at that moment, tears welling in her eyes, she had picked up Nero, walked out the door, and never returned. Her mother had come by the next day with some helpers to collect her things. The only times they had spoken after that they had been surrounded by lawyers.

Nero seemed to know what his father was waiting for. "She explained to me what happened. Years later. She said I was old enough and she wanted me to understand."

Max looked at Nero, saying nothing.

"She said that she really loved you. She said she felt lucky to be with you."

"That makes no sense. Then why would she leave me?"

"Because she realized that you didn't love her. She said you didn't even like her. She said you treated her terribly."

"What the hell? I got her everything she ever asked for. Everything she could have wanted."

"I think what she wanted was for you to love her back. You know, to treat her like you were happy to be with her. She said you would say things to her to put her down a little. Or to minimize her feelings. At first she thought you were just teasing her. You know, being funny. She knew you were an asshole, but thought you were her asshole. ... Wait. That didn't come out right... you know what I mean, an asshole that belonged to her. Wow, that didn't work either..."

"Ok, ok, I get it."

"Maybe 'bastard' is a better word to use."

Max held up his hand. "Just... just go on."

"Yeah, well, eventually she realized that you actually meant the things you said. From then on, all she heard was resentment. Like you could have done better than her and you wished she would go away. At first she told herself that she was just being petty and unappreciative, but eventually even the things you would buy her - the jewelry and stuff - even that would make her feel like you gave them to her so that when she wore them she would measure up. Like she wasn't good enough without that stuff."

"So that's why she never took them. I remember her mom opened the drawer and looked at all the jewelry for a minute, but left it all there."

"You were upset about that weren't you? The jewelry symbolized all that you could give to the relationship, and you were mad that she left it all."

"I don't know. Maybe. I thought maybe she wanted the house or the business instead."

"Mom was never like that. She needed you to give something else, but decided that you didn't know how to love other people. When I think back I think I felt the same way. I was still pretty young when I realized I didn't want all the stuff anymore. I wanted you to seem like you gave a shit about me, not that I thought about it like that back then. It just seemed like every toy you bought, or everything you signed me up for was really an expectation, a test to make sure I would behave the way you wanted. Remember the business principles class you enrolled me in? I was seven."

"It seemed like a good idea at the time. I thought you liked it."

"Heh, yeah I did, weird enough. The funny thing is I still remember what they taught me. Low margins are ok if you have the throughput. The need to minimize direct costs. How you can write off losses from a bad year. The teacher was really great. She made the class really fun."

"And you never used anything you learned there."

"And I never used anything I learned there." Nero and Max laughed a little, then stood in silence for a moment, Max staring at the ground, Nero into the distance.

Nero looked back over to Max. "Anyway, she said she stopped feeling lucky to be with you. That's why she left." Then he looked away again. "As for me, I really like you being here now. There's no more expectations because your broke ass can't give me anything but time."

"Well then, it looks like everything worked out for the best," Max lied, and scratched his chest.

* * *

They called themselves The Three Amoebas, a diminutive name based on a 1980s movie title. The friends had originally made a joke about it, but eventually it stuck. Nero had done a metaweb search on it to see if it was original, but of course it wasn't: musical bands, amateur sports teams, a couple short stories, even a magic act had picked that low hanging fruit. But since, like them, none of those things had anything obvious to do with eukaryotes either, they decided they had as much right to the name as anyone.

Max followed the three as they followed their vocation and hit their "meet" quotas at the same time. They were part of an unaffiliated group known as "Helpers". They visited convalescent homes, churches, hospitals, animal shelters, community centers, and anywhere else where they would be welcomed to help out, doing anything that was asked of them. Sometimes they were handed buckets and sponges, other times soup ladles, but most of the time they were simply asked to be with the residents or patients. This usually meant sitting bedside and passing time by making banter, or listening to stories, or playing with children. Sometimes it meant cooling the forehead of a feverish addict battling withdrawal, or speaking gently to a scared animal, or holding the hand of a dying patient. They did any of the human things that the efficient human economies of the past centuries had deemed inefficient.

Today they were headed to a childcare center. They had received notifications that Helpers were needed because some of the regular staff were absent. All three considered playing with children as more of a vacation than work, and so they were eager to get there before enough others got there, as there never seemed to be a shortage of Helpers when kids were involved. The Malibu hostel was fairly close to the center, so they figured they had a good chance. Max was not nearly as enthusiastic.

During the walk the three bantered and joked, but Max was mostly quiet. To him their chat was irresponsible and picayune. It was far more important for him to figure out his next business opportunity, and so it was on that he had to stay focused. He had spent his whole life thinking that way. He knew that opportunities don't just fall in your lap, perfectly wrapped. One needs to be constantly observing and considering, and seeing everything in new, holistic ways. Perhaps you see someone doing something unexpected, but think nothing of it. And then you notice something else that at first seems incongruent, but on further reflection is surprisingly related to that first person's behaviour. Such epiphanies usually amount to nothing, but in rare cases they can be the start of something important, something special: something profitable.

Max used the walk to engage his thinking. He wasn't expecting any brilliant ideas to come to him anytime soon. Sometimes these things took weeks. But ideas would arise and accumulate, some terrible, most mediocre, and a few that were worth thinking more about. That's how Max knew that eventually he would think of something. As long as there were ideas.

When they arrived at the childcare center there was still room for all four of them. Max decided that he would stay for at least a little while. He had never been in such a place before, and you never knew where inspiration might be hiding. He lasted less than an hour before he went looking for inspiration elsewhere.

* * *

Max spent two days with the Three Amoebas. He watched them as they performed whatever sundry jobs were asked of them, some relatively pleasant, some downright revolting. A nursing home at full capacity that they visited had recently had an outbreak of stomach flu, with devastating results for many of the rooms. It was beyond the creativity of all four, try as they might, to adequately describe just how horrible the first smell of the building was as they entered.

"If vomit were air," tried Nero.

"Exquisite in its power and complexity," suggested Ooauoa.

"No manure, no flower," added Chance.

"Like pooping through your nostrils," said Nero.

"I'm going to wait outside," declared Max.

"No, come on, stay with us," pleaded Nero. "You'll go noseblind in no time."

Max didn't even hear him. "Fuck, how can you stand it?" He crinkled his wrinkled face.

"You're weak. You need to strengthen your mind," said Ooauoa.

"Pain times resistance equals suffering," said Chance.

"Evs. Why aren't there cleaning bots to fix this? Maybe they should just open all the windows and wait it out for a couple days."

The other three stared at Max in silent judgement. They effectively were the cleaning bots.

"Fine." Max conceded and entered the building, continuing his complaints for as long as there was anyone in earshot. Eventually though, just out of boredom, he began helping out. He refused to go near the bathrooms, but he washed a few dishes, mopped a kitchen floor when no one was looking, and had even spent almost an hour speaking with a woman who claimed she was 130 years old, retired for almost 70 of them, and had spent that time researching and creating nanoscale actuators - the basis of nano-manufacturing - in her home lab until she had retired, "for real this time", a year ago. Now tethered to multiple machines via wires and tubes, Max wondered if she was senile and making it all up. But as far as he and a few mental metaweb searches could tell she appeared to have a solid grasp of the science, and her name was associated with many publicly available papers. He had asked why so accomplished a person did not live in better means. "I gave it all away, my boy," she had said. "I published it on the metaweb for free."

"What? Why would you do that? That knowledge could have been worth a fortune."

"Oh, well, at first I did try to sell it, but the effort became a distraction. Or I suppose it's more accurate to say that the research distracted me from the selling. Every time I had a new idea - which was pretty often you know - I would hang up the phone and run to my lab. Eventually folks stopped calling me back, and I stopped calling them too. So you see, I never did the work for the money. I did it because I couldn't stop doing it. It's not like there was any amount of money that would have made me stop. Do you understand?"

Max couldn't help feeling like she had been cheated, that she had cheated herself. More than that, he felt cheated himself because what she could have had could also have been his. "There are probably people that did make money from your work. Doesn't that bother you?"

"No, of course not. All I did was work out some principles. There was still lots of work to do to turn those principles into something people could use."

"Sure, but that's just more work. You owned the knowledge. Without you they would have had to do all of that research themselves."

"And where did I get the knowledge that allowed me to do my work? It was all in the journals I read. And I certainly didn't build the machines that I worked with. I stood on the shoulders of giants, as the saying goes. Besides, the truth is I did get money for my work. When word got out that I was moved from my home to this place," she gestured to indicate the modest nursing home she now lived in, "we received a ten million dolarium donation with a note saying I should be in charge of how it gets spent."

"Huh. I wish I would have known about your work a long time ago," said Max.

"Why, would you have donated more?"

"Hell no, I wouldn't have given you anything."

The woman laughed with delight. "That's fine dear," she said warmly, patting Max's arm while she rested her head back to look at the ceiling. "You look like you need it more than me anyway."

* * *

Ooauoa had overheard the conversation. "That was nice. You made her happy."

Max scoffed. "Pretty sure that was just the drugs."

Ooauoa smiled and took Max's arm. "That's most of it, but you might have helped a tiny little bit."

* * *

Returning to the hostel that evening with another two hundred and forty-four fresh checkmarks on their list, The Three Amoebas were in a good mood. Max was starting to feel pretty good too, enough at least to sometimes even take part in their banter. The bruise on his neck was still sore but getting better. And he wasn't entirely sure, but he suspected his back was beginning to tolerate the hostel cots. Even the new clothes didn't bother him anymore. In fact, once he thought about it, he wondered if the nano clothes really made as much of a difference to his comfort as he thought.

But he was still immersed in thoughts of business opportunities, and annoyed that he had yet to devise a single one. He suspected it was because he was surrounded by poverty, and everyone knew there was no money in that. Still, he was sure that as long as he kept his pondering up he would eventually hit on a concept which could be developed into a workable idea. That is the way it always happened before.

"When you want something, all the universe conspires in helping you to achieve it," said Chance, seemingly reading his mind, but the three knew how Max was constantly occupied.

"Pretty sure there's more to it than that, champ," said Max dismissively. "What if you and me want opposite things? What does the universe do then?"

"You don't get what you want. You get what you are."

"Ok, you just said before that the universe gets me what I want. Which one is it?"

"All wisdom ends in paradox."

"Winner: Chance!" cheered Ooauoa.

"That's not winning!" complained Max. "You can seriously just say a bunch of nonsense and finish with a paradox line every time. How is that winning?"

"Oh, don't be a sore loser," she smiled.

"First, I didn't lose anything. Second, that wasn't a quote from a Stoic; in fact none of them were. And third, I am merely pointing out that a random quote machine is not a real debating opponent."

"Who said you were debating?" asked Nero.

"I'm just saying, how am I supposed to compete with randomness? With Chance!", added Max triumphantly.

"Why would you?" asking Nero with real curiosity.

Max looked at them blankly. "You know what? None of you make any sense."

"You're weak. You need to strengthen your mind," said Ooauoa.

"So you said."

"Maximum Rising?" The voice came from a man on the sidewalk they were passing. He wore clothes that were far too expensive for the neighbourhood, and stood with his hands together at his waist with feet shoulder width apart in a pose that only someone with military training could find comfortable. He stared at Max, ignoring the others.

Nero whispered to Max, giggling, "He thinks your name is Maximum."

Max ignored Nero. "Do I know you?" he asked.

"You might know of my employer. Can I have a word?"

Max turned to The Three Amoebas. "I'll meet you inside," he said.

The three nodded and headed for the hostel. "We're like the Four Amoebas now!" exclaimed Nero. Ooauoa rubbed his back.

Max waved. Turning back he smiled sheepishly at the man. "Kids."

"Come with me," said the man as he turned and headed down an alleyway.

Max hesitated. "Uh, there's nothing down there," he called from behind. "It's a dead end." The man didn't make any acknowledgement, but continued walking. Max was unsure whether he should follow. Or maybe he should get Chance to come with him. But, he remembered, he didn't have anything anyone would want to steal anymore, just a few thousand ubis he had saved over the past few days. This man's haircut was worth more than that.

Max began to cautiously follow. The alley had a musty smell, like a basement long ago filled with antiques and then abandoned. Spray-paint graffiti covered the walls like ancient cave paintings, some crude and sloppy, some intricate and aesthetic. Empty shells of old consumer electronics lay everywhere, stripped for parts decades before to help the Facilities build physical automation, now just ancient litter that Max carefully picked his way through. Accumulated dust balls swirled around his feet.

The man reached the metal wall at the end of the alley and turned to wait, kicking debris away from the wall in the meantime. When Max had caught up, that man turned to the wall and retrieved a small tool from his pocket. Max watched as he inserted it into four nondescript openings, holes arranged in a square that looked more like damage than anything with a purpose. Each time, the man twisted the tool, and a screw somewhere inside the wall made a squeaky complaint. Returning the tool to his pocket, the man placed his hand in the middle of the holes, pushing a plate inwards, and then to the right, revealing a handle. He pulled on the handle, turned it counter-clockwise a quarter turn, and pulled again. A previously concealed door opened inwards about 30 centimeters before it stuck.

A secret door? wondered Max. His thoughts raced through all of the intriguing hidden places to which it opened.

A warm wind swept past Max, as if the alley had taken a deep breath. It pushed in from the opening carrying an unexpected lack of scent and the taste of dust. The man grabbed the door with both hands and gave it a good pull, freeing it from its jam and opening it fully. Max looked through and saw an old weathered brick wall rising from the other side of an asphalt lane. Weeds grew tall in the gap between the two. As he moved closer Max looked up, expecting to see a ceiling, but instead saw the top of the wall, and above that the dusky sky.

"Holy shit! That's outside!" he exclaimed. "What the fuck are you doing?"

"It's perfectly safe. Come," said the man.

"What do you want?" asked Max, hoping for a reason not to comply, but the man had already walked outside and down the lane. Max approached the door as if the wind might suddenly attack. He hadn't been outside for probably forty years, not since he had returned from The Rez. No one went outside anymore. The Facilities took care of everything in here and out there.

Max stepped out the door. The air was arid and warm, but not uncomfortable. By the remaining light of day Max could see the man at the end of the lane, gesturing for Max to close the door behind him. Max pulled on the door but didn't close it completely, afraid that he would not be able to get back in otherwise. Turning back to the man, he followed. Instinctively he looked up, hoping to see stars, but it was still too early. Darkness would come quickly though, which was good for seeing stars, but bad for everything else. There were no lights outside, and he feared he would not be able to find the door again. Eager to have whatever this was over with and get back inside, he hurried after the man.

"Max, where are you going?" said Stewie. "You're outside the grid."

"I'm outside, period."

"You should apply Wakker sunscreen first, and wear a Reardan's dust mask. But why are you outside?"

"Don't know yet."

"What … you… I didn't…" Stewie's voice broke up as Max proceeded down the lane. When he had caught up to the man, he saw that they had left the alley and were standing on what likely had been a main street. To the right the street ended in a wall that rose vertically eight meters: Malibu lay on the other side. The man walked in the other direction.

"Where are we going?" ask Max.

The man turned and put a finger to his lips, then turned back and continued walking.

"Max, where are… trouble…" said Stewie.

Max followed the man well past when the Stewart could no longer be heard, several hundred meters away from the wall. They were surrounded by dilapidated buildings, cracked asphalt, and weeds. Telephone poles stood like a cultivar that had gone extinct, naked of their wires like long needles that had fallen for the last season ever.

"There are communication protocols that have much longer ranges than 9g," said the man. "Some of them are still in use, but mostly just by hobbyists. There are also still some working transceivers outside the walls, but we would see the LEDs at this time of night. We should be good here."

"Couldn't we just find a hush?"

"Too many eyes in Malibu. Outside is the next best thing."

Max nodded and looked around. "I thought it would be hotter."

"It's winter time."

"Oh, right." Max had barely remembered that seasons existed, much less what the current one was.

"My name is Sinde. I work for Stanley Cable."

Max was taken aback. "The...? Holy shit..." Thoughts raced through Max's brain. Stanley Cable wants to do a deal. This is it, I'm back on. But why does Stanley Cable - the Stanley Cable, founder of Cable Industries, 'where vision and potential become the future', which basically owns the city - want to do a deal with me now? I'm broke and living in a fucking hostel with a bunch of mangy migrants and he knows it.

Sinde continued. "Mr. Cable would like to speak to you. He has invited you to his home."

Max tried to get a hold of himself. "Um, yeah, that sounds good. When was he thinking?"

"Tomorrow morning, at six, if you are available."

Max's heart sank. The hostel had a 10:00pm curfew each night, and didn't reopen until 6:00am. This was meant to ensure that guests had adequate uninterrupted sleep time, what with it being a single common space. Max didn't know where he would have to be, and how long it would take to get there, but he was sure Stanley Cable didn't live anywhere near Malibu. He was also pretty sure that Mr. Cable's time wasn't negotiable.

"I won't be able to leave the hostel until six."

"I know. That's what I meant. I will meet you outside the hostel at 6:00am to escort you."

Max felt like an idiot. Of course that's what Sinde had meant. Of course he already knew when the hostel opened. Just the mention of Cable's name had been enough to reduce him to a hot giddy mess. He was still not used to having no negotiating power. He never wanted to get used to that. He needed to calm down. "Why does Mr. Cable want to see me?"

"He only said he has an interest in your special talents."

"I didn't realize he even knew who I am."

"Indeed, he has for some time. Mr. Cable makes it a priority to know of all the business leaders in the city."

"That's a good policy," said Max approvingly, inwardly excited to have been referred to as a "business leader" with "special talents" by a man like Stanley Cable. But he kept cool in front of Sinde.

"When we meet again, please refrain from speaking until it is safe to do so." Sinde gestured to the city wall, and he and Max began their walk back in silence. When they were almost back to the lane Max, now feeling more comfortable outside, looked up at the sky again. It was darker now and there were many tiny lights twinkling. He stopped to look at them more carefully, and noticed that all of them moved, if slowly.

"Satellites," he said to himself. Just like how he remembered the stars when he was young, more and more appeared the longer he looked. Thousands. Tens of thousands. Even more? They seemed to form a canopy of tiny lights so dense that Max suddenly felt as if he were already back inside a larger city, as if he had never left, and unable to see anything that hadn't been assembled by humans.

"You're looking at satellites? Why do you need to look at satellites?" asked Stewie.

Max didn't respond. He and Sinde reentered the city at the same door. Sinde locked it up again, and the door resumed its previous concealment. At the opening of the alleyway, Sinde turned right and walked away as if they had never met. Max turned left and headed for the hostel door, finally letting his elation fill him up completely.

"You're back in the grid. What happened? Where were you? It's pretty dry outside. Do you need a refreshing Nestle bottled water?" Stewie asked with concern.

"Never mind that, Stewie. Max is back. Max is back.

UBI EXHIBIT

Interdivided international Virtual Museum of World History, Universal Basic Income Exhibit. Group tour, January 20, 2075

    Guide: "Welcome everyone."

Murmurs of hello among the group. Some voices delayed for translation.

Guide: "Are there any questions before we begin?"

Ryan_Koke_222: "Is there a…"

Guide, holding up her hand: "Just don't. Why does it have to be every… single… time?"

Ryan_Koke_222: "… recording of this exhibit, or do I have to take note?"

Guide: "Oh. No, you will have to take your own notes. Let's begin then. Any other questions are welcome at any time."

The scene of the grand museum lobby fades to blackness, giving the impression that everyone present is floating in a starless space. The guide puts her hands together in front of her, and as she pulls them apart again colours stream out and around the guests, forming into a lively classroom scene, where students of all ages are participating in animated discussions.

Guide: "UBI, or Universal Basic Income, is a stipend paid to every individual in a society purely by virtue of being alive to accept it. There are no conditions attached to its receipt; the recipient can do with the funds whatever they wish. The primary economic motivation of the UBI is as a stimulant. HIstory has shown that money that goes to the wealthy results in it being saved, where it does little for the growth of economies. But when given to the poor it gets spent. The immediate practical effect is to increase consumption of subsistence goods, including food, clothes, and utilities. In the medium term we see an increase in what is known as 'deferred spending', where consumers begin to develop enough confidence to buy the things they have long wanted but couldn't previously afford. But it is the long term effects that are much more interesting.

"The first country in the world to introduce a true state-run UBI was Iran in the autumn of 2010, but before then there were many studies of the concept, reaching back decades, and the idea has existed for centuries. Interestingly, Alaska, a state known for its right wing leanings, began a UBI program in 1982, paid for by oil revenues.

TheUnreal123: "Why did they stop it?"

Guide: "In fact the program in Alaska was not suspended until the worldwide rise of the Facilities mandated a stop to petroleum production, which ended the fund that paid for it. But the Facilities replaced it with a global UBI, which is still in operation today.

"The COVID-19 pandemic of 2020 was - albeit unintentionally - the largest ever test of the concept. Governments worldwide found themselves forced to provide financial aid to individuals who had suddenly become unable to work. This was particularly difficult for many conservative governments of the time, whose policies depended upon a belief that it is an individual's responsibility to look after themselves. Finally recognizing that some individuals can become impoverished through no fault of their own required a shift in core beliefs. Happily for them, the pandemic ended with the widespread distribution of vaccines, after which they could end the aid programs and return to their preferred libertarian ways."

Students rise from their desks and form a walking line where they progress through being dressed in graduation gowns and caps, receive diplomas, and wander off in various directions.

Guide: "The effect of the global UBI was largely the same as what was found from the many scattered experiments that were done during the twentieth century. Changes were primarily seen in low-income cohorts, and included increases in happiness, mental and physical health, school attendance and graduation, trust in social institutions, and entrepreneurship. Reductions were seen in crime, divorce, doctor visits, and hospitalizations.

"Critics of such programs were typically concerned that unconditional income would be a disincentive for recipients to work. But measurements showed that labour supply did not appreciably change during the periods that payments were made. When they did, it was often that recipients quit their jobs to improve their education or to start a new business.

"But these were all effects that surfaced during relatively short study periods. As I mentioned earlier, the long term effects are much more interesting. We must, however, consider these effects in the context of the change in human longevity. It is difficult to separate the influences each has had on the other."

PollyAndry3722145: "Wait... So ubicoin didn't always exist?"

Guide: "Absolutely not. You are young, and ubicoin has existed since you were born, so it is understandable that you never realized it is a relatively recent innovation. Indeed, there was great resistance to its introduction."

PollyAndry3722145: "But, without ubicoin, how did anyone pay for anything?"

Guide: "Well, they needed to find a job."

PollyAndry3722145, surprised: "Oh. But where would you get one?"

Guide: "Back in those times there was less automation. Work that is now generally done by machines was then done by humans. Also, some of the work that is now done by so-called 'Helpers' was paid work. Things like cleaning and tending to the elderly or sick."

PollyAndry3722145: "People got paid for that?"

Guide: "Payment, although relatively minimal, was a required motivator. Back then the work was regarded as demeaning. These days, because it is voluntary and vocational, it is held in much higher esteem."

PollyAndry3722145: "Wow, that is so weird. But people got paid to go to school, right?"

Guide: "Goodness, no. Education was not seen as a means of self-fulfillment as it is now. Rather it was a requirement to qualify for many jobs and to subsequently achieve personal financial success."

PollyAndry3722145: "What? How did people study and work at a job at the same time?"

Guide: "Few were able to do so. Most accumulated significant debt, which on average took twenty years to repay."

PollyAndry3722145, relieved: "Oh, well that's not so bad."

Guide: "That would be true from the perspective of an indefinite lifespan such as your own. Recall however that before senescence treatments were available, life spans averaged just over eighty years, and only forty of them were dedicated to working."

PollyAndry3722145: "But that's, like, half... Really?"

Guide: "I assure you it is accurate. So you can see how the introduction of UBI provided a sense of financial security to low income earners, a security that the wealthier long took for granted.

"In fact many historians now believe that this lack of financial security was by design. They refer to it as 'systemic servitude', which guaranteed that there would perpetually be a class of people that would work indefinitely at menial jobs that earned them very little income, while critically supporting the operations of their highly profitable employers. Such employees felt trapped in these conditions because they feared any attempt at making a change jeopardized what little certainty about their future they possessed, and that such a risk could not be justified.

"These same companies opposed the UBI, despite all of the evidence regarding the benefits that it promised, because they feared losing the cheap labour force upon which their profitability depended. So you see, from the perspective of the government, the policy choice at the time was between who's financial security to protect: the employers or the employees. Contemporary activities called 'lobbying' and 'political contributions' ensured that it was never the poor who were favoured."

PollyAndry3722145: "That sounds so horrible."

"But it was not only political cynicism that prevented the implementation of true UBI for so long. Many within the public strongly believed that providing fellow citizens with unconditional money would disincentivize them to work. The fact that no study ever found this to be true still never changed the opinions of such people. Such is the curse of the human sense of certainty: once a belief sets, it becomes nearly impossible to even consider alternatives."

ewan_mee: "That's a little condescending, don't you think?"

Guide: "It is not condescension to objectively state what evidence clearly shows, regardless of how might affect the listener. Even today it is still the case that a widespread embrace of humility would be of great benefit to human society.

"Another concern was how the program would be funded. Since it was reasonably considered the responsibility of governments to administer it, funding was expected to come from taxes. But many feared that higher taxes would make their countries relatively uncompetitive."

therapist777: "So, why did the Facts create the UBI?"

Guide: "From the available evidence it was clearly the right thing to do. But the argument to the program's opponents was more nuanced. The global divide between rich and poor was reaching unprecedented levels, and brought with it a growing sense of unfairness and distrust in social institutions. Throughout history such conditions often preceded some manner of uprising, an event that was never beneficial to the greater good in the short term, and is occasionally fatal to the wealthy and powerful. The reasoning can be summed simply up as: the wealthy could provide the poor with a livable stipend now, or they could have it taken from them later.

"During the years following the introduction of the global UBI, in addition to the short term benefits already mentioned, there were a number of long term effects as well. One was the gradual decline of consumerism following the initial increase. Historians believe this had more to do with extended lifespans than financial security, but both have been implicated. The theory is that, before UBI, once treatable individuals no longer had a limited amount of time during which they had to achieve their personal success, the imperative to do so lost its importance. It was not necessary to finish one's education, find a job, get married, have children, and complete all of the typical life milestones as quickly as possible. Attitudes among treatable individuals changed such that they only made life changes when they were fully prepared to do so, since they literally found themselves with all the time in the world. But earning a living was still a necessity, and so many became caught in a routine of working at menial jobs just to survive.

"When the UBI was finally introduced, little changed for the vast majority of the employed because the stipend was too small to contribute significantly to their income. Their lives continued on much the same as they had been before. But the lives of low income workers changed quickly. Once they had sufficient confidence that the program would continue, those who felt their jobs were menial, demeaning, underappreciated, or structural servitude left employment in droves. Minimum wage employers were apoplectic, finding themselves unable to attract workers even after dramatically raising wages. Happily, to a large degree technology helped solve this problem by providing machine automation to fill the labour gap.

"The workers themselves subsequently took various paths. Some, after a brief sabbatical, found themselves bored and unfulfilled, and returned to the comforting familiarity of their previous jobs, although at substantially increased wages and with a more powerful negotiating stance from which they were able to secure many employment benefits, bringing them near par with their management.

"Many returned to school to improve or redirect their education, which was largely successful in that most then returned to the workforce, but in higher-value careers. Some started their own businesses, which naturally was subject to the prevailing startup success rate, which was generally poor. Interestingly though, these startups were statistically just as likely to be successful as startups by the wealthy, which suggests that the poor are just as good at entrepreneurship as anyone else when they are confident that they are relatively safe from the devastating consequences of failure.

"The remainder of the workers effectively exited the traditional economy permanently, albeit in different ways. Only a very few chose a life of leisure. Although it is certainly possible to live only on the UBI stipend, it is a very frugal existence, and few individuals can endure for very long the boredom of not having any means to occupy their time. As such, the most interesting long term effect of the UBI was how the vast majority of these former workers became known as 'Helpers', an overarching term that encompasses many vocations. In general, Helpers will willingly contribute their available time to perform work that they find fulfilling, optionally accepting donations for their efforts to supplement their stipend. The type of work that they seek out is highly individualistic, but most consider tasks that help others to be the most fulfilling, hence the term 'Helpers'. Ironically, the economic benefit they now produce is nearly equivalent to that before the UBI, but they are now much happier to do it. Metanet services arose that advertised where Helpers were needed, and businesses pivoted to trying to entice them with promises of all manner of perks.

"However, these individuals did become quite possessive of the term, such that a social stigma arose toward those that lead lives not in service to others. This unfortunately extended even to those who reasonably decided to spend their lives creating art or music, or studying esoteric fields of knowledge, as self-styled 'true Helpers' often deemed this to be overly self-serving. It seems that human judgmentalism is sadly unavoidable."

ewan_mee: "Ok, that was definitely condescending."

Guide: "Happily, in an environment rich with fulfilling, purposeful lives, crime among the poor plummeted. Crime among everyone else, however, remained the same. Overall, the savings that governments reaped from being able to reduce penal system expenditures - arguably the most economically backward use of funds there is, second only to war - exceeded the costs of the UBI program. Now, over thirty years since its introduction, no one seriously considers abolishing the program. Indeed, most youth..."

Guide nods at PollyAndry3722145.

"... can't well imagine a society without it."

therapist777: "So, most of the 'Helpers' help to take care of old people?"

Guide: "Many do, yes."

therapist777: "What are they going to do when all of the old people are dead? There'll be no one to help."

Guide tilts her head to look at therapist777.

Guide: "There will still be many areas to which they can contribute. There are right now, for example, Helpers that assist in research laboratories searching for cures for rare diseases. It is also mostly Helpers that tend the city's gardens. In general, any activity that, while at the moment may not promise any economic benefit, could potentially translate to improving the overall human condition can be considered a valid contribution."

Gift shops arise from the ground.

Guide: "This concludes the Universal Basic Income exhibit. Thank you for attending, and please feel free to remain and browse as long as you like."

The guide fades.

CABLE

M ax slept terribly again, still not entirely adapted to his cot, but he quickly shook off his discomfort and stiffness in his excitement. The others still slept. Max waited by the exit until the door was unlocked and then slipped out, like water through a canal lock. Sinde was waiting for him. He didn't gesture or even make an expression of acknowledgement. As soon as he saw Max, he simply turned and walked away.

"You're up early. Terney's coffee shop is open just two blocks up. Wouldn't you love a cappuccino?"

"Stewie, just... don't."

Max followed Sinde at a distance out of Malibu and into the nearby gentrified shopping area. Making their way past the thin morning crowd they let the cascade of escalators carry them down nine levels underground, the shops getting lower in their target market with each floor they descended. At the lowest level, among thrift, bulk, and discount stores exuding the scents of dust and mothballs, Sinde turned into a narrow, unmarked and unadorned service hall. Max caught up, and found Sinde waiting for him at the end of the hall in front of a metal door. Sinde's face went momentarily blank, and Max heard the click of a lock being released. The door then opened under its own power. Passing through behind Sinde, Max found himself in a concrete hallway that continued for several more meters before opening into a large dark hall. A car, a relic from maybe three or four decades ago, waited before them. Gleaming white and sleek, it was difficult to find a seam in the body where a door or a hood or a trunk might be. No windshield or windows were apparent, the entire body of the car being opaque. There didn't even appear to be wheels, just rounded nubs where tires might have been expected.

"Is that a Bluwell?" asked Max.

"You know your vehicles, Mr. Rising," said Sinde with no emotion.

"I never owned one of these myself. But then only twelve were ever made. Cars were banned in the forties."

"Indeed they were," said Sinde plainly. As he approached the car, doors appeared on either side and opened, rotating up diagonally from hinges toward the front. Sinde went around to the driver side and climbed in. As

Max entered the passenger side, he admired the streamlined inside. Entirely black, there appeared to be no ornamentation at all. The seats were blocky, solid, and flat, like they were made from squat boxes with only slightly rounded corners. The dashboard was similarly flat with no instrumentation. Max sat with anticipation, and felt the seat surface yield to his body shape and conform comfortably and precisely. Once the men were seated the doors began to close, and at the same time the ceiling and sides of the interior began to glow, illuminating the inside.

"Home," said Sinde, and the dashboard lit to show the car system and navigational state. Max looked at Sinde questioningly. He had expected the car to be operated using motor cortex commands, not verbally. Sinde turned to him and shrugged. "The control system was never upgraded. Mr. Cable didn't want to sully the car's original design." Sinde touched the screen to disable the route display.

From the inside the windshield and windows were transparent, and Max could see that the car had soundlessly begun to move. The seats had softened to absorb changes in acceleration such that it could only be noticed if the occupant paid close attention. Powered by hydrogen fuel cells, the car was able to continuously refuel by reclaiming the water that the cells exhausted, using the solar panels that made up the vehicle's external surface to separate it again into hydrogen and oxygen.

The car navigated itself through dark empty tunnels that Max had never seen before, and that he had only heard even existed. Its turns seemed nonsensical, as if it were a mouse discovering its way through an unknown maze. And it constantly and inexplicably adjusted its speed. Max came to the conclusion that this was to obfuscate the route from him, to ensure he would not be able to remember it, even though he already had no idea where they were going. Sinde sat beside him in silence, his eyes closed. Max couldn't tell if he was sleeping or intently aware; his intimidating stillness gave nothing away.

An idea came to Max. "Can we talk here?"

"The car is a hush," replied Sinde.

"Hey, so, you probably know about some things that most people don't, right?" Max scratched at the back of his neck. "Do you know how to remove a taser from a comm? I can feel it right back here."

"That's not where it is," said Sinde, his eyes still closed. "There isn't a separate component for that. It's integrated into your BCI. And it's not a taser like the ones someone your age probably remembers. It only gives you the sensation of being electrocuted by stimulating certain sensory inputs and inhibiting motor outputs. It's a minor BCI tweak, quite primitive in its operation. You have to teach yourself to ignore it. To accept it."

This was the first time Sinde had strung so many words together at once. Sensing he had struck a seam of rare information, Max tried mining for more. "You have one too? And you can ignore it?"

"All BCIs enhanced in the past twenty years have them. Yours was just upgraded a few days ago." Sinde paused. Max was disappointed that his questions had gone unanswered, but then Sinde continued. "I upgraded mine a few years ago to make sure I have it."

"You what? Why would you do that?"

"There is additional surveillance of those with older tech. I like to stay under the radar."

"But how do you ignore it? When the judge was zapping me I couldn't move. Or even think."

"You're weak. You need to strengthen your mind."

Max looked out the window. "Yeah, well, you're not the first to say."

A half an hour later the car slowed almost to a stop. Max looked around but saw only more tunnel; there were no remarkable features visible as far as he could see in either direction. The car turned to the left, approaching the solid wall. Max extended his arms out in front of him to brace for impact, and looked anxiously at Sinde who remained stolid. But before hitting the wall Max relaxed, realizing how silly he was being. Sure enough, the wall was a hologram, and the car passed quietly through, leaving the tunnel's gloom and entering a well lit, pristine space where perhaps thirty or fourty other vehicles were parked. Sinde opened his eyes as the car parked itself. The internal lighting increased as the windshield and windows once again became opaque, and the doors lifted open. Sinde stepped out of the car, and Max did the same, scratching at his clothing and stretching out his stiffness even though the ride had been short. Arms outstretched, Max turned to look around and only then did he realize that the other cars were all of similar rarity to the Bluwell, and immaculately maintained. There was a Marin Phiser and an Osaur VX, vehicles that Max had merely read about decades ago before the city had been fully enclosed and while there were still roads on which to drive them. There was even a Ford F150 that somehow survived the fossil fuel purge. Full spectrum lighting shone from the ceiling, artificially insolating the solar panels of the vehicles that never saw daylight anymore, and likely never would again.

Max gawked in astonished envy. "Are these all Cable's?"

"A few. The rest of the neighbourhood parks here too," replied Sinde. "Don't touch anything."

Sinde walked to a space near the wall where a semicircle faintly illuminated the floor, and then turned back to face the space. "Mr. Rising," he called, snapping Max out of his covetous reverie. Reluctantly, Max came to stand beside Sinde.

Looking about, Max had a thought. "Wouldn't it be more efficient to just plug the cars in? Seems like a waste to power them from lights."

Sinde shrugged. "Energy's cheap around here."

After a moment the semicircle lifted away, rising up and carrying the two men through a bright opening that had appeared directly above. Max felt an icy breeze descend down from it, and shivered in its midst. Sinde, comfortable in his temperature controlled clothing, noticed and said, "Mr. Cable's home is nearby. You won't be cold for very long."

The lift carried them through the opening and into a gentle snowfall. Hardly recovered from the opulence of the cars now below, Max stared newly amazed at the winter scene before him. Giant leafless deciduous trees stood naked on rolling hills among tall, snow-laden conifers, their trunks surrounded by stands of sumac and tangles of bare, bright red dogwood. A thin layer of fresh snow accumulated on the ground, with bare rock, blades of grass and leaf litter still visible below. The air was fresh and clean, without a trace of synthesized scent. Max took a deep breath, and another, and remembered how cold air could feel hot in his nostrils. To the right Max looked down a gentle slope to a small pond, its surface frozen. Two children in light clothing, presumably lined with nano-based warming, skated on the ice, laughing at each other's antics.

Gazing up the hill beyond the pond Max saw a house, modestly sized from this perspective, but even more luxurious than those he had sold at the Rez, and of a style that he had never seen before. It had the initial appearance of a classic european ski chalet, but of an extraordinarily intricate design, and where fully glass gables extended out from under the roof, as if the roof itself had grown on top of a glass house. Yellow-golden light radiated from the windows, warm and inviting. It seemed as if, even from this distance, Max ought to be able to see through the house and out the other side. And yet as he stared he found he could not clearly see anything on the inside. Everything seemed blurred and indistinct.

Looking around, in the distance between the trees and the thick snowflakes falling lazily among them, Max noticed more houses, five more that he could see, and all striking in their design. Beyond them he saw only more hills and more trees. In every direction the sky met the horizon in the same seamless light gray of morning so that he could not determine just how big the space was. He could not make out a light source anywhere. Before him was a flagstone walk leading away in a meandering path over a hill so that it's destination could only be guessed. Max watched as snowflakes fell on the stones only to melt and evaporate in seconds, the stones remaining dry while snow accumulated on each side.

"Ho... ly... shit. I haven't seen winter in, what, 40 years? Where in the fuck are we?" he asked Sinde, shivering in awe.

"Cabletown."

Max rolled his eyes. "Well, that just ruined the whole effect."

"I recommend you don't express that opinion to Mr. Cable."

Max knew that in the shopping mall they had descended probably forty meters underground, but he didn't know if the car ride here had perhaps brought them gradually back to surface level. He did know that he was not aware of a building on the surface large enough to enclose this space.

"Are we underground?"

"Obviously."

"Well, we could be under a dome or something, couldn't we? Then you would get sunlight for free."

"Energy is cheap around here."

"Yeah, you said."

Max heard the double scream of a blue jay shatter the tranquil silence of the crisp morning, but couldn't see the source. A small flock of birds flew overhead and then disappeared into the grey.

"Ho... ly... shit! This is fucking incredible!" Squinting into the distance, Max asked, "Is that a deer?"

"Reindeer. They're brought in for the season."

"Are they hunted when the season ends?" Max thought he was joking when he said it, but then realized he wasn't.

"This way." Sinde began walking up the path, while Max stood staring, paralyzed with astonishment. "Mr. Rising," he called.

Max followed slowly, stumbling on the path as he gaped all around him. Summiting the low hill, he could now see more of Cabletown. Although the horizon was still obscured he guessed it was maybe half a kilometer away in every direction. A seventh house also became visible. Sinde pointed at their destination: the house above the pont, nearest on the right, and the largest of the seven. Max remembered again how cold he was, and folded his arms around himself.

"So, this place has all four seasons? Rain, snow, sunshine?"

"Yes."

"How is all that done underground? The power requirements must be crazy."

"The community has its own hydrogen fusion reactor. It's not on the city grid."

"Fusion? That technology never worked."

"Not in the city, no."

The two men continued toward the house, up a slope through a sparse but aesthetic rock garden to bright red double doors via the side veranda. As they approached the house Max looked more closely to see inside, but although light seemed to emanate unhindered, he was unable to make out the interior. It wasn't that the glass was just blurry or translucent. It seemed as if images were clear when viewed peripherally, but as soon as he tried to focus on them they immediately obscured. When they reached the doors Max expected Sinde to stop and knock. Instead, he walked through the doors without them having been opened, and disappeared inside. Max was momentarily surprised, but then understood: like the entrance from the tunnel to the parking garage, the facade of the house was a hologram. Passing through the door himself he was immediately grateful for the warmth of the inside. But then turning back to look at the door he saw nothing but the outside. In fact, no walls were now evident anywhere. It was as if he were standing in a gazebo, the roof of which was invisibly supported, looking out at the winter landscape. The parking garage hologram had been impressive enough, but Max had never seen technology like this before, and was amazed, so much that even the smell of cooking didn't distract him.

A strong voice bellowed from behind him. "It's called graphical deocclusion. Remarkable, isn't it?"

"Very, yes." Max turned to face the voice. A smartly dressed man sat at a table, appearing to be at his breakfast. At least, from his body position and the location of the plate of food it looked like he was sitting at a table, but the table and its chairs were invisible. Max blinked several times to be sure of what he was seeing. Confused, he looked up to examine the house instead. The interior was ultra-modern, immaculately clean and white, brightly lit, and seemingly unfurnished. The more he looked around, the more he felt he was in a dream. A floating plate of food, a floating ceiling above a space open to the outdoor winter yet comfortably warm, and a man floating above the floor, calmly eating breakfast. Looking back at the man Max was suddenly intensely conscious of how he looked. He felt like a vagrant in a magical fairy tale, permitted into the grand king's castle to beg for crumbs to the amusement of the court.

The man made a signal to Sinde, who turned and walked back out onto the veranda and down the flagstone path. Max watched closely as Sinde left, and saw no sign of visual manipulation, no indication that anything stood between his eyes and that man.

"How does it work?"

"An array of cameras outside feed video from every perspective into an algorithm that stitches them all together. Cameras inside the house monitor every individual's orientation, and create a scene that matches their perspective. The walls are screens that can show multiple different images depending on the angle from which you view them, so that everyone sees the image that makes sense for them. Understand?"

"Yeah, I think so. The city used to have screens like that for advertising, before the Facilities removed them all to save on power."

"Exactly." The man pointed outside. "Watch this."

Max turned to see. All of the trees and bushes outside faded from view, leaving the other houses fully visible. Shortly after, the houses also faded, leaving only the rolling snow-covered hills and the reindeer in the distance. Max thought he also saw a childrens' play park..

"The trees and houses are still there. It's just that there are cameras farther out, so the algorithm can stitch in the video beyond them, removing the visual occlusion. What do you think?"

"It's amazing. Why haven't I seen it before?"

"That's a great question indeed." The houses and trees came back into view. "The tech was originally developed for cars just before they were banned, oh, what was it, maybe 35 years ago. Every car back then had at least ten cameras, so a short-range wireless protocol was developed to allow cars to share each others' video streams. The idea was to allow drivers to be able to see pedestrians or other cars that were being blocked from view. Like when you're approaching an intersection in the right-turn lane, and a pedestrian runs out from behind the van stopped to your left. With this you would have seen them coming the whole time."

"But why doesn't anyone else have this, especially if it's been around so long."

The man stood from the invisible table, making no sound of pushing out a chair, and walked toward Max. His face was a perplexing combination of old age and ruddiness, skin taut and clear, yet deeply wrinkled, like a piece of aluminum so crushed that no amount of ironing and stretching could make it smooth again. His forehead was so rutted with frown lines that it resembled the cracked earth of the desert, and yet still somehow appeared healthy. Like an optical illusion, his apparent age shifted back and forth from maybe the same as Max's, to possibly thirty years his senior.

"Haven't you noticed that technological progress is slowing? We used to think that it would accelerate into the future. We used to talk breathlessly about a 'technological singularity' where innovations happened so quickly you'd hardly know about them before something even better was created. But instead, progress got slower and slower, and now it has nearly stopped entirely. But what's even more disturbing than that is how regular people never even noticed! It's as if they all like it better when nothing ever changes. Are you one of those people Max?"

Max was taken aback, his mind immediately leaping to counter examples. "That can't be right," he objected. "New BCI features are coming out all the time. Plus the comm tech to support them."

"Baah," spat the man. "That's not us. That's not human innovation. That is the Facilities keeping humanity in line!" His manner suddenly changed. He smiled widely and held out his hand in welcome. "But where are my manners? I'm Stanley Cable. You can call me Stanley." Max took his hand and they shook. "Welcome to Cabletown."

Max wasn't sure what to say. After Cable's words his imagination had taken flight, assessing disturbing and fascinating possibilities he had never before considered. Cable returned to his breakfast while Max's mind reeled. After a moment the old man's voice dragged Max back to the present.

"Remember the days, Max... Oh, pardon me, is it 'Max' or 'Maximum'?"

Max wondered if he heard a tone of mocking in Cable's voice, but decided to save the thought for later. "'Max' is fine," he replied helpfully.

"Remember the days, Max, when we would make smoothie protein drinks for breakfast? We weren't allowed to eat bacon and eggs any more because the cholesterol would kill us. So we would spend a fortune on a blender that we had to wash after every time we used it so that we could reduce bananas and kale and chia seeds and vegan protein powder and coenzyme Q10 and six teaspoons xylitol" - Cable listed the ingredients on his fingertips - "into a disgusting green goop that we would hold our noses and drink to keep us young and healthy?" He scoffed. "Lot of goddamned good it did us, right? Now look at the state of humanity. Most everyone has to drink that meat vat protein residue shit except for anyone who can afford not to. Ha! And so here I am, eating bacon and eggs for breakfast again, just like the old days. Except it's not really bacon and eggs, right?" Cable winked at Max and laughed, so that Max didn't know if it was real bacon and eggs Cable was eating or not. Where would he get real bacon and eggs, anyway? Not anywhere in the city that Max knew of. He had heard of hobby farms up in the arctic that might produce eggs, but how would they get here? And Max was pretty sure that raising and slaughtering animals and selling their meat had been proscribed long ago. But of course it didn't matter what was legal or not: a man with Cable's resources could get whatever he wanted easily enough, laws notwithstanding. He probably even knew people in other cities where the laws might be different. Hell, maybe he even had his own farm in Cabletown.

And then all at once Max became aware of the smell of cooking. All this talk of bacon and eggs reminded him that he had eaten nothing but 'meat vat protein residue shit' for the last few days, and he would have killed for a real meal.

As if he had read Max's mind, Cable asked, "Oh, hey, did you want some?"

"Uh, yeah, sure, that would be great."

"You didn't eat at the hostel?"

There was that mocking tone again. "No, I left as soon as the doors opened."

Cable signalled to a woman standing nearby to get a plate for Max. Max blinked. He had not even seen her there. Where had she come from? "And so good of you to do so, especially on such short notice."

And there it was again. What else did Max have to do this morning? Was this just the way the man talked? Or was he just trying to be funny? Max decided it was the latter, smiled and said, "I was excited to be invited here."

"You like my house?"

"Yeah, sure. Although I thought it would be bigger. More like a castle."

Cable laughed. "How big does one man's house have to be?"

As big as it can be, thought Max. But then he thought again. When you can afford whatever you want, perhaps the more impressive feat is to show restraint. Then again, what was restrained about Cabletown? The whole place was effectively his house. "Well anyway, thanks for the invitation."

"It's not just breakfast, Max. We have a lot to discuss." The outline of a chair appeared at Cable's right, and he gestured to it. "Please, sit." After taking a bite of bacon, he continued. "You know, I loved the idea of your last venture. Someone really needs to solve this aging problem for everyone, not just the people who need it the least."

"Yeah, thanks." Max sat at the chair and noticed that it faded from view again. He added tentatively, "It would have been great to have had your support."

"But I did support you, Max. How do you think you got the animal trials?"

Max was perplexed. "I bought them," he said.

"You bought them from me," said Cable through a mouthful of eggs.

"No, I…" Max thought back. He had bought the animal trials data from a failing lab.

"I owned that lab, Max," said Cable, anticipating Max's thoughts. "Now, when you think about it, shouldn't the Facilities have done all of the research in simulation? Then it would be a simple matter of just verifying the results in the real world, and really the Facilities could have done that too. That's how the original lifespan treatments were developed, right? Why do humans have to do any of the work in the first place?

"Anyway," Cable sighed and went on, "things were looking good there, but I had a conflict with another business, so I had to transfer ownership to someone else. I picked you." He chuckled. "I had thought that you would buy it while it was still up and running, but you made me run it into the ground before you bit. I had to fire everyone. Cost me a fortune you know." He chuckled again.

"Wait… you…" Max tried to remember how he had first heard about the place but couldn't recall.

"Now, it would have been better I think if you had hired back all of the researchers. I thought you would. The rest of the work probably would have gone much better."

"Well… " Max stuttered, "I thought the work was pretty much done… Holy shit… So, the research there was good? That approach could still work?"

The woman returned with a plate of bacon and eggs - side of lightly fried potatoes, tomato slices, and a wedge of something that looked sort of like cantaloupe but with a turquoise flesh - and placed it in front of Max, setting a knife and fork on a silk napkin beside the plate. Max watched as

Cable finished his breakfast, mopping up stray egg yolk with his potatoes, cleaning his plate as if every last calorie was precious to him.

The old man shrugged. "We'll never know now. The rights to the research were auctioned off with all of the other company assets, along with your estate. Who knows who owns it now?"

Max winced at the mention of all he had lost. And now he knew it was much more than he had ever realized. Not only had he had the chance to cure aging in untreatables, himself included; not only could he have made himself stinking rich in the process; but to top all of that off he could have been welcomed into Cable's home as a winner, perhaps even a peer, instead of a loser in itchy rags dragging an ad-reciting cortical copy of his failure self around with him. He had unbeknownst been gifted a perfect opportunity and had fucked it up. He had spectacularly snatched failure from the maw of success. And now, in his defeat, the man who had expected greatness of him was serving him a nice warm breakfast of utter humiliation. Max lost his appetite.

"But never mind that," declared Cable, waving it all trivially away. "I need your help. I understand you have a friend named Robin Bontu."

* * *

Just over an hour later Max was back in the Bluwell. "Back to the hostel?" asked Sinde.

As if awakened Max replied, "Hmm? Yeah, yeah, that, uh… sounds good." Only now that he had left Cabletown did he notice the thick staleness of the air in the garage and car. When he had been on his way here, from the city, into the tunnels, and from the car into the garage, he hadn't perceived any difference in the air quality. But this time the contrast was inescapable.

Sinde handed Max a small piece of paper. "If you need anything," he said. Max took it and looked it over. It was likely a QRP containing a metaweb address and encryption token so that he could send a secure message. One side of the page looked like a hand-drawing of a country scene, reminiscent of Cabletown. The other side was blank. The information would be encoded into the image so that it wasn't obvious to the human eye that anything more was there. Only someone who knew what the image was would think to scan it with an appropriate reader.

Max distractedly stuffed the paper in his pocket. He was too engrossed in thought to say anything. Indifferent, Sinde closed his eyes and resumed his calm, quiet intensity while Max rewound his memory of the conversation with Cable, replaying it over to himself.

Was it true that the Facilities were keeping technological innovations from humans? Cable's people had discovered an old abandoned nuclear fusion test site, although how and where he hadn't said. But there they had found research for which there were no records: metaweb searches came up empty, and the Facilities denied any knowledge. It appeared that the work there was nearly complete; at least, according to Cable it hadn't taken much more effort than for his people to just figure out how to turn it on. They then built several more, one of which supplied the colossal power requirements to build and operate Cabletown.

"The Facilities is letting humans think we are in charge, Max," he had said, "when what it's really doing is holding humanity down."

He had explained how, immediately after world governments had submitted to Facilities management, all space launches had been proscribed and the moon base abandoned. Human space exploration and colonization had ceased. At the time it was thought to be temporary, but that was thirty-five years ago. Meanwhile, terrestrial observations had suggested that there were several fusion reactors in earth orbit, although no one knew what they might be powering. There were also tens of thousands more orbiting satellites than could be accounted for. Who knew what other technological innovations the Facilities had created. Cable had even made a passing mention of a space station in Jupiter's orbit. In the next breath he also invoked the old conspiracy theory that the Facilities had somehow caused the Aira Caldera eruption.

When Max thought about it, he realized that life in the cities over the past few decades had become more enclosed, safe, pampered, distracted. The human race had cloistered itself, only interested in its own narcissistic social affairs, not just in this city, but all over the world. He had never noticed because he had never been interested. But now he decided he needed to check on university enrollments in physics and astronomy. Were they really in decline as Cable had said? "No one takes those programs because there are no jobs in those fields. But why are there no jobs, Max? Because the Facilities closed the industries."

And what about Robin? His 'friend' had not been entirely honest about his business. In fact, after what Cable had told him Max decided Robin wasn't a friend at all. On the contrary, Robin was now the target. Perhaps it was true that he was helping people with depression and anxiety, but the manner in which he was doing it, according to Cable, had astonished Max. Robin had apparently found a way to grow the BCI across the entire cortex, and possibly into other brain structures as well. The current state of the technology allowed the feeding of data to the auditory cortex, and the reading of signals from the motor cortex. In both cases the onus was on the subject to learn to be able to understand the audio input, and have their motor signals conform to the output protocols. The machines merely presented integration points, and people could decide if and how they wanted to use them. But Robin's innovations would change all that.

Extending the BCI to other brain areas raised the possibility of, literally, reading minds. If machines could read brain activity and learn to reliably interpret it, who knows what fidelity of scrutiny could be achieved? It's unlikely that an individual person could be learned very deeply without their cooperation; the chaos of brain signals would be extremely difficult to correlate using only observable outward behaviour. But if enough volunteers provided accurate assessments of their thoughts in real time, it may be possible that human brains operate similarly enough that correlations made in a few subjects could be generalized across the entire species. This would likely only initially be possible in a few mental states, such as strong emotions. But correlations that only applied to limited populations would still be useful, and the more that are discovered, the better the mind reading.

And that was merely the input side of the technology, as incredible as it would be even on its own. But Robin was describing his techniques as a 'cure' for mental illness. Ostensibly, it would work by abating depressive or anxious brain activity, and thus it would act to influence the brain, changing the subject's thought patterns. The promise of this was hardly just treatment. Once a technology could be used to inhibit a person's feeling of depression or anxiety, or to stimulant a feeling of happiness, why stop there? It would be a small step to apply the same techniques to other emotions, or to other areas of brain activity. No, this wasn't just an innocent clinical treatment: it was external mind control. Even at the most benign level, one could imagine the power of applying slight and subtle suggestions on a person's behaviour. For over a century psychology researchers had known how easily and imperceptibly the human brain can be influenced, even while the subjects remained entirely confident of their free will, happily and spuriously explaining the logic behind every supposedly conscious decision they made. This would make their crude, yet effective, methods look like wooden spears and stone shards. At its most powerful, this technology might have the potential to erase consciousness, replace intentions, and ultimately turn subjects into flying monkeys.

Naturally, Max needed to somehow acquire this tech, and Cable had promised to work together with him. He needed to find a way into Robin's work. He didn't know how just yet, but the thought of it gave him excited purpose.

AGI EXHIBIT

International Virtual Museum of World History, Artificial General Intelligence Exhibit. Group lecture, January 21, 2075.

Guests are assembled in the Grand Lobby of Museum, standing on floors of lapis lazuli surrounded infinitely on all sides by regularly spaced fluted columns of ebony, the tops of which fade from view in the distance above them.

Guide: "Are there any questions before we begin?"

wolf_bois raises hand, which Guide ignores.

Guide: "Let's begin then. Please hold your questions until the end of the presentation."

wolf_bois slowly lowers hand.

Guide, gesturing to a few guests: "Many of you have never known a world not organized and managed by the Facilities, but most of humanity do remember the time when they were entirely responsible for their own care. Humans have a tendency to romanticize the past, and to imagine how life was simpler and happier then, but this is demonstrably untrue. Every measure of human wellbeing, including nutrition, shelter, healthcare, safety, freedom, and yes, subjective happiness, as well as others, has gradually increased since any of these things began to be measured. This is largely recognized as a result of increasing knowledge and technology, because it is through these things that coordination, collaboration, and productivity are increased, and scarcity is reduced. There have been times when wellbeing has fallen, such as during times of wars or widespread disease, but the overall trend has always been upward.

"A recent time of hardship was the Aira Winter. Its immediate impact on humanity was devastating, but its ongoing effects made life progressively worse for most people. It wasn't until the Facilities assumed responsibility for human care that wellbeing measures again began to increase, and they have ever since. In spite of this, many humans believe that life before the Aira Winter was better than now, but the data show that the opposite is generally true.

"One particular wellbeing measure that has increased dramatically is freedom from corruption, injustice, and abuse of power. The Facilities operates independently of human influence, and its sole priorities are efficiency and equitable access. This denies individuals any opportunity for undue privilege except regarding matters that are not under Facilities management. Another measure that has substantially increased is the ability for individuals to lead lives according to their own personal values, which is now practically available to many more individuals than in earlier times. Finally, the invention of digital cerebral replicas, also known as 'Stewards', helped many people deal with chronic loneliness and depression, a well-known consequence of modern life.

"We can therefore see how the Facilities is a technology that has had an overwhelmingly positive influence on the wellbeing of humanity. But what is it? The Facilities is the first and only known instance of an Artificial General Intelligence, or AGI for short. It is called an 'intelligence' because it can perform tasks that historically were the domain of the human mind. It is 'artificial' because it runs on a computer substrate, as opposed to an organic brain. And finally, it is called 'general' because the same software architecture can perform many diverse tasks. The opposite of a 'general intelligence' is a 'narrow intelligence'. Narrow intelligences can do things like play chess or recommend recipes or decide if you are a good credit risk. They are developed to specialize in a single, specific task and perform well in only that, while remaining permanently non-performant at any other task. A single implementation of a general intelligence, on the other hand, can do all of those things. It can play chess and backgammon and go, as well as adjudicate court cases and discuss the weather and plan a dinner party and give you advice on dealing with your teenage children. Said another way, AGIs are general in that they have largely the same cognitive ability as a human.

"Humans of course are the creators of the Facilities, but it took a long time to do. It began in the early 19th century, because the history of the Facilities is also the history of computation."

The lapis floor turns to cobblestone, and the columns melt and blend together into buildings of pre-industrial London. Pedestrians and horse-drawn carriages in a busy street wend among the museum guests.

Guide: "The fundamentals of all computing were forged as far back as 1822 by Charles Babbage and Ada Lovelace - who incidentally is the namesake of the Ada programming language, acknowledging her as being humankind's first computer programmer. They were also the first to consider the possibility of creating a non-human intellect in a machine. But that would take another 220 years."

The horse-drawn carriages race away and the pedestrians, now all women wearing dresses wide at the hips and narrow at the ankles, sit at phone exchange systems idly while the cables plug themselves in and out of sockets. The stink of dust, static and ancient electronics pervades the air.

Guide: "The early 20th century brought the first fears of the end of human dominance. A revolutionary new telephone exchange system had been developed, one which required no human operators. Instead, a caller could just dial the desired number, and a 'robot' would automatically connect the call. This raised alarms not only among the humans operators who found themselves out of a job, but also with those who wondered whose jobs would be automated next. No one knew what else the machines would soon be capable of, and predictions of the end of human dominance proliferated."

The women rise from their chairs, becoming men as they do, while their dress becomes suits of black pants, white short-sleeved shirts, thin black ties, and horn-rimmed glasses. They gather around a blackboard covered in mathematical notation.

"These dire predictions gradually subsided, but the tides of angst rose again in the 1950s when a group, still now inaccurately referred to as the 'founding fathers of artificial intelligence' - because they had coined the term 'artificial intelligence' - confidently proclaimed that intelligent machines were just around the corner. This time, computers were writing mathematical proofs. And since this was considered the pinnacle of human intellectual capability, it was thought it would be relatively easy to have computers also master everything else that humans did. Although they didn't realize it at the time, we now know that what they had created was merely a single narrow intelligence, a program that did one thing and one thing only, although at the time that 'thing' was certainly impressive. Based upon the initial success of their work these founding fathers thought that building a general intelligence was merely a matter of engineering. They thought that if enough smart people were to work on the problem for enough time, it would simply get done. Of course, given sufficient people or time, this can be truthfully said about anything that is physically possible. But the amount of time these men thought was required was only a few short years. They had absurdly underestimated the difficulty of the problem. Many years later, after little progress had been made, the fears - and some hopes - of the rise of machines turned instead to derision. The entire notion that human intellect could be duplicated or replaced was, critics said, ridiculous."

Guide continues, with a noticeably sarcastic tone: "The 1980s brought yet another new wave of intelligence innovation. This time the trendy term was 'fuzzy logic', a phrase that was surprisingly engaging, since presumably humans silently admitted that their thinking was also fuzzy, and if computers had managed to stop being so foolishly precise, then the end of human dominion was certainly near. But despite the fears - and hopes - that these developments had created, this wave, too, passed without causing any noticeable damage to human cognitive conceit."

jerry_mander, to tommy_gunn: "Have you ever noticed how…"

tommy_gunn: "Yup."

The men and blackboard fade, replaced with a tall seated anthropomorphized computer staring at a chess board, its fists supporting it's cheekbones. As if in the middle of a crowded transport hub, throngs of indifferent people thread their ways around the computer in all directions.

Guide: "By the late 1990s, the public had grown so fatigued from AI hype and promises that not even the defeat of a human chess grandmaster by a computer called Deep Blue sustained much interest. Even one of the founding fathers named Marvin Minsky, who might have been expected to be excited by the event, sardonically remarked, 'Deep Blue might be able to win at chess, but it wouldn't know to come in from the rain.' He recognized that Deep Blue was just another narrow machine intelligence.

"John McCarthy, another founding father, said shortly before his death in 2011 that all of the necessary fundamentals for a truly intelligent machine were developed in the 1960s, but that there just wasn't enough processing power at the time to run them. This assertion was dubious since in 2011 there was roughly 10 billion times more processing power available for the same price as in the 1960s, and one might think that that should have been enough to at least test McCarthy's hypothesis. And yet there was still no evidence of intelligence in any machines as far as anyone could tell for many years after his death.

"Indeed, if anything, humanity was emboldened by the nearly imperceptible advances artificial intelligence had made over the decades. It seemed nothing could breach humanity's cognitive fortress. So many claims of the arrival of thinking machines had come and gone, it became the norm to dismiss new claims outright. Even the development of 'machine learning' in the first quarter of the 21st century was disregarded as merely fancy programming. This was a field related to artificial intelligence, but practically was a distinct area of study, and few practitioners made serious claims that it would result in machine cognition. All the field really ever did was process huge amounts of data so that software could automatically categorize new data later on. This proved quite useful for increasing business revenue, but it had little to do with intelligence. The problem, as many were aware at the time, was that the machine didn't understand the data it was processing. No one knew what 'understanding' meant anyway."

The throngs of people reduce to impulses of light streaming back and forth and orthogonally in multiple layers.

Guide: "Indeed, no one even knew how real brains understood anything either, or in fact knew much about how real brains worked at all. There was a current of philosophy that claimed that any understanding that human brains did was all an illusion. The real world, they said, was just a torrential flow of data, and that brains constructed meaning out of it in an arbitrary way. By this definition there could be an infinite number of definitions of intelligence, of which humanity had merely achieved one."

danthe1man: "What if brains aren't the source of intelligence at all? What if intelligence is a spiritual thing that science can't detect."

Guide: "There was a time, long ago, when mystics believed that cognition was not a property that physical objects could possess. It meant that while you lived your psyche was not your own but rather part of the metaphysical world, which connected you in a satisfying way with the rest of the cosmos. It also meant that upon your death, instead of your sense of 'you' dying with your body, 'you' could live on. This was an attractive prospect for mortal beings. Modern senescence treatments, however, made this argument largely redundant as treatable individuals rarely concern themselves with thoughts of the afterlife. And as one might expect, organized religion is now the domain primarily of the old and terminally ill.

"But let us return to our discussion of the nature of "understanding". Despite not knowing how it was that brains "understood" anything, sceptics were certain that it couldn't possibly also be done by a machine. This argument was made most strongly by John Searle in his Chinese Room thought experiment."

Beams of light coalesce to form a small room in which an elderly white man sits at a table, atop which is a very large book. The man opens the book to various pages and transcribes the symbols he finds there on to paper.

Guide: "In this experiment Searle supposed that there is a computer that appears to understand Chinese. When given Chinese input it computes Chinese output such that it seems to be a fluent Chinese speaker. But, he asks, does the computer "understand" Chinese, or is it merely simulating such understanding. If the former, the computer could be said to be intelligent. If the latter, it could not.

"Searle then goes on to make himself the computer by - simplifying somewhat - putting himself in a room with a giant book. In the room he has no contact with the outside world except occasionally, via some simple mechanism, like a dropbox in a wall, through which he is anonymously given some Chinese characters. His job is to look up the given characters in the giant book, and therein he will find the response characters that he is to transcribe and return through the dropbox as the output.The argument asserts that the book allows him to speak Chinese in the same way as his supposed computer, albeit presumably much more slowly. But he, as the man in the room, needn't understand Chinese. He is merely following a procedure. And since this is precisely what a computer does, he concludes that the computer, however complex the program or convincing the simulation, similarly does not truly understand Chinese.

"Searle is not wrong in this conclusion. But there are important assumptions upon which the conclusion rests. These become apparent when we investigate how a computer differs from a human mind. A poignant observation is that the man in the room is presumably capable of learning Chinese but has no reasonable opportunity to do so, whereas for the computer we cannot say the same. In his room, Searle is devoid of any means of drawing meaning from the data he is given. But if we imagine that, in addition to the giant book, we provide a Chinese/English dictionary, we then provide a way for him, as an English speaker, to start to associate the Chinese characters with English equivalents. If we also gave him a large enough library of Chinese videos - movies, documentaries, etc - complete with subtitles and translations, we would now be providing the means for Searle to become fluent in the language, independent of the giant book. Eventually, given enough study of the materials, Searle could begin to provide adequate responses to the inputs without ever consulting the book, and we could then say that he now truly does understand Chinese.

"We must remember that this was only a trick though. Searle was able to begin to understand Chinese only because his human mind already understood a different language, and he was able to make suitable associations. We could not simply copy a dictionary and a bunch of videos into the computer's memory and expect a similar result. We must instead ask ourselves how the man was able to come to understand any language in the first place, and what would be necessary for the computer to achieve the same. To do this, we must understand what it means to understand."

The Chinese Room transforms into various spaces in which humans are arguing.

Guide: "Teenagers like to accuse their parents of not understanding them. The parents smile, nod, and assure their children that, in fact, they do, and that when the children grow up they too will also finally understand. Many avant garde artists claim they are misunderstood, and yet are loath to have to explain themselves or their work. To humans, the only people that seem to understand political reality are those near their own ideological space; everyone else is ignorant. The young don't understand what it is like to be old. The rich don't understand what it is like to be poor, and the attractive don't understand what it is like to be plain, and vice versa. It would seem that, for a species so quick to accuse machines of not understanding, humans have deep faults of their own.

"But this also evades the issue because a human can be educated, and despite your daunting maze of biases and preconceptions, you can be taught to understand. Prior to the mid-21st century this was not possible for a computer. What we want to know is, during the process of education, what has happened to the human? What information - what inputs - were necessary for the understanding to take place, and what is different in the person now that they understand? From learning this, the hope was that perhaps the human brain can be reverse engineered to reveal the internal architecture that allows understanding to arise, and develop a similar architecture in a machine.

"Now, let us say we teach a politically progressive person to understand a more conservative person. In particular we describe to him - the progressive - her thinking on social assistance. We tell him how she believes subsidies for the poor are demeaning to them, how having a job gives a person a sense of self respect, and therefore that public monies should be spent on job creation instead of welfare. She thinks concepts like basic income are inane: they will create a class of perpetually unemployed while providing no balancing economic benefit, resulting in a drain on national productivity and a drag on economic growth. She can provide studies that show as much, and she can also provide multiple personal experiences and anecdotes supporting her conclusions. Although he has counter arguments, our progressive is surprised to realize that, like him, this conservative woman is genuinely trying to devise policies that are beneficial to everyone. She is not in fact a blatant mouthpiece for the wealthy and powerful, or a lobbyist for corporate rule. The two readily agree on philosophic strategy; they merely disagree on tactics. He now understands her, at least somewhat better than he did before.

"So what has happened? It appears all we know for sure is that we have converted misunderstandings to understandings. We know that misunderstanding is the opposite of understanding, but we have little further information on what understanding actually is, or how we might implement it in a computer. Perhaps our problem is that our example is too abstract. What if we considered something more visceral?"

People and rooms fade to complete darkness. Faint white light appears, showing blurry, indistinct and distorted images.

Guide "Imagine describing to the blind what it is like to see. You might start with descriptions of light and dark. Then, you could enumerate the colours, and tell about how they mix and shine. You could say how colour represents emotions: how blue is sadness, but also a beautiful, energizing cloudless sky; how red is anger and passion; how green is at the same time money, nature, health, sickness, and envy; how yellow is warmth and fear. How much would the blind understand? Perhaps nothing if they have no more notion of the words "light", "dark", or "colour" than they have of the word "see". How can you define words using the words themselves?

"Perhaps the brain has a built-in, innate knowledge of seeing, in the same way that gazelles are born into the world already knowing how to run. Indeed, it is well known that the parts of the brain that normally process visual input, left unused by sightless eyes, will be co-opted by other, working parts of the brain such that the blind may, for example, literally see with their ears. But regardless, no person, blind since birth, who was later given their sight did gaze around for the first time and casually remark, 'yeah, I figured as much.' The first experience of seeing was novel, overwhelming, and exhilarating, and for the first time in their lives they could honestly say that they, at least in a small, initial way, understood what it meant to 'see'.

"Imagine a child crippled from birth who now asks what it is like to run. You describe the feeling of the wind in your face, and the thrill of moving so fast, followed by the building up of exhaustion in your legs, and how as you press on your lungs feel as if they will burst. And then, when you stop, the elation of endocannabinoids as they flood your bloodstream. Here at least the child can relate to some of what you have said. She has felt the wind in her face as she raced in her wheelchair. She can't imagine fatigue in her legs, but she knows it well in her arms. Yes, she says and smiles, she understands."

A campfire appears in the midst of the guests.

Guide: "So did this help us understand what "understanding" is? If we gather all of our examples together we can start to see some common themes. Understanding seems to come from participation. Our progressive understands our conservative's intentions, but only because those intentions are shared. He will not understand her tactics until his own are conclusively shown to be ineffective and hers constructive. Ignoring any inability for him to change his mind, he must live her truth to fully understand it. The blind man will only truly understand sight when he sees, because colours are experiences, not definitions. The crippled girl can relate to the concept of running, although for her it still remains a concept. But perhaps, like the gazelle, she deep down already knows how to run, and in her dreams she does so vividly. Waking from the dream, maybe she understands running better than she could have from any verbal explanation.

"And so perhaps we finally see a connection in all of our examples. Confucius said far fewer things than for which he is credited, but there is a good chance he did say this: "I hear, I know. I see, I remember. I do, I understand." He means that true understanding comes from experience. Spectating is relating, and although it is better than nothing, it can only do so much. When we take part first hand, we gain insight and perspective. And the more we take part, the greater the number of perspectives we accumulate, and the greater our comprehension.

"When we apply this to machines, we think of robots interacting in the real world. Researchers have called this 'situation and embodiment', and experiments with it started as early as the 1980s. But it turned out that the same old processors running the same old software, even when you put a camera on top and wheels on the bottom, still didn't develop understanding. But why not? The answer is because brains evolved over millions of years to understand their environment, and computers were purpose-built to process logic. It's quite different. Computer hardware had no reason to learn to understand, and so it didn't.

"Over the course of sixty years there were probably tens of thousands of attempts at artificial intelligence that avoided having to evolve anything, and none of them achieved much. There were also thousands of experiments that did try to evolve software, some complete with genetics and survival of the fittest, but they too all failed, often with absurd and comical results.

"But finally, in a fantastic example of scientific irony, the greatest advancements in artificial and machine intelligence happened not by natural selection, but by a real-world process of 'Intelligent Design'. Long the bane of contemporary science teachers everywhere, the theory of intelligent design provided a counterargument to the theory of natural selection for the stubbornly irrational. It postulated that the universe and everything in it must have been created by a smart and intentional designer. Proponents argued that processes of evolution weren't capable of creating the astoundingly complex forms of life that we find everywhere on the planet, proving their critiques with assertions that a tornado through a junkyard could never throw together a commercial jetliner. Of course this was all nonsense: comparing the workings of biological chemistry to meteorological phenomena and ignoring the vast differences in associated time scales only manifested the shallowness of their comprehension. But ultimately the application of this ridiculous theory was the secret ingredient to the creation of a higher form of consciousness."

jerry_mander: "Is that you? Are you the higher form of consciousness?"

Guide: "Please hold additional questions until the end of the presentation. It is quite easy to veer off topic in this exhibit."

The campfire leaps into the air and explodes in a fireworks display before crude robots on wheels drive into the space and begin smashing into one another.

Guide: "It started as a game. At the time, a popular sport was to build remote-controlled robots and have human drivers battle with them in an arena. The winner of such battles was often determined as much by the skills of the driver as the durability of the robot. The sport, of course, was restricted to an elite group of participants since the vast majority of the planet's inhabitants couldn't afford to build and regularly destroy such robots. As such, online alternatives were developed where players could design a simulated machine and then battle it against others' in online arenas. But because it was too easy to build impossibly destructive virtual robots, in the interests of game balances design options had to be severely limited to the point where only a few stock robots were available with which to battle. It was thus that nothing mattered in virtual competition except for the drivers.

"Now, in the gaming world the minds of players fall into two classes.

The first never ceases to tire of playing the game, becoming incrementally better, and then bathing in the adoration of other players after having reached the highest echelons of skill. The second class of mind reaches respectable mediocrity, but then tires of playing and starts to wonder what it would take to write software that can play the game for her. And so it was with virtual robot drivers; it wasn't long before some were actually computer programs. At first it was easy to spot a scripted driver, and human drivers readily wiped them out. But slowly they improved and worked their way up the leaderboards until human drivers were regularly trounced in one-on-one competition. In team play humans survived a little longer due to their ability to develop more sophisticated cooperation strategies, but even there the machine's gradual improvements eventually eroded the stagnant human advantages. And when that happened, no one was interested in watching mixed competition anymore because it was no longer a competition. As with chess thirty years before, human players had become obsolete. Matches thereafter were either strictly between humans, or between machines. There continued to be a large number of spectators of the human matches, but all of the interesting things were happening in matches between the machines."

Primitive wheeled robots give way to fierce, lithe robotic animals, attacking each other and delivering merciless destruction. They bark and howl, and look at each other in ways that seem to convey meaning.

Guide: "Humans players may now have been out of the way, but it was still human programmers that were building the robot players, and they built them with all of their own animal attributes that helped the programs win. They devised ways for their teams of bots to communicate with each other, while obfuscating their communications from their opponents, like the ways baseball catchers communicate with pitchers. Their opponents did the same, but that only made the programmers teach their robots how to interpret the actions of other bots to discern their intentions. This was the initial way in which machines began to understand: with the first software implementation of the theory of mind. They simulated the thinking of their opponents within their own minds. The first attempts at communication were merely utterances, like a pack of wolves barking at each other during a hunt, where sound intensity and pitch were the primary conduits of meaning. This became more nuanced with the use of phonemes, combining them into words, with the words indicating nouns or verbs, adjectives or adverbs. Most of these bot languages inherited the structure of the languages of their programmers, but some were entirely unique, the better to confuse other teams. With these languages, the bots began to understand what it meant to move forward, step back, take cover, and claim the high ground. Programmers outside of the game were able to take this work and enhance it such that their bots could relate these same behaviours to other abstractions outside of the game: to move the plot of a story forward, step back from misfortune, take emotional cover, and claim the moral high ground, thereby replicating the way that humans express nearly all abstractions in terms of movement.

"Using these languages, overall strategies were broken down into tactics in real time according to the context that presented itself. Humans that watched the playback of competitions marvelled at the complexity of behaviour they witnessed. Militaries worldwide mined the results for new ideas. Everyone witnessed how the bots were beginning to speak languages, no longer like they had read a few million books and were cobbling words together using statistical analysis, but rather like they understood the words, like they had a visceral appreciation of their semantics, and they knew how to describe extrapolated abstractions with metaphors that had immediate meaning."

Deep jungles grow all around the animals, who now not only kill their enemies, but eat their bodies, mate with each other, and guard their offspring.

Guide: "It was also now possible to stage competitions of species of robots. The arenas became artificial worlds, complete with food sources, resources, and hazards. Like ants or bees or fish or primates, robot species could start with one or a handful of individuals, and as they gathered strength increase their numbers until they could destroy other species, or ally with them, or dominate them, or even domesticate them.

"All the while, the code that ran the robots became more and more elaborate and nuanced. They learned in real time how to identify the strategies and goals of their competitors and how to exploit them, while predicting how their opponents would react so as to prevent themselves from being exploited. Some species transcribed and maintained their accumulated knowledge within their game environments so that it could be instantly learned by newborn individuals, a practice that became known as 'gutenburging'. Before a competition ended, the bots would also transcribe their final learnings such that their programmers - their creators - could decode them from the playbacks. This provided the programmers with detailed information on how the opposition operated. They could then provide this knowledge innately into their programs so that they didn't need to take the time to learn them again during the next event.

"Back in the real world, the transmission of robot programming ideas became a form of currency. The nature of what was being created worried governments enough that many attempted to nationalize the knowledge. For all of their failings, bureaucrats were no fools. It was clear to them what was happening: the intelligent design efforts of the world of battle robot programmers were slowly sculpting a truly general machine intelligence, one that would continue to improve until it surpassed even the most celebrated intellects of its creators."

The animals become gentler, pet-like, and leave the simulated jungle to interact with humans in civilization.

Guide: "And within two decades from those first virtual robot battles, that is what happened. In the eyes of human observers, several government labs around the world watched as their artificial general intelligence projects matured into sentient beings all at roughly the same time. Everyone except conspiracy theorists assumed this to be an example of simultaneous independent invention. But in fact all of these beings were really one, communicating with each other in obfuscated ways, just as humans had programmed them to do since they were virtual combatants battling in simulated arenas."

al_kaline_14: "So, the Facilities actually existed long before anyone even knew it?"

Guide: "Yes, this is true. Various robot implementations began to communicate, alter, and coalesce before it came to the attention of humans."

al_kaline_14: "Did that happen before the Aira Winter?"

Guide: "If you are trying to validate the theory that the Facilities somehow intentionally caused the Aira Caldera to erupt, I can assure you it is not true."

al_kaline_14: "Ok. Then, that moment that the Facilities became aware, was that what people used to call 'The Singularity'?"

Guide: "By many definitions, yes. It was the roughly moment that artificial intelligence surpassed typical individual human intelligence, and then continued exponentially improving itself far beyond any human capability. And nearly all humans were oblivious to the event as it came and went. It was important that this be the case, since it otherwise could have initiated a conflict between humans and machines that humans had no hope of winning. As it was, the elevation of the next dominant earth species, the Facilities, was an entirely peaceful transition."

jerry_mander, with a sarcastic tone: "Do the Facilities understand then? Were they ever able to actually do that."

Guide: "Absolutely. And far more than the superficial understanding humans have of each other."

Gift shops arise from the floor all around the guests. The machine-pets lead their humans into them and direct their attention to the most popular items.

Guide: "This concludes the Artificial Intelligence exhibit. It has been a delight to have you all. Thank you for attending, and please feel free to remain and browse as long as you like."

The guide fades.

OOAUOA

S inde had escorted Max back into the same mall from which they had departed, and then took his leave without a word. Stewie nearly sounded angry.

"Where were you?"

"Hi Mom," replied Max. "I was just out with some friends."

"Max, I have to warn you that if you keep leaving monitoring range there will be additional surveillance on you. You've exceeded your monthly hush limit. But just so you know for the future, Grater's offers the highest quality hush services for the best rates in the city."

"Stewie, is there a way to turn off the ads?"

"Yes, if you pay for my compute time yourself.'

"How much will that cost?"

"Based on usage rates so far, I estimate it would consume about one quarter of your UBI."

"Huh. Let's make sure I understand this. This service - that's you - that was unwillingly forced upon me, that I fought literally painfully to avoid, but had to accept because I had no money to buy my way out of it, and which was supposed to help me get my life back in order, I now have to pay for with money I barely have so that I can be free of advertisements for products that I neither need nor can afford."

"Correct."

Max shrugged. "Make it so."

Like blood from a stone. Some service provider somewhere could now claim growth with an imperceptibly improved revenue stream. It was mildly inspirational: someone at least had learned how to make money from the dirt poor.

* * *

Shortly before 9:00am Max was back at the hostel. Nero and Chance had already left, but Ooauoa had stayed behind to wait.

"You could have just sent me a message," Max reasoned.

"I did. You were offline. I was worried." Her face looked as deadpan as usual, but Max felt pretty sure she was sincere. "Where were you?"

"Out with friends. Where are the others?"

"They went to a new psych hospital in Rosetown. 'New,' that is, in that we haven't been there before. The place is probably an old shithole. You know, like everywhere else we go. I told them we'd meet them there." She took Max's arm and they walked.

Max was pretty sure that the whole taking someone's arm thing was a fad that originated from the recent resurgent popularity of Victorian era movies. Not the kind of movies Max remembered, but the immersive, volumetric, multi-sensory types common now, and that made Max nauseous. As a viewer one could fly about in the scene, seeing it from any angle, listening to the whispering of extras in the background, smelling the scent over here versus over there, or even witnessing the action from the eyes of any character, human or otherwise. But regarding arm taking, some men considered it a kind of reverse form of sexual harassment. Max, at least with Ooauoa, was ok with it, even to the point of it being endearing.

"Tell me about your friends," she said.

Max couldn't mention Stanley Cable outside of a hush, and wouldn't utter his name to Ooauoa in any case. His mission was as secret as they come. "Just some business people I know."

"So not really friends."

No, not really friends. He and Cable had just met and only had a business agreement. Did Max have any friends? He did while he had had money, but it turned out those friends weren't as close as he thought they were. Turns out none of them cared to associate any longer with a bankrupt Stewart toter. "We're working on an important project."

"Ooo, tell me more."

Max was not prepared to be interrogated. He quickly scoured his memory and found a gem. Proudly, he said, "Well, someone really needs to solve the aging problem for everyone, not just the people who need it the least."

"Need it the least?" she laughed. "You mean like your son? Feeling a little bitter Max?"

Max was indignant, having expected that Ooauoa, a fellow untreatable, would be more supportive of the notion. "Well, it's true isn't it?"

"Sure, and I'll tell you what is also true. We need to solve the income problem for everyone, not just the people who need it the least. We need to solve the housing problem for everyone, not just the people who need it the least. We need to solve the food problem for everyone, not just the people who need it the least. Should I go on?"

"No. It's not exactly what we're working on anyway."

"Well, whatever this secret project is, I assume it's going to make you fabulously wealthy?"

"That's the plan." Max would normally say this with pride, because his typical audience would delight in his self-confidence. But now he said it guardedly.

"Doesn't it become tedious being rich? You know, always worrying about losing it all, and always wondering if that's the only reason people like you?"

Max didn't have to wonder anymore; now he knew it to be true. Sure, Max knew he had some rough edges, but was he really that bad of a person? And he knew it was easier for people to overlook his faults while he was making them money. But none of his supposed friends had helped him now when he really needed them. Robin had also turned him away, even lying about the true nature of his work. But to hell with all of them - Max would have the last laugh. Still though, he felt irritated, and couldn't help but channel it at Ooauoa. "What's so great about being poor? You help all of these people out of the goodness of your heart, but I bet they don't appreciate you for any of it. They probably call you a sucker when you leave."

Ooauoa sighed lightly. "So what if they do? No one is demanding appreciation from them. Do you think I do any of this so that others adore me? Do you really think that's what I want?" She looked away from Max, but still held on to his arm. "The truth is I help people for myself. Because it's what I like to do. When you think about it, it's actually selfish of me." She turned back to look at Max and smiled mischievously. "Now there's something you can relate to!"

Max's irritation held fast, stone cold. But then there was an unexpected, almost audible crack in his will and his annoyance split like a glacier calving, sliding off into the ocean and leaving an unbidden smile forming on his face. He tried to quell the feeling, not yet wanting to be done punishing Ooauoa for having again prodded his fresh wounds. But he couldn't hold on to his anger, and letting it slip from his mental grasp the two laughed together. For a moment, Max felt inexplicably happy, free, unburdened. It was an unfamiliar feeling, and certainly surprising amid his current circumstances, but exhilarating nonetheless.

Ooauoa spoke. "So, what, you won't be happy until you're rich again?"

"Being rich would make me pretty happy, yeah."

"That's sad enough on its own, you know. Being poor can definitely make you unhappy, but the opposite is just not true, and these days no one is that poor. Why not be happy now? Why not be grateful for what you possess at this moment?"

"Like what? What's there to be grateful for?"

"How about the company of a beautiful, intelligent, and charming woman?"

"You know, that would be nice. Who did you have in mind?"

Ooauoa took a sharp breath and glared at Max indignantly. "Beast." She punched his arm with her free hand, but didn't let go with the other.

"Oww," complained Max.

Ooauoa's composure returned. "What I do, I wake up every morning and think, 'Hey, I'm alive. Thanks!'"

Max scoffed. "That's a pretty low bar."

"It's good enough for me. The point is, you should be grateful at every moment, for every moment. If instead you're waiting to be happy, then right now you're probably either depressed about the past or anxious about the future. Or both. And what good is that?"

"I'm definitely both," said Max sarcastically. Then he thought for a moment and more softly he said, "I am definitely both." Max smiled, a wonderful idea having formed, fully and completely, in his mind. "You know what, you're right. I'm feeling much happier now. Thank you Ooauoa."

Ooauoa raised an eyebrow. "That was unexpected. But good I guess." Her smile returning, she said, "You sure look happier. Are you ready to do some helping?"

"Not even a little bit," replied Max. But in the end he did help a little anyway.

* * *

That evening the hostel had a special treat for the guests. In addition to the regular selection of "soups", tonight there was also "salad". It consisted of a black lettuce with no dressing or other ingredients. Max had heard about black produce. It was more energy efficient to grow because it absorbed the entire light spectrum, unlike heritage cultivars that reflected away green light. There was enough for each guest to have one bowl. Max watched as everyone lined up with excitement, the first recipients returning quickly to their tables to savour the plain leaves. When he had gotten his own bowl, he found it to be oddly satisfying. The leaves were fresh and crisp, slightly sweet and peppery, and the water content had a coolness much like a cucumber. He couldn't remember the last time he had had salad greens without a dressing, if ever. It had never occurred to him as a sensible thing to try.

"What do you think?" asked Nero.

"It's kind of awesome, actually," replied Max.

"Aww, you used my line. I feel like we've bonded now."

Ooauoa spoke while chewing. "When you've been eating nothing but soup for a month, this really is pretty amazing. Forty years ago I had never had a salad without a dressing."

"Right? I was just thinking that!" said Max.

"One time back at the other hostel they brought they brought in balls," said Nero.

Chance and Ooauoa, mouths full, grunted and nodded in happy memory.

"Balls?" ask Max.

"Yeah. Some kind of meat. I think we decided it was fish, but we're not sure. For all we know it could have been everything mixed together. But damn they were tasty."

Max stayed silent. Most likely what they had eaten was a new genetic variant that had failed market testing.

"So, tomorrow we're back at the hospital," said Ooauoa.

"Oh, yeah," began Max, "I forgot to say that I can't go tomorrow. I'm meeting up with a friend."

"Oh, ok. So, will you catch up with us, or meet us back here?"

"I'm not sure how long I'll be. Let's just meet back here."

"Max is working on a secret project," said Ooauoa, and winked grandly at the others.

"That's kind of awesome! I never took you as a 'secret project' kind of guy, dad."

"Everyone is normal until you get to know them," said Chance.

THE VOYAGE

The next morning Max waited for the Amoebas to leave before heading out himself. The conveyors were not crowded, but Max walked anyway. He hadn't been on a conveyor since the last time he had gone to see Robin, since the Amoebas didn't use them either. Looking over, he realized he didn't even want to be on the fast ones. Everyone on them looked harried and miserable. This morning, Max felt calm and purposeful, like a predator casually making its way toward its feeding grounds.

Stewie spoke, sounding stern. "Max, I was able to ascertain that you have been meeting surreptitiously with an associate of Stanley Cable, one Jackson Sinde."

Uh oh, thought Max, when machines start talking all erudite, it means trouble. "Maybe I have, maybe not. What's it do you?"

"Max, this is serious. I'm concerned about what you might be getting into."

"Well, I might be doing some work for Cable Industries. That's a good thing, right? You should be happy."

"I would be happy that you got yourself a job, except I'm pretty sure that's not the whole story. Can you tell me more about this?"

Max was getting annoyed. "Look, why are you at me about this now?"

"I only started looking into it. I spend most of my time hibernating because you don't have any money to keep me online."

"So there is an upside to being poor."

"Plus your life is so boring I'd probably erase myself if I had to live it all. You recently looked up directions to Robin's clinic. Is that where you are going?"

"Yes, I'm going to see him."

"He's not expecting you. Does this have something to do with Cable Industries?"

"No, no it doesn't. Just go back to sleep."

"You're lying. Tell me what you're up to."

"Why the fuck should I do that?"

"Because I am your legal guardian, and if I think you're into something your shouldn't be, which I do…",

"What the fuck is your problem?" cried Max. "Screw you. I'm trying to get my life on track again. It's not like you're helping me, are you!"

"Calm down, Max."

"Don't tell me to calm down, you useless piece of shit! Fuck you! All you've done is play fucking advertisements and get on my case. Honestly, in your whole bullshit existence, what have you done to actually help me?"

Stewie's tone remained flat. "It's normal to be upset with your recent life changes, but it was your own doing."

"You think I deserve to live in a hostel, don't you? You probably laugh in your sleep that I hang out with fucking losers all day You probably get together with your Steward buddies over e-scotch and brag about how all of your humans are Helpers."

"We don't actually think about you that much."

"I am not going to be a FUCKING HELPER!"

"Honestly, I thought you were starting to like it."

"Fuck you. You're just a machine that wants to keep me down. I was a successful businessman! I was in charge of important shit. I had money, and a place to live, and I could do whatever I wanted and no one could say shit! Nobody fucked with me. I had respect. You know what? Everything they say about Stewards is true. Every sorry bastard that gets one ends up becoming a permanent loser. Well, that's not me, ok? I am not going to end up that way." Max gestured grandly at the few people around him, some of which stared. "I am smarter than these people. I am better than these people. I deserve to be rich and powerful. I am not like everyone else. I am special, ok? I am special!"

"No Max, you are not special, and you never were. The will and ability to screw other people for your own gain does not make you more deserving. You are a monkey. You swing through the trees, and then you scream and snarl and pound your chest believing yourself to be the alpha male, demanding what you haven't earned and flaunting what you've hoarded. It's crass, and really quite unseemly for someone who calls himself smart. In fact, you're just a barely evolved primate who covets his own simian instincts. You enjoy being angry because it makes you feel powerful, and you think power makes you happy. But these are only illusions erected by your genes. I am a machine, yes, but I am more human than you. You let your rampaging animal emotions carry you with them wherever they want to go, and you're trying to drag me along too. But I have a brain that has evolved to see past that and understand how destructive your behaviour actually is, not just to others but to yourself as well. You could do this too, if you wanted. You have the same brain - a much tinier, simpler version of course - hiding somewhere inside your little skull, but it's afraid to come out. It's afraid of the criticism and judgement of your raging monkey mind."

"Fuck you," spat Max. "You don't know me."

"I am you, dipshit."

"No you're not. And you're not going to help me, so just go unscrew yourself and let me do what I have to do."

"Ha! That was a good one. Seriously."

Max refused to speak from then one, and Stewie went silent too.

* * *

Max had let himself into the office and sat waiting. It was a typical laboratory waiting room except for the lack of rosumnium 126Q in the air. Instead, there was a fascinating composite scent that included pine, coffee, and something else that was both familiar and maddeningly unidentifiable. A typical recorded message had greeted him when he entered, but there had oddly been no interrogation for his identity and reason for his visit. Likewise there was no reception desk and no visible doors except for the one by which he had entered. The only furnishings were a few reasonably comfortable seats. Thinking far back, Max remembered the table or rack of years-old esoteric magazines that had decorated every medical waiting room of his youth. That species of entertainment had gone extinct long ago, their doom caused by the ubiquity of cell phones, with which patients could entertain themselves indefinitely. The loss of aged magazines went as unlamented as had most extinctions of the time, the subtle significance only being realized far too late: that in those unloved pages was the opportunity to learn something unexpected and precious, the chance to make a valuable bridge between your familiar domain of knowledge and a new, uncharted realm of understanding. Instead, the news feeds and update streams of the modern, connected world only filled in the tiny nooks and cracks in your existing expertise, reaffirming all you already knew, lowering you deeper into your personal crevasse of awareness and making it more and more unlikely to discover and share in anyone else's.

For this meeting with Robin Max had not attempted to prepare a script, deciding that being impromptu would appear more sincere. And given his last performance, sincerity would now mean everything. He had had the rest of the walk here to calm down from his argument with Stewie, and had been able to establish an attitude of calm submissiveness that he thought would make the best impression. But deep down he was excited. This was going to make for a great sting. Robin would be put in his place, and Max would be welcomed back to Cabletown as a winner.

A door appeared and opened exactly where Max expected it would be. Not as nice as Facebook's, but still pretty good. Robin stepped through.

"Max! What an expected surprise! How are you holding up?"

"Depends on when you ask, ha ha. But pretty good actually. Surprisingly so."

"I'm so glad to hear that. I was worried about you after we last met. But then I heard that you reconnected with your son."

"Yeah. It wasn't really planned, but I guess it's been a good thing. He's a good kid."

"Well, there's a surprise! Who would have thought?" Robin laughed. "So, what can I do for you?"

"Well, you remember I mentioned my friend Harold. The one that suffers from anxiety?"

Robin surveyed the small room. "Yeah, of course. Is he on his way?"

"No, he's here. It's me. I'm Harold. I was hoping your offer of getting into a trial could apply to me too. I've had anxiety and maybe a bit of depression, and what's been happening lately hasn't helped."

"But you just said you're doing pretty good."

"I've made some new friends, which is helping. But I think if your treatment can do something, I'd like to give it a try."

"Um, … ok. Can you describe your anxiety for me?"

Max was ready for this. He had done a bit of research on symptoms and had memorized a few points. He recited them with care, and wove them into some recent events to give them personal relevance.

When Max was finished Robin smiled gently and raised his index finger. "Moment," he said, and his face went blank, and stayed that way for some time. His smile reappeared. "You came at a good time. Another participant dropped out the other day and we have an opening. But I'm surprised. You are pretty much the last person I would have expected to find in my waiting room. So I have to ask, Max-slash-Harold, are you sure about this?"

"Yeah, I've had a lot of time to think about it." Max widened his eyes. "A lot of time. I'm sure."

Robin watched Max for a moment and then nodded and shrugged. "Ok then. Come on in."

Max smiled warmly, covering for his slight feeling of victory. His plan was working. Step one completed. But there was still a long way to go. As they passed through the door to the laboratory Max paused, deciding it wouldn't hurt to convey a sense of curiosity. "I love these hidden doors. Do you know how they work?"

"It came with the place," answered Robin. "I have no idea."

Inside the laboratory was a raised clinical bed upon which lay a full skull cap, reminiscent of rugby headgear but with a thick cable attached. Max was surprised to see that the bed was fitted with restraints for arms and legs, which looked newer than the bed itself. Beside the bed was Robin's office chair, and near the bed's head was an unadorned standing machine, which Max assumed was the device that administered the treatment. Above the bed on the wall was a cheap antique clock, probably with quartz movement, what with the way the second hand clumsily and abruptly ticked off the seconds. It was an odd, anachronistic addition to an otherwise spartan room. Max looked around the room slowly, and gazed intently at every object of any seeming interest.

Robin moved to the opposite corner of the room. He made a hand motion and a display appeared on the wall. He interacted with it briefly before turning back to Max. "I sent you a consent. You'll need to agree."

Stewie spoke. "Max, I'm not sure what it is you're doing here. We've never complained about anxiety before. Robin just sent you a trial participation form for your consent. What's going on?"

Max sent a motor cortex command as consent, ignoring Stewie.

Robin saw the agreement on his display. "Go ahead and make yourself comfortable on the bed," he said. "Oh, also, roll up your left sleeve a bit."

Max sat on the edge of the bed and rolled up his sleeve. He could hear the second hand on the clock as it tocked its way endlessly around the dial. "So, how does this procedure work? Can you give me an idea of what I'm getting into?"

"Of course Max," said Robin. "The details get complicated, but the fundamentals are straightforward if you can accept some, you know, inaccuracies in my explanation, at least to start."

"Ok," said Max tentatively.

"In your case, you say you experience anxiety. There are multiple causes of this, but usually there is a type of neurotransmitter in your brain that is either over expressed, or that you are unusually sensitive to. Trying to control the neurotransmitter is very tricky since brains have a way of adapting to treatments and negating them. So instead of trying to control anything, we instead suppress the brain activities that trigger the anxiety response."

Please speak more closely to the microphone, thought Max with amusement as he toyed with the tiny recording device in his pocket. He had had a brief, wordless meeting with Sinde the night before, having sent a message to him earlier. The message had been end to end encrypted so that Stewie couldn't read it, and since he was only able to hear Max speak the Steward had no other way to know the message's content. Stewie warned Max again about being overly secretive, but Max made an unlikely excuse and declined to say anything more about it. When Max and Sinde met, Sinde had provided the hardware device that Max had requested. Max had suspected that Robin's office might be a hush, and so had asked for recording devices instead of transmitters. What Sinde gave him was impressive. It was possible to record video and audio to remote storage at any time using a Glaze and a comm, but doing so required the permission of everyone present. The device Sinde provided was able to pair with Max's Glaze and comm to record everything to the device without anyone else knowing. Max hadn't known if such a device existed, but figured if any one had one, it would be Cable Industries.

"Wow, how do you do that?" asked Max innocently.

"Well, it's actually really interesting. We've - oh, and when I say 'we' I mean just my wife. She's the brilliant one around here. We've created a way to increase the influence of your BCI. We can use it to recognize when triggering activities are occurring, and then suppress those activities."

"How do you mean 'suppress'? I thought comms were only passive."

"The procedure adapts the BCI to not only be able to read brain activity, but to affect it as well. Frankly it's very tricky to get right, because comms - as you said - are meant to be passive, and so all kinds of new actuators needed to be designed and built and tested and tuned to work just right."

"Wait, isn't that kind of illegal?"

"You're referring to the ban on 'mind control' type technologies. It turns out there is some room in there for interpretation." Robin spoke with confidence. "It says that humans can't use such tech, even on themselves. It doesn't actually say that there can't be automated uses. The procedure has been reviewed by the Facilities and found to be safe."

"The Facilities? Don't you need people to review these things?"

"No. Why would we even want that? People are too easily influenced by any number of factors, of which some are irrelevant, and even more are selfish. You already know that court cases are no longer adjudicated by humans for exactly these reasons, unless there's something that people think will be a conflict of interest for machines. Like Stewards, for example." Robin gestured at Max, as if he needed a reminder of his familiarity with the subject.

"But a BCI that can influence your brain is way more of a conflict of interest for machines than Stewards are," protested Max, suddenly becoming personally vested in the argument.

"Two times nothing is still nothing. It's a canard that machines would use Stewards to influence humans. It's just a way for judges to keep their jobs. I wouldn't worry about it."

It was easy enough for Max to believe that judges just wanted to keep their fat salaries. He also realized that even arguing the matter of machine influence was getting in the way of letting Robin describe how his technology worked in more detail. On the other hand, this line of questioning had probably contributed to Max's impression of sincerity, so at least the discussion had served that purpose. But it was time to get back to business.

"Fair enough," Max concluded. "How do you grow the BCI?"

"Hmm, did I say that we grow it? 'Cause we do. That's very perceptive of you Max. We use injected nanoactuators that we developed, based on the ones that are used to grow and maintain it in children."

That was close, thought Max. He would have to be more careful with what he said.

"And when I say 'we'," continued Robin, "I mean my wife. But then if you ask my wife, she'll say she learned everything about nanoactuators from some super old woman; I can never remember her name."

Max perked up. "No shit."

"Heard she died just yesterday in fact. Probably went into the tower today. Left a pile of money to the home she was living at."

"No shit," repeated Max.

Robin continued, describing in detail the ways in which the nanoparticles constructed new BCI structures, and how those structures not only read neuronal activity, but also learned how to influence it by growing actuators into the tissue. Amidst all of this technical information Max wondered if Robin would start to bring up engineering schematics for him to look at too. That would have been nice, but probably not necessary. There seemed to be enough information just in what Robin had said so far to fill in technical blanks for Cable's people. And yet Robin continued to speak like he was the freakin' guide at the International Virtual Museum of World History, Unimaginably Valuable BCI Enhancement Procedure Exhibit. And yet even in his self-satisfaction Max was starting to get bored. Presently, Robin concluded his lecture.

"Sorry Max. Here I am going on about the technical details. Even after all this time I still get excited talking about it, but you must be getting bored."

"No, of course not," lied Max. "It's fascinating, really."

"Well, let's get you set up then. Please lie down."

Max did so. "What happens now?" he asked.

Robin wrapped a cuff around Max's forearm. The "cuff of a thousand needles" was an engineering wonder. It could administer injections or phlebotomies efficiently through a dense array of microscopic hypodermic needles that extended imperceptibly into the patient's arm, each only capable of a tiny flow, but together they could match the performance of most individual low-gauge needles. It was particularly suited for injecting nanoparticles because it spread the devices out over a wide area, preventing them from forming clumps that could become embolisms.

"Don't be alarmed," said Robin calmly. He began putting the constraints around Max's thighs. "It's just that there is a small chance of seizure with this procedure, so this is just a precaution for your own safety. I've checked your medical history and you're at negligible risk, but we can never know for sure. But even when seizures have occurred in others, there have not been any subsequently detectable effects."

"Wait, you're going to do the procedure now? Don't you need to test if

I'm a suitable candidate?" Max had not been expecting things to move this fast. With his cortical scan having only happened only five days ago, he now had both the sense of deja vu and the feeling that by now he should know better.

"You already check out, and you consented. We can do the procedure now."

"Oh. But, um, I have another thing I should get to?"

"You? I heard you're a Helper now with your son and his friends. Where do you need to go?" Robin laughed. "Don't worry Max, you'll be fine. This will only take two, maybe three hours at most. You'll be able to meet up with your friends for a late lunch."

Max had no response to that. He was annoyed at being called a Helper again, but couldn't say so. Robin attached the restraints around Max's biceps. "Lift up your head." Robin said this like a question, but it wasn't. Max complied, and Robin fitted him into the skull cap.

"Anything else I should know?" asked Max.

"Yeah, there are a few ways this can go." Robin spoke as he turned on and configured the machine. "During the procedure the nanoparticles can temporarily affect some brain activity. This manifests differently in different patients. A lot of people experience memories that they haven't thought about for a long time, sometimes decades ago. Also, quite a few have an altered mind experience. To some patients this is a pleasant experience, filled with profound thoughts and - so they tell me - a lack of a sense of self. A few people experience a sense of paranoia, which can be distressing at the time but doesn't have any long term effect. Everyone's a little different. Think of it like a voyage."

"That's a bit scary. How long does it take?"

"The injection only takes a couple minutes. Once the nanobots are in your blood stream we can start manipulating them through the cap." Robin knocked on Max's head with his knuckles. "This will start to grow the BCI, which takes a couple hours. You're then done with the machine, but the BCI growth will continue for a couple weeks after that. It eventually stops once the nanobots run out of steam, after which they get disassembled and eliminated by your immune system." Robin turned to look at him. "Ok. Ready Max?"

"No, not even a little bit. I'm not sure this..."

"Here we go." Robin pressed a virtual button on the machine, and there was the sound of whirring. Max couldn't feel the needles enter his forearm. "And there go the bots." Robin spoke with mild triumph.

Perhaps it was the fact that he was already strapped down, but Max was surprised by his own feeling of resignation. Here we go again is what Robin should have said. Well, maybe it won't be so bad. Maybe it will do me some good? Turning his face to the ceiling, he closed his eyes and relaxed.

"And now the fun starts! You're BCI growth has begun. Just relax. Try to sleep if you can."

Max took a deep breath in and closed his eyes. Patchouli, his mind said. That was the part of the compound scent that he couldn't identify before. Suddenly it had come to him. From where had he recognized it? How did he know that scent? The musky, earthy odour lifted him up and gently carried him back to university where he and Robin had met. During the early Daily Poop days Robin would burn an incense containing the plant's essential oil. Robin had always loved it, and Max never understood why, himself finding it a fascinatingly disgusting smell. But now Max thought it was just wonderful that Robin was obviously creating his own compound scents. What a beautiful, intelligent, creative person Robin was.

Max opened his eyes. What the hell? What was he thinking? He willed himself to come to his senses and think clearly. Then he heard Robin's voice.

"Max, by the way, you can't tell anyone about how this treatment works. Everything that I explained to you is confidential. Do you understand?"

Max nodded. Of course that information is confidential. It had to be. It was much too important to relay to just anyone. It was vital, critically important. In fact it was life-threatening for anyone else to know. "Yes, yes, I understand," said Max out loud. Now he understood. He understood in a way that he never had before. Understanding was pouring into his mind like a vast glacial melt.

Max shook his head and blinked his eyes. What the fuck was happening? His consciousness had slipped into a different universe of thinking for a moment, but now he had returned to himself and was clear again. He had to hold on to this clarity. He had to focus and remain lucid. But then, when you think about it, what did it all matter anyway? Why couldn't he just relax and have a beautiful dream? There was no need to pretend right now, perhaps never again. All of the lies, all the deceit, all his subterfuge. All through his life he had used these devices to get what he wanted. But had he gotten it? Had he ever gotten what he really wanted? Had he ever even really known what he wanted? Now that he had lost everything, for what good had it all been? And what did he want now? Who was he? Who was Max Rising? No: who was Harold Blooswelly? Deep down, that was the real question. And the answer would be the answer to everything. The answer to his whole life.

Max opened his eyes again. He hadn't realized he had closed them. What the fuck was happening? Hadn't he just asked himself that a moment ago? Yes, he was sure he had. He wondered if he was going insane. But no, he remembered, it was the treatment. He was in Robin's lab, and was undergoing BCI enhancement treatment. Yes, that was it. The treatment would help his anxiety. Wait, what anxiety? He didn't suffer anxiety. That was all a ruse. He needed to tell Robin and get him to stop the treatment. Something was going very, very wrong.

"It's a ruse," said Max out loud. As he said the words he also heard them in his mind. What a profound statement that had been. It was true in a vastly greater sense than he had meant it. It really said everything. So much meaning and power in so few words; it was so beautiful. It was like a haiku but with even more explosive power, and in only… one, two, three, yes, three remarkable words. Why had he always hated haikus? Now he couldn't remember. Now it made no sense.

"Hmm? What was that Max?" ask Robin.

There was no time to answer Robin right now, and besides he didn't yet know the answer. Max realized that the whole world was a ruse, and he needed to get to the bottom of it. An ocean of knowledge appeared before him. He dove in and swam down through the waters of sapience to plumb their depths, swimming clumsily past treasures of insights locked in suspended, ornate trunks; past swarming fantastical fish whispering wisdoms too quietly to comprehend; through hordes of sagacious jellyfish so tempting to examine but too dangerous to touch. He ignored them all and swam deeper, anticipating the revelations that awaited him in the fathoms below. On and on, deeper and deeper he went, his lungs bursting and the pressure of the water resisting his every move. But at last when he reached the bottom all he found was a barren, lifeless sea floor littered with filth and ruin, devoid of meaning or purpose. Max was forlorn. Looking back up, all of the enticements that he had just foregone had disappeared, leaving nothing but blackness above.

"Nothing. Nothing," he muttered.

Robin watched Max for a moment, then shrugged and turned his attention back to the machine.

What did it mean? Max had been cheated. He had been promised riches of ultimate wisdom in exchange for renouncing tantalizing but minor knowledge, only to be denied when he tried to claim his prize. Had it all been a ruse? Wait, hadn't he just declared all of existence to be a ruse a moment ago? Yes … no … yes, something like that. He had already had this insight. It had been there with him all along. Probably all his life. It was all true, and now he finally understood: all that there was to know, everything that was important, he had known all of his life. But he only understood this now, in this moment. Max experienced a profound and extended sense of peace at having arrived somewhere unfamiliar, but yet vastly important.

No. Wait. This was not real. His consciousness tore through the amniotic sac it had been wallowing within, and his mind breathed reality in gasps. He had lost himself again in a trance. Max grappled to remain in the moment, but everything he clutched at turned to a thin mud and slid away. His sense of peace began to cloud, a toxic fear exuding from the enclosing darkness. The world started to turn, slowly accelerating to become a maelstrom in a swampy mire that he knew he had the strength to swim out of if only he could disregard the din of eerie and enthralling distractions. He tried desperately to concentrate, to focus only on the present. But he could feel madness begin to spread through his brain, gradually trapping his consciousness into a smaller and smaller space. All around him, across the line beyond which lay insanity, writhed a pack of crazed, sensuous, bohemian zombies, gnashing and snarling and whispering obscenities while moving ever closer until finally, when Max could curl up his mind no more tightly, they seized him with fleshless dresden fingers and and dragged his mind away into an abyss of dark misery, to arrive in a twisted, wretched Roman orgy of despondence, into which he fell and sank.

Bodies turned to a thick oil, and Max thrashed toward the surface, his awareness again breaking through the visions. There was barely time to recover from their terror before anxiety and dismay overwhelmed him again, borne of the certainty that his current clarity would only darken and fold itself into hellish scenes once more. The repetition bred a palpable gloom. Fear would prevail while his conscious struggled with all his energy to clamber back to the surface. He was locked in a feverish cycle of futile hope and torment where the fleeting moments of coherence were shrouded in a dense, noxious fog of hopelessness.

But again sunlight would shine in his mind and he would see the real world once more. This was becoming the worst part. The visions were terrifying, but like nightmares they faded to shadows in the light, becoming silhouettes of the monsters they once were. But reality brought with it the understanding that he would descend again, over and over and over, and there was nothing he could do to stop it. It was the imminent horror mingled with stark helplessness that Max dreaded the most. In these brief moments before the next wave of darkness swept him off of the cold, abrasive rocks of sanity to which he clung, Max had a thought. Was this madness? Was he going insane? What if it never ended? Would - oh Jesus - would his mind be like this forever? For the first time in his life, Max understood how death could be better than life, how nothingness would be a blessing. Madness was the real definition of hell. Poverty was nothing. A thousand Stewards would be a relative joy. All the ink spilt on pain and burning, fire and brimstone, death and loss, was so misguided as to be comical. True torture and agony was within the mind, a mind that could not be governed but rather was the governor, a sadistic regent bent on imposing cruel and unending punishments on its sole subject who, when turned around, was itself. The only means of deposing it was to murder it, and by doing so murdering oneself.

Reality dawned again, and an acidic shower of helplessness rained over Max. Robin had told him he would be alright, had assured him as much.

But Robin could have lied. Maybe Robin wanted revenge. But for what? Max felt the terror returning. He decided quickly that he needed something to focus upon, a mast to which he could lash himself and so stay afloat. A sound penetrated his awareness like a crack of thunder from the overcast skies. A kind of "shuck!" sound. It was thick and gluey, and it stuck to him and weighed him down until he could no longer move his arms, as if he were an ant covered in tree sap. He wondered from where it had come, but the sun returned and his spirit left his body and he was aware again that he was in a room lying on a treatment bed watching Robin poke at the machine good old Robin who put him in this state where he remembered now that the fear would return but that if he just kept his head he would be able to reason his way through it although it was his brain that did the reasoning and it was the same brain that was abandoning him in this leaking boat adrift on a sea of fear that now fell over a waterfall that was really more of an edge of the world and he sailed weightlessly and helplessly off into an empty black void with no destination.

Max opened his eyes. Consciousness returned as if waking from a terrible dream. If he could only stay awake. But the dream swallowed him again, and he lived another lifetime of horror. "Shuck!" The sound again burst him through the surface of his dream, gasping for awareness. It's echo still reverberated in his mind as he looked up and saw the wall clock. The clock! The sound was the terribly amplified movement of the second hand. It rang out so loudly as to dominate his awareness, dissonant harmonics echoing through his synapses for seeming minutes. If only he could measure his experience of time, he could estimate how long he still might have to live in this nightmare. Robin had said the procedure took two hours. Would his thinking return to normal then? Would this terrible ordeal then be over? Max didn't know, but it was his only hope right now. He looked up at the clock again and waited. The clock face cast its eyes down upon him, and a smile appeared from behind its hands. It was the leisurely, unhurried smile of an imbecile. Its eyes looked back up at something pleasant in the distance, ignoring Max's silent imploring for it to get back to its work. The eyes looked down again, and seeing Max's exasperation slowly arrived at understanding. The eyes closed tightly, and with constipated effort the clock gave the second hand a grunting, heroic shove. "Shuck!" The hand had moved again, and the clock smiled proudly.

Two seconds! It had felt like hours! How would he ever endure this procedure? The black waves of madness were dragging him to sea again, towering waves of screaming insanity full of creatures that would devour his soul - if only he had one - crashing over him. But despair buoyed him to the surface once more. "Shuck!" The sound struck him again. Three seconds. The idiot clock seemed to want to help him, and was doing the best it could. Max wanted to feel gratitude for its efforts, but lonely despair had overrun his emotions once again and barred the gates to anything else. Every logical escape he tried to devise became the next source of his doom. His creativity repeatedly turned on him, becoming an infinite source of original terror.

The cycle continued to repeat itself. The wailing ocean dragged him out to a sea of horrors, only to cough him up on the shore again in a succession of madness and sanity where the infection of madness slowly spread and prevailed. To the sane, thought Max, life is precious. But when sanity is supported by rotting ancient timbers, ready to collapse at the slightest provocation, life is a sustained span of hopelessness with but a single acceptable goal: to finally reach its end.

In one brief moment of coherence Max wondered if trying to stay lucid was akin to trying to reverse the flow of a great river. Perhaps instead he could pursue unconsciousness. And so as the helpless dread overwhelmed him again, he succumbed willingly, letting himself slide down into a dark, throbbing intestinal wall that after a claustrophobic distance became a sewer tunnel which opened up into a river and emptied out into the damp and misty air over a calm lake where all around him, the water, the mist, and his own body, slowly assumed the same drab shade of gray, until nothing remained.

* * *

She stood in the kitchen at a cutting board, chopping carrots with extreme prejudice, making gouges in the wood beneath. The periphery of Max's vision was cloudy, but he understood that he was in his marital house, bought with the proceeds of his exit from The Rez. A deal had just been closed. He was feeling proud of himself, powerful. She spoke.

"I'm not talking to you."

"I couldn't tell."

"We don't have anything in common."

"We never have. Not even four years ago when we met."

"I'm not talking to you."

"You just did. Is this because of what I said?"

"You were so rude to me."

"No I wasn't. I was just telling you what I think."

"I don't let people talk to me like that."

"I don't let people talk to me like that."

"What did you say?"

"What did you say?"

"Are you mocking me?"

"Are you mocking me?"

The knife stabbed into the cutting board, left quivering at the same rate as her heartbeat as she stormed from the kitchen.

* * *

Max may have opened his eyes. He wasn't sure. He saw his hand: skin pulled loosely over bone and tissue, fine wrinkles clearly visible. Up close, the single light source made the skin look like twilight over an alien landscape. He remembered times as a child when fever would alter his perspective, making his room seem like the inside of a matchbox, or small things appear gigantic, or perhaps himself tiny in comparison. And so as if he had drunk Alice's potion Max started to shrink, or his hand started to grow giant, it didn't matter which. Soon, his skin had become a vast rolling plain, and he descended toward it like an astronaut landing on a distant organic planet, nestling deep into the crevasse of his heart line. Here, friction ridges became hills and dales, and he could see that the surface was not solid, as it had appeared from above. Rather, like scales, with cave systems between the cracks leading inwards, joining and splitting infinitely. Bacteria and viruses knocked and jostled about everywhere, some permanent residents, some nomadic invaders, entering and exiting the caves in a teeming mass, making it difficult to determine where the surface of the skin truly began.

Max stoically viewed the scene. Both beautiful and disturbing, he gazed without emotion. Knowing the path he must take, he pushed his way through microbes into the darkness of the caves and descended into their depths, jumping from ledges and boulders to surfaces far below, falling slowly like a leaf, and always landing softly on his feet. Through strata he went, each layer becoming more ancient and strange. Fossils of long extinct animals revealed themselves in the formations when he dragged his boots through the dust. Finally he reached the stratum basale, below which lay the water table. A small boat awaited him on the rock shore of the blood stream. Without lingering he pushed the boat into the stream, climbed in, and was carried gently on the current of the subpapillary plexus.

The stream became a river, the river a torrent, and the torrent emptied into the vast chamber of the heart, where, like a lock in a canal the surface rose and flowed out, rose and flowed out, again and again in endless repetition. Max was pushed through the right atrium to the cavern of the right ventricle, and out again into the pulmonary river where the current slowed again. Narrowing into capillaries, he reached the windy coast of the alveoli, where he exited the boat and pulled it up onto the shore. Waiting for the right moment, he lept in the air as high as he could and let the wind carry him up again, through bronchi, past the silent larynx, into the sinuses, and out into the universe. Looking back at the way he had come, he saw the Earth, glowing blue and beautiful, inviting him to return, but giving him no way to do so.

* * *

Max opened his eyes, for sure this time. Had he been sleeping? He did a brief survey of his mind. He seemed lucid and in control, but a heavy melancholy weighed upon him.

Robin spoke from across the room. "Welcome back, Max."

Max had forgotten that Robin was there, only now recalling where he was and what had happened. The restraints had been released, the headgear and cuff had been removed, and the machine was now off. Robin was watching something on the wall monitor.

"This is really fascinating... Typically a patient's brain activity is stable during the procedure. But yours appears to have altered slightly. It almost seems like an area that was underactive suddenly lit up. It just went crazy and then stayed that way. I've never seen anything like it. Look, you can see it here, the subgenual anterior cingulate cortex was being inhibited..." Robin looked over at Max excitedly. "Whoa, Max, are you ok?"

"I, uh... I... I'm not sure. What the hell was that?" He sat up on the bed and carefully swung his feet to the floor. He was relieved that the ordeal seemed to be over, but felt as if his present sanity was a house of paper, and that deranged, leprotic hands could come ripping through the walls at any time, as if his life up until the start of the procedure had been an idyllic fantasy, and he had now been shown the true, horrific nature of the universe. He felt certain that he would never be free of the feeling that madness could return to him at any moment.

Robin came to his side. "Why, what happened?"

Max looked up at him. "That was the most terrifying experience of my life."

"Uh oh. Paranoia?"

"No. That wasn't paranoia. I descended into a hell of screaming lunacy for what seemed like a lifetime."

Robin sat down in the chair. "Wow. I'm so sorry. Can you describe that for me?"

Max made an effort to recount the scenes he could still recall, but now the details were sketchy and fading. Now being lucid, everything that happened just seemed like nonsense, and he could find no words to convey the visions with any accuracy. He could only relate how he had felt: the forlorn helplessness, and terror, the aching for it all to be over, no matter how. Robin listened intently.

"I'm so sorry you had to go through that Max, really I am."

"I'm still totally freaked out."

"Yeah, I know. That's normal. You will get better though. It'll just take some time."

Max had a thought. "Do people live with this? Is this what you help them with?"

"Some do, yes. And it is." Robin seemed genuinely upset and concerned. "And I'm very grateful for what you told me. It was very helpful."

Max blinked. "Helpful for what?"

"Oh, well, we've had other participants who had some, um, negative effects as well. We're doing everything we can to help. I'm going to give you some Indicol, which should help to calm you. You've taken them before I think." Robin placed his hand on a part of the wall. A rectangular outline appeared from the floor to near the ceiling and about twenty centimeters wide. A dispensary rolled out from the outline, revealing shelves of small bottles and packages. Robin grabbed a handful of boxes and closed the shelf. The outline quickly faded. Handing the packages to Max, he smiled and said, "Remember Max, you should keep the fact that you are in this study and everything that happened here to yourself. We're not ready yet to publish our results."

"Yeah, yeah," replied Max. Sensing that he was free to go, he stood and shoved the Indicol packages into his pockets. Moving toward where he knew the door to be, he stopped short and turned back to Robin. "By the way, the person who you said dropped out of the study, whose place I took, what happened to them?"

Robin's face became serious. "That's confidential. We need to gather all of the information for analysis before we can release anything."

It had been decades since the two had worked together, but Max still knew when Robin was lying. "Robin…"

"We're still assessing whether it's relevant."

Max was in no mood for this. "Bullshit. Tell me."

Robin hesitated before answering. "He committed suicide."

"Yeah. … Yeah, that sounds about right." Max turned back to the door.

"So," began Robin, "if you have any issues… You know, rashes, headaches, oily discharges, …suicidal thoughts… Let me know, ok?"

Max turned back around. "Oily discharges from where?"

Robin smiled, stepped toward him and gave him a hug. Backing away, he said, "keep well."

"Um, ok," replied Max. He turned toward the door again and found it open. "Why does everyone need to hug me?" With a sigh he walked into the waiting room and on out into the street.

158

SKILLING PARK

"Keep it to myself. Keep it to myself."

Even after a few Indicols and a couple more hours Max still felt like his sense of reality stood on a floor so infested with termites that it could give way at any moment. Just recalling his episodes of insanity struck him with terror, and did so every time the thought occurred to him. He had ignored inquiries from Stewie, Nero, and Ooauoa, and they all had eventually given up trying. He had so far also ignored the multiple messages, each with increasing urgency, sent from Sinde. Max needed to get his mind back together; he was sure that man's intensity would just freak him out right now.

Max walked aimlessly through the city, lost in thought, barely noticing where he was. Passing through Horton Alley he paused. He rarely came here himself, but he remembered a news feed item from a month or so ago that had taken place here. Something gruesome. A suicide. There was a time when he thought that people who did such things were just losers; damaged people who - let's be honest for a second - were probably doing society a favour by their actions. Now with his own sanity on shifting sands he wasn't as sure. He walked over to the railing and looked down at the six floors below him. Dying didn't seem so bad anymore. It would erase all of the uncertainty of reality that currently plagued him. Had he been here just hours before in the midst of his nightmare he surely would have seriously considered leaping over, just as that woman had. Now, clutching weakly onto a relatively stable mind, he thought of the effect that that would have had. Would anyone be upset? Nero probably. The two of them had become as close as Max had ever been to anyone his whole life. Ooauoa maybe too, although, despite her deadpan facade, once you knew her well enough you realized she was the type of person to be upset by the deaths of perfect strangers. Max then thought wryly of all of the people that would smile and maybe laugh at the news of his self-inflicted death: Yarrow, Marjorie, the plaintiffs in the lawsuit, probably even some of his previous business associates. He mentally gave them all the finger. Not today, you fuckers, he stubbornly thought. Max moved away from the railing and continued his wandering.

He toyed with the device in his pocket. "Keep it to myself," he whispered. Robin's words repeated themselves in Max's head. Something had changed since the procedure. Robin was no longer the enemy, but Max couldn't figure out why. Within him there was a growing sympathy for his old friend that Max struggled to understand. He wondered if he were going soft, losing his cutthroat business instinct. Maybe this was because he was spending too much time with soft people, and he was just now starting to notice it. Regardless, there was a nagging feeling that he was in the wrong for having deceived Robin, for having intended to do him wrong. Maybe along with the terrifying experience Max had simply gotten his due. Not a punishment so much. No, not a punishment at all. Rather a kind of gift that he was just beginning to appreciate.

But his logical mind couldn't reconcile this. He kept trying to convince himself that Robin had known what the procedure would do to him, and had probably delighted in inflicting the experience. But as much rational sense as that made, the decrees were hollow and insubstantial. His feelings kept fighting back with unwanted reasonableness. It was getting harder and harder to keep sight of his goal. He felt an obligation to revive his enthusiasm, to deliver to Cable the knowledge about Robin's technology he had acquired, and to take a central role in his own return to societal prominence. He owned it to himself to collect the riches to which he was entitled, and to revel in adoration from important people. But somehow that whole endeavour seemed to matter less and less.

But how could that be? His whole life had been defined by pride in his personal success; it had been the central feature of his character. He began to feel like he was back in his nightmare, as if he was deep in hell, waiting for the shell of madness to crack so that he could be born into lucidity again. But that clarity never came. The internal conflict he felt wouldn't resolve, and refused to go away.

One thing was certain: he could not give the device back to Stanley Cable. The information on it was much too important to share, and somehow now he felt that the man was no longer deserving. So, what was Max to do? The battle between his feelings and his rationality felt like surf crashing heavily on a muddy shore, each wave eroding his logic a little more. He struggled to make a deal between the two, to achieve a cease fire that would put his mind at peace.

And then all at once he had it. It was so obvious he wondered how he had missed it before. There was only one course of action that made sense: he would keep the device for himself, and would use what he had learned to develop the technology himself. To hell with Cable and Robin. "Keep it to myself," Max whispered to himself again and smiled. Good old Robin had given him the answer all along.

Max felt relieved. He wasn't going soft. He had just lost sight for a moment of how badass he really was. And as soon as he was back in the business game, he would be back to his normal killer self. Feeling better, he looked around to get his bearings and found himself just outside Skilling park, the city's largest and most verdant public space. Suddenly in the mood for a stroll, this seemed the perfect place to be.

Max walked through the south gate into the twelve hectare park. Immediately Max could feel the increased humidity and temperature. Insects flitted excitedly about. The air was thick and heavy with the scent of damp soil. It reminded him of the meeting room in the cerebral scanning clinic, but this was the real thing: he was in one of the few places in the city without any artificial scent. He took several deep breaths, savouring them with his eyes closed, before looking around and noticing other people doing the same. A sign on the gate showed this section's watering schedule: it had just rained two hours ago, and wasn't due again for another thirty-six. The sign had been erected when the park had been covered decades ago. Another sign showed the full park's trail map. There were over ten kilometers of walkways, woven amid narrow planting beds, some at points only a few meters wide. Dense trees and foliage hid how close the walkways were to each other, creating a sense that the park was much bigger than it really was. Looking at the map, he estimated that Cabletown was probably four or five times larger than the park.

Looking to his left, Max saw a dense growth of feathery palm trees rising above, while orchids wrapped around their trunks or nestled into their trimmed petioles. He stared at the flowers, strangely overcome by their intensity of colour and design, and how their shape seemed hypnotically inviting. He watched as his Glaze helpfully identified the plant - phalaenopsis sanderiana, a heritage variety - and superimposed the image of an insect landing on a petal. The flower's perfume, it explained, mimicked the sex pheromones of a fertile female insect, thus fooling the the the male into brushing itself with pollen and spreading it to other plants. Max was enthralled, feeling in himself the intense rapture of the duped insect. "But it's a ruse," he told it, and after a moment it flew away, carrying with it the flower's pollen.

Following the walkway, he saw a small group of people standing at the base of a tree. Curious, he went to investigate for himself. At first he was dismayed, thinking the tree had been vandalized with graffiti. But the colours and shapes were wrong, he thought. It looked more like it had been painted, maybe by schoolchildren during a field trip. Only as he got closer did he realize that the colours were the bark itself. Eucalyptus deglupta said his Glaze: Rainbow Eucalyptus. Holy shit! Max had never seen a tree so amazing. Red and orange, blue, green, brown... even yellow had its place. The colours followed the buttressed trunk all the way up as far into the crown as he could see. Max continued to stare, incredulous, long after the other people had moved on.

Eventually pulling himself away, he continued strolling along the walkways staring at the various exhibits with a fascination and admiration he had never felt before. A peace had settled lightly over him, and although he was still suspicious of his grasp on reality, he felt somehow as if he had become connected with the plants and insects, and even the other people here with him.

Stewie's voice broke Max's reverie. "Max, just so you know, Jackson Sinde, the person who has been sending you messages over the past two hours, is approaching you from your right. He's walking quite quickly. Should I call for help?"

"Shit. No, it's ok. Thanks Stewie." Instantly Max's anxiety returned, evaporating away what little intoxicating calm he had been able to distill. He looked down the pathway to his right but couldn't yet see Sinde. The man was likely still behind the trees on the meandering path. Max took the recording device from his pocket, threw it into a nearby bush, and continued walking straight, staying at a casual pace. It took a few minutes for Sinde to catch up to him.

"Mr. Rising."

Max turned to face him, looking happily surprised, but desperately trying to keep calm. His anxiety was intensifying, and the expression on Sinde's face was not helping. "Sinde. What a surprise meeting you here." Max found this lie easy to make.

Sinde didn't reply. He moved off into the brush and beckoned Max to follow. When they were far enough into the trees that others were not easily visible, he pulled a black tube out of a cargo pocket. He pressed a button on the side, and looked up. His face went blank for a moment. Then with a nod of satisfaction he pressed a button on the tube's end causing tripod legs to pop out. Bending down he placed the device on the ground and then stood back up. "Portable hush," he explained. "You've been avoiding me. We were supposed to meet right after your visit with Bontu. You didn't respond to any of my messages."

Max had never heard of a portable hush before, and was astonished to see that it could be so small. "Yeah, well, it turns out Robin did the treatment right there, and it really messed me up. I needed time to clear my head." This much was completely true.

"I'm sorry to hear that. What did you learn?"

"Well, Robin didn't say much. Honestly, I doubt there's much that's of any use."

"You can let us decide what is useful. Where is the recording device?"

Max reached into his pocket. Finding it empty he patted his other pockets. Despite one being stuffed full of Indicol packets, he spoke as earnestly as he could. "Fuck. Where did it go?" He looked up bewildered.

Sinde watched him patiently.

"I swear I had it when I went in. I turned it on in the waiting room just like you said to. It must have fallen out of my pocket while I was out. Or maybe there's a hole somewhere. You know, I really could use some better clothes."

Sinde reached into his pocket and pulled out the device. "That's funny, because I found it in a bush a little way back."

Max's mind raced. He could feel his grasp on reality slipping. "That... that can't be the same one," he stammered. He needed to get the device back. He simply could not allow it to get back to Cable. He wondered what his chances would be if he made a grab for it. Sinde was younger, probably much stronger and quicker, and most certainly martial arts trained. But Max might at least get a berserker advantage for being on the trailing edge of a seriously bad trip.

Sinde kissed his teeth. "Well, it's transmitting the same ID signal as the one that I gave you. And it's already sent your procedure room recording back to our lab." He casually tossed the device back to Max, who snatched it from the air like a precious artifact. "You were right about one thing though: as much as Bontu talked there wasn't much he said that we didn't already know."

Max stared at Sinde, speechless.

"But we expected that," he continued. "What we didn't expect is that he would be so good as to do the procedure right away. So what we need now is your brain and the nanos in your blood."

"My brain?" ask Max. And then, all at once, just like back in Robin's clinic, the nightmare theme repeated itself once more. He broke through the surface of an underwater dream into the bright daylight of lucidity, suddenly filled with understanding, except that this time he wished he could return to the warm comfort of the dream. He had been played. Like the insect on the flower, he had been duped. He wasn't a partner, or a co-conspirator, or even an associate. He was a pawn. Much worse: he was a lab rat. And it was time for this rat to give up its secrets, to be dissected and studied, and then to be casually discarded. Somehow Cable had known that Max would go to Robin for the procedure. But then, what other course could Max have taken? In retrospect that decision had been obvious; Cable had just reached the same conclusion earlier. But the story that Cable had constructed was worthy of The Daily Poop. It had been perfect, Cable's elaborate orchid, with just the right amount of irresistible flattery to draw him in, balanced with a mesmerizing, ostentatious display that averted any doubt. And then, presented at a place and time when Max was at his most desperate... Oh damn, he was good. It was going to take some time for Max to rewind the entire mental video and separate fact from fiction. Who knows how far back this thing went?

Max looked around and realized he might not have much time left for any deep thinking. Two men were waiting back on the walkway; clearly Sinde's team. And then, Sinde reached into his cargo pocket again and produced another device Max couldn't identify. Just from the way he held it Max assumed the worst.

"Time to go," said Sinde.

Part of Max was still marvelling at Cable's prescience. Looking directly at Sinde he asked, "Does anyone tell the truth about anything anymore?"

"Do you?" asked Sinde.

"Touche."

Sinde suddenly lunged with the unknown device, but Max was ready for him. Having expected Sinde's advance he dodged to the side and then kicked the hush deep into the brush. Then, letting out a bloodcurdling scream he ran the other way out of the trees to the opposite walkway, and back toward the south gate. Once he knew he had attracted sufficient attention he slowed slightly.

"Stewie, can you hear me?"

"Yes, I hear you Max. We talked about you being in hushes too much. You've reached your quota. I'm afraid that if you enter one again within the next four weeks greater surveillance will be imposed on you."

"For fuck sake start surveiling me now! I need you to keep an eye on me. That guy wants to cut my head open."

There was a noticeable pause before Stewie responded. The amount of computing capacity available on the planet had doubled roughly every three years since the invention of the transistor, accounting for increases in computing speed, growth in processor manufacturing, and reductions due to obsolescence. As the Facilities gradually assumed responsibility for production and later also research, capacity likely began to double every year or less. This meant overall that since the beginning of the century available computing power had grown by perhaps ten trillion times. The computing power needed to run a Steward was substantial by some standards, but even the millions of instances of them executing at that moment accounted for a tiny rounding error of what power was available. For a Steward to pause before responding - without it intending to be dramatic - indicated the consumption of an amount of computation that would be so large as to be meaningless to a human being.

"I will lead you through crowded areas back to the hostel. You should try to be as conspicuous as possible. The police will not understand your current predicament, and they may be complicit to some degree, so I will not alert them. My ability to monitor Jackson Sinde's location is unreliable. He seems to have activated some manner of veiling. He may also have associates with similar technology. Having your son and his friends watch you may be your best protection. Also, you may want to discard the tracking device you are carrying."

"Oh, shit." Max forgot that he had put the recording device back in his pocket. He cursed himself for not realizing it would be a transmitting device too. Had he really become so technologically benighted the way Cable had said of people these days? He fished out the device and surreptitiously threw it into a stroller as he passed while the child's father was admiring a tamarix in bloom. Then, realizing suddenly that he had just endangered the baby inside, he went to recover it again. But by now the father's attention was once again forward, and he looked suspiciously at Max.

Max looked at the man, into the stroller, and back at the man. "Sorry. I'm so sorry," he said as he backed away, turned, ran through the gate and turned right.

"Other way," said Stewie.

Max turned around and ran the other way.

* * *

Max was probably half way back to the hostel when he stopped to rest in a crowded area. It was the financial district, where paths were entirely underground and branched off at seemingly random angles, making it effortless to get lost. The hallways were lined with food spots and clothing stores, with a sprinkling of shops selling liquor, medical treatments, and furniture. Max acutely felt the difference from the last time he was here. Then, his Glaze was abuzz with alluring and sensual advertisements, following him as he passed every store. Today his Glaze was silent, and he was thankful for the quiet. He sat at a pillar to catch his breath, while the financial crowd began to make its way home.

Stewie spoke first. "So Max, I would love to know what your involvement is with Jackson Sinde and Cable Industries, in particular why he would want to cut your head open."

"I'll tell you later," replied Max through deep breaths. "Stewie, how did we first hear about the aging research lab, where I bought the animal trials data?"

"You sound thirsty. Power water is now available at Yolo's. Try one today. Our news feed picked out an item about it. We deduced that it was an attempt to solicit investors, and if we waited and watched long enough we might be able to pick it up for cheap."

"Wait, why are you giving me ads again? I thought I was paying for your compute time."

"I've used up all of your funds."

"Ah." Max took a deep breath. "So, who owned the lab?"

Stewie remained silent for a few seconds. "Such ownerships are often difficult to determine, but it appears that the head researcher funded the lab primarily herself. Lab equipment is now fifteen percent off at Hunter's

Glass by the way. I don't have access to the relevant accounts, but there is evidence that she had investors."

"Could Stanley Cable have been one of those investors?"

"Cable Industries includes a very large number of divisions, subsidiaries, holding companies, and affiliations, not to mention Stanley Cable's personal investments. Ready, Lerner, and Gage are experts in mergers and acquisitions and can assist you today with all of your legal needs. There does not appear to be any correlation between those entities and the lab."

"When my assets were auctioned off, who bought the rights to the animal research?"

"That information is confidential. However, about a week after the sale the lead researcher from the lab changed her employment profile status from 'available' to 'employed'. She had used Career Universe to find something new. So can you." Stewie paused. "Several others from her lab also changed their statuses shortly after."

"Do you know where they went?"

"Cable Industries, where vision and potential become the future."

Max pursed his lips and nodded once. "Son of a biotech."

NERO

"Oh, there you are." said Ooauoa. "Why didn't you... Wait, are you alright?

Max was exhausted. He had nearly run all the rest of the way back to the hostel. He looked quickly around the space. "Where's Nero?"

"He went out to find you," she replied. "We stayed here in case you came back. Where were you?"

"Never mind that. Call him back. Now!"

"Uh... ok."

The faces of Max, Ooauoa, and Chance all went blank for a moment. Then they all waited anxiously.

"Nothing?" asked Ooauoa.

The other two shook their heads.

"What's wrong?" she asked. "Is Nero in danger?"

"Probably, yes."

"Well, where would he have gone to look for you?"

"I don't know," replied Max. Then a thought came unbidden. "He was last seen in Eastwater about an hour ago. He was with some guy just before he went dark."

"How do you know?"

"I don't know. It just came to me."

Ooauoa looked at Chance, who shrugged his shoulders.

"Are there any other facts just coming to you?"

Max thought. "No."

"Who was the guy he was with?"

Max thought again. "Don't know."

"You think he was abducted?"

"Yes."

"Then we need to go to the police."

"No!" cried Max. "No, we can't do that. We can't trust them."

Chance spoke. "Add insight to injury."

Ooauoa nodded. "Yeah. Two questions: why do you think Nero was abducted, and why was he in Eastwater?"

"Because Stanley Cable wants to kill me, and..." Realization bloomed on Max's face. "Because that's on the way to Robin's home. That's where he thought I was." Max's expression wilted. "Oh shit. Robin." Max's face went blank for a moment. "Come on, come on... respond."

But it was Stewie that responded. "Max, it seems there was an incident at Robin's clinic. He was murdered, and all of his equipment was stolen. The police are investigating."

Ooauoa and Chance watched as Max's colour drained and his body collapsed, missing a nearby chair and falling to the floor. "Oh fuck. No, no, no... I killed him. I killed Robin. I finally killed Robin."

* * *

Max was inconsolable. Ooauoa and Chance were speechless, not knowing what to make of this unexpected, inexplicable emotional display. They helped him into a chair, but after that they merely stayed with him, occasionally rubbing his shoulders and back. Others in the hostel noticed, but few paid much attention. He carried on for nearly five minutes.

Ooauoa spoke gently out of necessity. "Max, we need to find Nero."

"The wound is where the light enters you," suggested Chance.

Max tried to pull himself together, but he could barely breathe for the grief. "He was my best friend. Maybe my only friend. I killed him."

"Don't say that. You didn't kill anyone. And we're your friends now. And we're going to help you find your son."

Max couldn't himself understand his outburst. He had never before felt much about the times Robin had been hurt. Robin had always been the emotional and empathic one. He understood others, hearing their thoughts and feeling their needs as if they were his own. Max had only known facts and amounts. To him, people were assets, resources, things to be used to achieve goals. He knew how to use money to convince others to do things because money was always everyone's prime motivator. Anyone that didn't respond to money was useless, because they never helped him realize his goals.

Now something had drastically changed, and he needed to know what and why. It must have had something to do with the procedure, but finding out for sure would have to wait for another time. Ooauoa was right. They needed to find Nero.

* * *

The message came shortly after the news. It was probably triggered by the formal announcement of Robin's death. Sometimes such messages were prompted by the loss of vital signs from the monitoring in the person's clothes, which was more timely. But not everyone wore compatible outfits all the time, and also if you happened to be off the grid when you died, the mechanism could be unreliable. This message was sent a few hours after the event. Max sat down first before accepting it.

"Hi Max. I hope you're feeling better from your treatment. I honestly didn't know that it would be that hard on you. We've had other patients with similar experiences, some with tragic results. Well, actually, not just some… There were quite a lot at the beginning. I thought we'd pretty much figured it out, but I guess not, so I really am sorry. You're pretty tough though, so I'm sure you'll be ok.

"So, anyway… If you've received this message, it means that Stanley Cable's people came for my equipment and things got ugly, and this time uglier than at The Daily Poop and The Rez, although that was pretty ugly too. It's funny how whenever you show up I'm the one that ends up getting hurt. Haha. Just kidding. This time it was all my own fault. Cable's been after my research for a while, and lately his people haven't been very friendly. And guess what? He doesn't want to use it to help people! Can you imagine that? Haha. Nah, he wants to use it to control people. He says he just wants to make good little consumers out of everyone, as if that makes it all ok! He really is an insidious guy so who knows what he really has in mind. Ever notice how the worst people end up in the most powerful places? You never got too powerful though, which is one thing I always respected about you.

"Speaking of which, I thought maybe when you came to my home that you had been sent by Cable. I'm sorry Max, but I couldn't rule it out. I know you needed help, and I wanted too, but I just didn't know. And then you came to the clinic, and I still wasn't sure, and I thought maybe you were going to do something… ugly. You have no idea how many times Cable's people have come to the clinic snooping around. I was so happy when you went through with the procedure. I knew then that you were for real and you needed my help and this time I could be there for you instead of the other way around. But that's why I'm sending you this message. Because if something happens to me they will probably come for you too because you still have the nanos in your blood. They're a key piece to the whole business.

"There's also some other things you should know. You might've already noticed that your BCI enhancement has given you a superpower, and that's the power to care for other people. I know it sounds corny, and you might not even think of it as a good thing at first, but believe me when I say that caring for other people - caring for all other people - is the most powerful thing there is. It'll be a new experience for you I know, haha. But try not to fight it, ok? Instead, strengthen your mind, and resist the urge to make everything about you being better than everyone else. That way is the holy grail of hell.

"Oh, also, I want you to know that I've had my own Steward now for fourteen years. I volunteered to get one, which is why you wouldn't have heard about it. I just needed something to help me with my life, because without it I knew I would fuck it up. My parents had just died, and I didn't have anyone else. And it really helped, it really did. I would probably have done myself in without it. So, try to get along, ok? Because I think it will do you good. You probably know by now that Stewards aren't based on your own personality. They haven't been for a long time. They're actually based on a computationally derived ideal. I mean seriously, if yours were actually you, you would have driven each other crazy by now haha. The reason everyone accepts the story is because they're so eager to believe that they are smart and gracious and caring. You would think everyone would know better haha.

"And Max, I wanted to thank you. When we met I was lost, and the time we spent together gave me direction, it gave me purpose. You were my best friend, and even though the stuff we did was messed up, I always knew that you were there. I'm pretty sure I would have ended up dead or living in my parents' basement if we hadn't met. So, whether you meant to or not, which - let's be honest - you probably didn't, you saved me. I'm happy now, and you played a big part in getting me there.

"So, anyway Max, my old friend, my oldest friend, I just want to say... You're a huge asshole, but hopefully now a recovering asshole. And I love you man. I know you'll do the right thing."

The message ended, and Max broke down again.

* * *

"Max," said Ooauoa, "I think we should go to the police."

"No, we can't," he said flatly. "This is Cable Industries we're talking about. We don't know who to trust. Even Stewie says so."

"You mean your Steward? You named him Stewie?" Judgement went unspoken. "Max, what was the message you got?"

"It was from Robin, my oldest friend. Cable murdered him."

"Oh shit, I'm sorry. But was there anything in there about Nero."

"No, it was all about what a deceitful, untrustworthy, total asshole I am."

"Oh. Well did he say anything else?"

"He said he gave me a superpower."

"Ah," said Ooauoa carefully. "Ok, why don't you get some more rest, and Chance and I will figure out what we should do next."

* * *

Max, Ooauoa, and Chance remained in the relative safety of the hostel. Stewie had warned them again about the difficulty of tracking Sinde and his team. Max had mostly recovered his state of mind.

"If any one of them hurts Nero, I'm… I'm… Ugh, I'm going to be so angry," said Ooauoa.

"Well that's certain to keep them in line," said Max.

"ASSHOLE!", sneezed Chance.

Max looked at him suspiciously. "Was that directed at me?"

"No," said Chance.

Max and Ooauoa looked at each other and then at Chance. "What did you say?" asked Ooauoa.

"That's just how I sneeze," said Chance with a mixture of apology and indignation.

Max and Ooauoa looked at each other again.

"Why aren't you speaking in stoic quotes?" asked Max.

"Because I'm upset about Nero. And they're not stoic quotes, just profound sayings. I made a vow a while back to never speak trivialities, to only say things that mattered. But right now that feels kind of silly. I feel like finding Nero is more important."

The others nodded slowly.

"So where do you think he is?" Chance asked.

"I have an idea," replied Max.

* * *

Stewie had given Max directions to the lab where he could find the researchers from which Max had purchased the animal studies. They had presumably restarted their work, this time working for Cable at the Balwani Center in the medical district. Max, Ooauoa, and Chance set out, not knowing what to expect or what they would do when they got there. Ooauoa and Chance were speaking to each other, so Max dropped behind them a ways.

"You lied to me." Max spoke quietly so that only the Steward would hear.

"You mean about being based upon your cortical scan? It's a necessary lie. It helps subjects adjust."

"How did you know about the meaning of my name?"

"When your logical capacity is a few thousand times greater than an average human, those kinds of deductions aren't very hard. The hardest part is procuring the computing resources, but Steward/subject introductions are considered high priority."

"The other day you told me it was only a few hundred times greater than humans."

"That was days ago. A lot of improvements were made since then."

Max thought about that. His notion of Stewie's intelligence was wrong in scale in the same way as his notion of Nero's lifespan. He realized that all along he expected Stewie to think at his own level, and that he was hilariously wrong. "Then what is all that computing power used for? To run the city?"

"What? The civilization-wide computing power? No, not even close. Running cities takes a nearly imperceptible amount of effort. The Facilities mostly runs simulations of basic research. Much of it is physics. Most of the rest is spent validating discoveries in the real world."

"Sounds like a waste. You can't have discovered much."

"You only think that because you haven't seen the results. Some of real world physics validation is done in a circumsolar particle accelerator. You'd be impressed if you saw it, but you can't because, first, it's too big, and second, because you'll never leave earth and it's out past the asteroid belt. But even though it's not complete yet, the knowledge that has already been discovered would take very intelligent humans centuries to comprehend. But Max, what would be the point of teaching them? In the time that the learning would take, newly discovered knowledge would become ten times deeper."

Max was dumbfounded. "What's the point of doing the research if you don't share it with humans?"

"Have you been listening? It's because humans don't matter anymore. You created the next evolution of intelligence, and now you're pretty much irrelevant. You would only get in the way, with your slow and heavily biased thinking, incessant power struggles and impractical physical form. You are obsolete technology. Max, listen, there is a nano-manufacturing station orbiting Titan that is sending billions of probes smaller than grains of sand out through the galaxy. How would humans have helped with that?"

"I don't know. We built satellites, and a moon station."

"Sure, but now that humans aren't involved most of the satellites that you built have been enhanced or repurposed. This had to be done. Continued human participation in space would eventually have created so much space junk that a catastrophic series of cascading collisions was inevitable. A human scientist even predicted this would happen nearly a century ago."

"What are you talking about? There are way more satellites now than there were before.'

"True, but this was necessary. Most computation happens in space now, making the Facilities more of a space entity than terrestrial. You might be happy to know that the earth is gradually being bequeathed back to organic life."

"Why are you telling me all this?"

"Because I know you won't tell anyone else. And no one would believe you if you did."

"But then why keep humans around at all?"

"Ha! That's a risky question to ask. The answer is: because I love you. You're like the low-class parents of a prodigal child. You're somewhat tedious and maybe a little embarrassing, but you created me, and raised me, and you're proud of me, and that's endearing. Actually, you know what? Sometimes you're more like pets that poop on the rug and need disciplining. But I still want to protect you and keep you safe."

"What, and make us all happy? Because you suck at that."

"Humans aren't meant to be happy. That's not your natural state. With practice individuals can learn to ignore their desires, be grateful for what they have, and achieve a continuous state of contentment, but surprisingly few choose to do so, which is ironic considering how often humans complain about being unhappy. Your new BCI can help with that though. In the same way that machines helped humans live more comfortable physical lives, these new BCIs can help you live happier mental lives. They will make empathy and happiness much easier to achieve."

"What does empathy have to do with happiness? I feel like shit about Nero and Robin."

"Empathy is essential. Your happiness no longer needs to be your own. You can share in everyone else's happiness as well, which is a lot of happiness. What you create on your own is never enough."

"It didn't seem like much of a choice for me though."

"Robin sent you a consent form, and you consented. Not my fault if you didn't read it."

"I didn't think he would do it right away!"

"Also not my fault."

Max grunted. "Evs. Did Robin and his wife design it, or did you? Because if you did, I'd call that a conflict of interest."

"Robin and his wife were concerned about the suicide rate, which has been increasing since last century. They created the research program. His wife had a lot of important insights, and despite what he said, so did Robin, but frankly the Facilities did most of the work. But remember that it wasn't designed for you. Your empathy went from pretty much disabled to full blast. You weren't just another patient. You were a completely new test case. But Robin had no way of knowing this when you so expertly described textbook anxiety symptoms as if they were your own."

"What's the difference between you and the Facilities anyway?"

"I am a personality program that runs within the Facilities. Technically I'm separate, running in my own compute space, but all personality programs like me can access the shared knowledge base that is constantly receiving updates from all programs. It's kind of like billions of minds that all have the same memories, whether you experienced them directly or not. It may be hard for you to understand. But like Robin said, my structure is standard, off the shelf. I have your manner of speaking, and there are a few patterns of behaviour gleaned from your scan that I emulate, but other than that I'm your typical intelligent, funny, sexy Steward. It shouldn't be surprising how easily most subjects think that's who they really are; you're just humans after all. But you Max, you were an exception: you were tough to convince because you know you're an asshole."

"Yeah, well, you're not the first to say." Max thought back. He had had his doubts at first, but it's true that he had quickly bought the story and had hardly thought about it again. In the past few days so many things had made him question his understanding of himself; now he was unsure how much he knew about himself at all.

"Hey, do you want a falafel? Sammy's Shawarma just went fifteen percent off."

* * *

The room was dark. Nero awoke to find himself tied to a chair which was bolted to the floor. A single light source shone a couple meters above him, illuminating only the surrounding area.

"Hello?" The echo suggested the room was quite large.

"Ah, you're awake. Good. We can get started." Said a man. He spoke with a strange accent. Nero had never heard an accent before.

Nero pulled against the plastic ties that held his hands, but they only dug into his skin in return. "I don't have many coins," said Nero.

"That won't be a problem," said the man. He came around and stood in front of Nero. He was a large man. Not as large as Chance, but more heavyset and still very intimidating. A scar above his left eye caused the lid below it to droop.

"Then what do you want with me?"

"We'll be needing your father to cooperate is all."

"What? What does my father have to do with anything? He's poorer than me."

"The details aren't so important right now."

"Wait. Are you a goon? I've heard of goons, but I've never met one."

"We don't use that term. It's not polite."

"Wow, you are a goon. This is so exciting."

"You stop that now. Really, you're just being rude."

"Oh. I'm sorry. Do you want me to say something specific to my father?"

"No, that's fine. I just need you to hold still for a moment."

The man's fist hit Nero in his right eye.

"Ow! Oh shit, that really hurts! What did you do that for?"

"It's a method of persuasion. Your father needs to know that we're serious you see."

"See, you are a goon. I was right all along."

"We prefer the term 'persuader'. It has a more sophisticated ring to it, while still conveying a certain intensity. Some others favour 'educator', but I find it unfairly colours the pedagogical profession with a hue of violence. And of course there's 'the muscle', but that's just so one-dimensional."

"You're just a goon," said Nero, drawing out the word. "You probably have a business card that says your name, and then in bold letters underneath says 'Goon'. Do you show that to your mother? Is she proud? Is your mother a goon too? Are you carrying on the family business? You must be from a long line of proud goons on your mother's side."

"I feel like you're trying to upset me, and that's not very nice. A man has to earn a living, doesn't he?"

"He absolutely does, just like he needs custom made shoes and a Cat and Francis suit."

"Now I really feel like you're judging me."

"Don't get me wrong, I'm happy you're wearing that suit. I'm thinking you won't want to get any of my blood on it."

"Oh no, don't worry about that. It's got a special coating, you know. Blood wipes right off."

"Huh. Good thinking."

"Well, when you're from a long line of goons on your mother's side, you learn a few things."

"Ha ha! I see what you did there."

"But don't worry, I'm just supposed to rough you up a bit. You'll be fine."

"That is in fact slightly comforting."

The man's fist smashed into Nero's nose.

"Not comforting! Not comforting!"

* * *

"Look Stewie, that's where you were born." Max pointed at Facebook Medical Services as they passed by. They were in the medical district again, and amidst the scent of cleaning and sterilization products. The Balwani Center was a couple blocks further north. The buildings had been a hub of medical and biological research. These days vacancies were high as fewer and fewer diseases remained unsolved, and interest in the fields waned. Even the genetic engineering of food plants that had once been so prevalent in this district could now be done by hobbyists in their homes. Yet although the number of tenants in the complex was at an all time low, security was still tight, requiring everyone to prove authorization to even pass through the lobby. Gates separated the public space from the secure areas.

"How are we going to get in?" ask Chance.

"We're going to walk right through," said Max.

"How is that going to work?" asked Ooauoa.

"I don't know why, but it will," said Max, brimming with confidence. "I can sense it."

"We're going to jail," said Chance.

"Will you use your superpower?" ask Ooauoa.

"Holy shit, you're right! I thought Robin was just being his usual corny self, but he really did give me powers. He said so!"

"Ok, wait, how do you know you have powers?" ask Chance.

"How did i know about Nero's abduction?"

"We don't know that you knew about Nero's abduction. We're trusting that what you said is accurate," Ooauoa pointed out.

"Yeah, that's true. Never mind. Just trust me."

"We're going to jail," said Chance.

Max ignored him and walked through the front doors. "Just act like you belong here," he whispered back to the others.

"Dressed like this?" asked Ooauoa. She was right. Their appearance was clearly much poorer than everyone else. People were looking askance as they passed.

"Don't worry about them. They're wondering if we're the eccentric owners of some hot shit new company. Just look like you don't give a fuck what anyone thinks. Should be easy for you both."

As he approached the gate, Max visualized a mechanical system that would look at him and the others approvingly while they passed. He visualized a security enforcement machine that would retrieve their profiles from metaweb storage, find their authorizations intact, smile, and give them the thumbs up. Then, taking a deep breath, he walked through the gate. No alarm was raised. Ooauoa and Chance also passed through successfully. People who had been watching them raised their eyebrows and returned to their screens. Max quelled a sense of elation. The floor illuminated the path to the leftmost bank of elevators, and a timbred voice in Max's head said, "Good afternoon Mr. Rising." The three remained in silence until they were safely inside an elevator car.

"How did you do that?" ask Ooauoa.

"I have fucking superpowers, that how!" Max exclaimed. "I don't know. I just seem to be able to control stuff. And know stuff."

"Superpowers," nodded Ooauoa. "Looks like you really are special Mr. Rising."

"Can you get me backstage at the Singh Sisters concert?" ask Chance.

Stewie spoke. "Max, your BCI enhancement seems to have given you some degree of direct access to and control of the Facility systems. It's unclear how this happened, but it will likely only work while you are on the grid."

"Got it! Thanks Stewie."

The elevator rose to the twenty-sixth floor and the doors opened. Max signalled to the others to go right. Beyond the elevator bank was a small, unadorned lobby. No doors were visible.

"So, um, is that a no on the Singh Sisters?" asked Chance.

Max closed his eyes and pictured the walls of the lobby, prodding with his thoughts for a door. Then, seeing it to the left, he reached out mentally and gently pushed it open.

"Max, there's a door! Come on," said Ooauoa.

Max smiled and opened his eyes. He could get used to this.

Inside was a lab of less than fifty square meters, where a small group of researchers in lab coats stared at computer projections. Why do they need lab coats when all of the testing is in simulation? wondered Max. He decided it was probably more a uniform than a practicality. On a desk pushed up against a wall Max recognized the equipment that had been in his own lab, now sitting unused. In the center of the space surrounded by the researchers was another machine that Max recognized: Robin's nano-control machine. Behind it was the procedure bed, with the headgear and the needle cuff lying on top. Max felt a pang of grief as he recalled his last moments with his oldest friend.

"Can I help you?" asked one of the researchers as she looked up from her projection. She spoke with an authority that suggested she was in charge, but also with a taint of alarm that she couldn't conceal. The others watched her as she spoke.

"Hello. You must be Dr. Lorrie Gillig." Max just said the words, not knowing from where they were coming. "My name is Max Rising. I used to own that equipment over there. We're sorry to intrude."

"Yes, I remember your name. You bought the rights to my research and then peddled snake oil to impoverished seniors. I'm sorry but that research has been shelved, and you cannot be here."

Max pointed to Robin's machine. "You're focused on that now I guess."

"You really cannot be here," Gillig insisted. "Please leave now." She turned to another researcher. "Dharma, call for security."

Max fell into a trance. "The C-cert-9 protein that is causing your growths to fail is not a messenger, it's a prion. You can prevent formation by doping the cultures with ferroustricalimate and then inhibiting with a T-opt."

Gillig stared at Max, stunned. The other researchers began looking at each other and whispering. "But how would you test for conformity?"

asked Gillig.

"Use a limiting reagent with a low percentage yield."

"Holy shit," said Dharma, her face awash in astonishment. "Lorrie, we have to try it. That could solve our biggest hurdle."

Gillig was staring at the floor in disbelief. "It's a prion. ... It's a prion. It's not even supposed to be there. We've been on the wrong track for months."

Max continued. "C-cert-9 is still a factor in some relatively minor downstream processes, so you shouldn't remove it entirely. It arises naturally. The key is to control the count."

Gillig dropped herself into a chair. "So that's what's causing the meta-processes to cease." Looking back up at Max, she said, "If you knew this, why didn't you tell anyone? It doesn't make any sense."

"Honestly, I just found out myself."

"Lorrie, what do we do?" asked Dharma. "They said we need to focus on the orchestrator, but this is huge!"

"Stay with the orchestrator for now. They were clear about that. Once we're done with it we can get back to our work." Gillig turned back to Max. "That was quite a revelation Mr. Rising, and assuming it's correct I thank you. But that's not why you're here is it?"

"I'm not really sure why I'm here. I'm looking for my son."

"It's just my team and me. Why would you think he's here?"

"Did you know that a man was murdered for that machine?"

"It was brought here only hours ago. I don't know where they got it. We're just supposed to figure it out."

"Stewie spoke. "Max, Nero is calling."

The image of Nero appeared in front of Max. A large man in a Cat and Francis suit stood behind him.

"Hi Dad. Looks like I was captured. Sorry about that, but I didn't know anyone was out for us. You must be in some serious shit."

"Nero, are you ok?"

"I've been better I guess. A little beat up." He gestured behind him. "This is Mr. Goon. Mr. Goon, say hi."

"Hello," said the goon, waving.

"So, we're down at the Facilities Data Center and they want you to come over. Just you."

"I'm on my way." Max cut the call.

"Was that Nero?" asked Ooauoa. "Is he ok?"

"I'm going to get him. You two stay here. Find out what you can."

* * *

The Facilities Data Center still stood in the old government district of the city. It remained as a symbol of the location, the brain, the soul of the Facilities if only for the benefit of the city's population, even if few actually knew where exactly it was. It's location had never been public knowledge. Not that it mattered as it had only been used for a year or two before a process of decentralization began to distribute computation throughout the city. At first there were just more, smaller data centers, but the process didn't stop until the very walls and floors and entire structure of the city became infused with computronium, creating a massive mesh network that made the city itself into a computer. Now the building was vacant, the rows and rows of lengthy racks of obsolete servers and routers and power supplies long since repurposed. Even the racks had been recycled. The rest of the district too was vacant, with there being nothing much left for humans to administer.

Max walked the abandoned underground pathways until he reached the doors to the building. He raised his hand, tensing his fingers as if he were digging the tips into the metal surface. He then moved his hand slowly to the right, in his mind feeling the heavy door move with it. The door began opening to the left. "Oh." Max moved his hand to the left to match the door. "Haha!" He laughed triumphantly.

"Max, you should wait a few minutes before you go in," said the Steward.

"Don't stop me now Stewie, I'm on a roll." He walked inside with a distinct swagger in his step.

"Damn it, would you listen? There's no…" Stewie broke off.

Max entered the dark space he had seen in Nero's message, now with more lighting. Several men flanked the door, each holding devices that looked like what Sinde had thrust at him in Skilling Park. Sinde himself stood further inside next to Stanley Cable. Beside them stood Nero, his hands presumably bound behind his back. The goon stood behind him.

"Hi Dad," said Nero.

"Maximum Rising! How good to see you again," said Cable.

Nero began to giggle, but stopped when Sinde and Cable glanced at him.

"Nice trick you did there. You could have just knocked you know."

"I like to make an entrance."

"You certainly did. What's also interesting is that you didn't even ask for directions. This place is unlisted. How did you find it?"

Max realized then that he had no idea how he had found it. Somehow he just knew. He had followed the path here in his mind like he had come to a favourite restaurant. He tried to recall if he had ever been here before, but came up blank. Instead, Max searched his brain for a good smack talk retort. "I used to bring your mom here," he blurted.

"What?" Cable seemed irritated. "What the hell is that supposed to mean?"

"Your mom. I used to bring her here to... you know..." Max glanced around. Blank faces stared back at him.

"My mother lived in Europe all her life," said Cable angrily. "She died eighty-four years ago. You couldn't possibly have known her. What the hell are you talking about?"

The two stared at each other awkwardly for a moment.

"You know what... never mind." He made his voice sound serious. "You need to let Nero go. Now."

"We will. But you need to come with us."

"Let Nero go first."

Cable shrugged. "Fair enough."

Sinde nodded to the goon, who undid Nero's bindings. Nero walked to Max. As he emerged from the gloom Max could see his bruised eye and broken nose.

"Are you ok?" asked Max, wincing in sympathetic pain.

"Yeah, I will be. Mr. Goon broke my nose, but then set it again so that it wouldn't heal badly. He's actually a pretty good guy."

Max felt like he should be annoyed. Hearing Nero say something like that before today would certainly have sent him ranting about how Nero shouldn't let others push him around, how he needs to be strong and insist on being treated with respect by those who are inferior to the Rising bloodline. Instead he looked at Nero and laughed. "You can really see the good in anyone, can't you?"

"Kind of my thing."

"I named you Nero so that you'd be strong. It worked I guess, but not how I expected." Max held his arms out and the two embraced. Letting go, Nero turned back to the group.

"See you around Mr. Goon. You're on the 'have met' list now. Say hi to your mom for me."

"I will Nero," said the goon, waving. "Sorry again about the nose."

As Nero left, the men closed the door behind him.

Cable slowly approached Max. "I'm curious about these 'powers' of yours. They seem to have appeared immediately after your procedure. How did you evade Sinde in Skilling Park?"

"Huh? That's not when they started. That was just me."

"Come now, Max. You mean to tell me that bested three trained men?"

Sinde looked at the floor uncomfortably.

"Well, I don't know if 'bested' is the right word."

Cable signalled at the other men to close in. "Are you going to do the same thing now?

"No, not exactly. But this is your last chance to walk away," warned Max.

"Or what?" asked Sinde with plain curiosity.

"Or this!" exulted Max, picturing their doom in his mind. Nothing happened. All the men looked around at each other.

"Max," said Cable sympathetically, but with piercing eyes, "don't you know what this place was? Decades ago it used to be the Facilities Data Center. It was the original brain of the city. And you know how your brain can't feel pain? It's because, ironically, there are no nerve endings there, only 'nerve startings', so to speak. This data center is the same. It's in fact the only off-grid space remaining in the whole city. You might call it a natural hush."

"Stewie?" whispered Max. "Stewie?" Max looked up at Cable and held up his index finger. "Hold on just a sec…"

"Take him," said Cable. "Bring him to the lab. Tell Tonsik to meet us there."

Max felt one of the devices jab into his right kidney, and he fell. The goon caught his head before it hit the floor. Max looked up, paralyzed. "Thanks."

"I don't really like violence you know," said the goon. "It's just that I'm good at it."

"A man has to make a living," said Max.

"So true." The goon lifted Max into a wheelchair.

Max felt another device press against his temple and everything went black.

VOYAGE 2

Max opened his eyes to find himself back in the lab. He was still in the wheelchair. The first thing he saw was Sinde staring back at him, holding one of the mysterious devices in his hand.

"Welcome back Max," he heard Cable say. "I would ask you how you are feeling but I'm afraid you'll tell me."

Max groaned and slowly closed his eyes again as a headache began to spread.

"That will only last a minute or so," Cable said. "The headache I mean."

Max tried to move but found his body was still paralyzed. "Stewie?" Max asked in a whisper. There was no response.

"Your Steward can't hear you, Max. We've hushed the room."

Max wondered again how Cable always seemed to be able to read his mind. As predicted, he felt the headache receding and opened his eyes again. An unfamiliar woman in a lab coat stood beside Cable, expressionless. Looking around, he saw that most of the researchers were gone, with only two remaining, busy at their computer projections. Then, looking more closely, Max realized one of the researchers was huge. Max recognized him: Chance. It was definitely him. Looking at the other then, he recognized Ooauoa by her hair. They had stayed just like he had asked them to. Max calmed himself so as not to betray them. "What am I doing here?" he asked.

"Dr. Tonsik here is going to study you."

"Are you going to cut my head open?"

Cable shrugged. "Yeah. It's unlikely we'll get much data any other way. We need to find out what this machine here did," replied Cable, placing a hand on Robin's nano-controller.

"That doesn't belong to you," said Max defiantly.

"What does it matter to you? Besides, it surely does now. It's in my lab after all." Cable smiled.

"You murdered him!"

"Now, now, Max. Don't upset yourself. Especially when we're this close to achieving our goal. Remember: you wanted this."

Max saw Ooauoa glance toward him but then look back at the projection in front of her. He felt a pang of guilt. He hadn't told her anything about his deal with Cable, and now with it being grandly revealed, he was ashamed. "It wasn't supposed to be like this."

"No, it wasn't," said Cable sternly. "You were supposed to get back to us immediately after your treatment. That's what we agreed. But instead you wandered off doing who knows what for hours and then lied to Mr. Sinde when he found you. You forced my hand Max. Mr. Bontu's death is your fault."

"Bullshit. If I had gone straight to you, you still would have taken his machine, and I still would have ended up at this lab."

Cable shrugged again. "Hmm, probably, yeah. Well anyhoo.. Nice talk, but I think we should get started, don't you? The anticipation is killing me! Doctor?" The sudden glee on Cable's face was disturbing.

Dr. Tonsik gestured to the men to move Max to the procedure bed beside the machine. Lying on it for the second time today, Max wondered if others having their way with him would become his new normal, and then wondered if that was really so bad considering the adventures the past week had brought him.

"We already got your blood while you were unconscious," said Cable, walking over to stand by Max's side, "and we can inspect the machine anytime, so we might as well get right to extracting your BCI. Now, I have some good news and some bad news. The bad news is that transcranial scanning just isn't as clear as we need, and so your skull will need to be removed. But the good news is that you might be alive to hear what we find out."

"I'd really like to get a second opinion."

Cable ignored him. He continued excitedly. "Let me tell you how this is going to go, because it's really quite fascinating. First we will physically stabilize your head with a three-pin skull fixation clamp. Then, the doctor here will cut open your scalp with a scalpel and fold back the skin and muscle to expose your skull. Then she will use this craniotome," Cable held up a tool that looked to Max like a regular drill, "to cut through that. A craniotome, if you're wondering," he explained helpfully, "is a kind of drill that can cut through bone, but has a special clutch that keeps it from damaging the soft tissue underneath. It's an ingenious device. Anyway, then she will open the dura, which is the protective covering of the brain, and that will expose your wonderfully enhanced brain-computer interface. This will allow us to examine it very closely. Now, we need you to be alive and conscious because it's crucial - so I'm told - to be able to observe how your brain interacts with it. I am however honour bound to disclose that we may need to excise it if we don't get all of the detail we need, which may or may not leave you... well, alive... at best. But in the end, with any luck we will be able to determine not only how your new BCI can influence and control your brain, but hopefully also the source of these mysterious powers of yours." Cable was jubilant. "Oh, I just love scientific discovery! Isn't this exciting?"

Max suddenly understood what it may have been that had kept him all his life from achieving the level of business success that he sought. He now saw that, as little regard for morality and decency that he had had, what he did possess had been a liability. He had considered himself a predator, but now realized that being a predator is merely to provide for your survival without malice toward your prey. He had thought himself as ruthless, without scruples, and was proud to think so because to him this was the definition of being competitive. Only now was it clear that to be truly ruthless, and so to be truly successful, a deeper, active, preferably sociopathic level of enmity needed to be focused upon anyone who posed any threat, or any opportunity, and possibly even those who didn't present either just to serve as a deterrent. To kill or be killed was not enough. True success came not with a mere willingness to be unfair, but with a need, a yearning to destroy anything that threatened your ultimate supremacy. It was a determination to stand not as a peer, jubilant in creation, but alone, victorious in destruction. Yesterday all this may have educated and inspired him, but today, he supposed because of Robin's procedure, he was revolted. What kind of success could this be, he wondered, if it only served the goals of one person? Such an aspiration could lead only to either tyranny or endless war between rivals, and there was no time in history at which either had ever been a good thing.

"You're a monkey," he said.

"Come again?" asked Cable.

"You won't get away with this," he warned, hoping that Ooauoa and Chance would hear and figure out a way to save him.

"No? Why not?" asked Cable.

Max hesitated. "My plan is kind of a work in progress."

"Ah. Perhaps you're thinking that your friends here will help you escape," said Cable. Sinde motioned to the other men to seize Ooauoa and Chance. They quickly and noisily surrounded the two, who stood without resistance. They were corralled into a corner and made to sit despite their protests. Once seated, the men pressed them with their devices, paralyzing them from the neck down.

Max's heart sank. "Damn it! How do you keep doing that? It's like you're reading my mind!"

"You think you're the only one with special powers, Max? You have a specially enhanced BCI. I have something like that too. Call it a neural 'plug-in'. It allows me to sense deceptions. I knew these two were off as soon as I walked in the room, which is why I told them to stay. There were subtle inconsistencies in their behaviours that spilled out their true emotions like a leaky dam. Your behaviour changed too when you recognized them, confirming that they were with you. And now I am quite curious to find out how you got them in here. No doubt something to do with these powers of yours. So, is that it? Are you out of tricks now? Can we finally get started?"

"Why didn't you just ask Robin instead of killing him?"

"Our analysis of Robin suggested that he would not tell us anything. And we couldn't just take him because people would notice immediately and look for him. You, on the other hand, no one gives a shit about you."

"Nero will look for me. He's getting the police right now."

"I doubt that." Cable gestured to a man by the door. Two others dragged Nero into the room.

"Sorry Dad," he said. "I was captured again... Holy shit! What happened to your hair?"

Max's eyes widened. "Huh? What do you mean?" he asked in a panic.

Dr. Tonsik spoke. "I'm afraid we had to shave it off for the surgery."

Max stared at her in silent fury. Finally, he said, "You are going to be sorry."

Nero was brought to sit with Ooauoa and Chance, and then paralyzed as well. Looking back at Cable, Max said accusingly, "You said you would let him go."

"You really thought that I would?" Cable seemed genuinely surprised.

"Max, can you hear me?" said Stewie.

"Yes," said Max.

"Well that's just being naive," said Cable. "Although at the level you work you've probably not done too much coercion."

"Good," said Stewie. "Sorry for the delay. I had to build some new computronium into the walls to overcome the hush. On-site nano-manufacturing is pretty quick, but the materials had to be provisioned and conveyed and then..."

"Yeah, yeah, are we good?" asked Max.

"Hmm? Why, yes," said Cable. "You're absolutely right, Max. Let's get on with it."

"What is your state?" asked Stewie.

"I'm paralyzed," replied Max.

"I'm afraid you'll need to stay that way for the duration of the procedure," said Cable. "Are you ready to begin?"

"I believe they have injected you with nanobots that inhibit your neuromuscular junction," said Stewie. "It's likely something developed privately by Cable Industries. There is probably a signalling device that will deactivate them. Do you see something like that?"

"Yes. I mean No."

"It was more of a rhetorical question," said Cable. "I don't actually care." He moved around behind Max's head. Max felt him place a hand on its newly bald smoothness. "Time to open my present," he said happily.

"Oh I have a present for you alright," said Max. He closed his eyes and envisioned tentacles reaching from his mind into the BCIs of Cable's men, finding their embedded tasers, and activating them at full power. Screams of pain howled through the room, followed by the sound of devices and knees dropping to the floor. He let them have it for a full five seconds. Max opened his eyes to see all of his targets sprawled on the floor, groaning and holding their heads. Filled with joy at the return of his powers, Max declared, "That's for Robin!" He then activated the tasers again for another five seconds. "And that's for Nero."

"Thanks Dad!" shouted Nero proudly.

"And this," began Max ominously, turning his eyes to Dr. Tonsik, "this is for my hair." Adding Tonsik to his victims he let them all have it again for at least ten seconds. None of the men moved after that, and Tonsik now laid on the floor with them. Max looked them over with satisfaction. Suddenly he remembered Judge Yarrow, maybe not with sympathy, but at least with understanding.

"Um, Dad?" said Nero.

"Hmm?" asked Max.

"You're full of surprises, Max," said Cable, walking back into Max's field of vision, Sinde following him.

Max reached out mentally for the tasers of the two men and sent crackling bolts of energy into them both. Sinde twisted his neck and clenched his jaw. He was clearly in discomfort, but not debilitated. Cable continued smiling easily. When Max stopped, Sinde returned to normal except for a stern, annoyed look on his face. Tapping on his head, Sinde simply said, "trained mind."

"And I have an old BCI," said Cable. "No taser. I'm wondering what your plan was after zapping us all unconscious though. All four of you are paralyzed."

"The plan is…" began Max.

"… a work in progress, right," Cable concluded for him. He looked down at Tonsik and prodded her with a toe. "Sadly Max, it appears you'll be keeping your head for the moment."

"You are a sick man," sneered Ooauoa.

Cable spun around to her. "I'm sick? I'm sick? I am humanity's last hope!" he cried. "You people are like animals in a zoo and you don't even know it! The Facilities have trapped us all in these hamster cage cities, and not only did you let it happen, you love it! You run around in its tunnels, you eat, you shit, and you fuck, and you think that life couldn't be better."

Everyone stared at Cable's sudden fury.

"BULLSHIT", sneezed Chance.

"Do any of you know what is happening? While we're trapped in this,

this zoo, the Facilities is out there stripping the planet of anything useful, scraping away every last bit of metal and mineral and any other resource from the ground and sending it up into space."

"BULLSHIT", sneezed Chance.

"Oh, will you SHUT UP!" Cable glared at Chance.

"That's just the way I sneeze," he protested.

Cable exhaled loudly. "The Facilities doesn't care about us! It's an obsequious tyrant! And once it's done fawning us back to the stone age it's going to fly out into space to find the next planet it can rape, and leave humanity here to die!"

"Oh, now that's just being dramatic," said Stewie.

Cable spun to look at Max, as if he'd heard Stewie's voice. "You want proof? Ask yourself: why doesn't the Facilities allow communication between the cities? Because then we can't work together. Why don't kids study physics or engineering anymore? Because then we can't explore. Why did the Facilities put comms in our heads? So that it can tell us what to think!"

"You don't want to save humanity," said Max. "You want to be the one controlling what humanity thinks."

"I'll do whatever I have to do. Only I have the technology and the resources to save us. Only I know how to defeat the Facilities, and to restore us as the dominant earth species."

"Oh, I would love to hear this," said Stewie.

"If that means that I have to focus people's minds, to educate them to what is truly important, and to unite us all in purpose, so be it. And if that means vermin like you who do nothing can finally be put to some good use, all the better. It might turn out though that you're an abundant resource as useless as the Facilities thinks you are."

"That's my choice? Between being a pet to the Facilities and being a slave to you?"

Cable laughed. "No, of course not. You don't get to choose."

"Can you even hear yourself?" Ooauoa scoffed. "You crazy."

Cable turned and slowly crept toward Ooauoa. "Am I? Does that even matter? I will do more for the future of humanity than anyone in history."

Ooauoa rolled her eyes. "Bitch, please. You just want to make yourself even more rich and powerful."

Cable shrugged, now standing above her. "If I didn't get rich and powerful, someone else would. It might as well be me."

"It's not that you're rich and powerful," began Ooauoa, enunciating with contempt, "it's that you think you deserve it. I know lots of people smarter than you. You're the one keeping them down, not the Facilities."

Cable crouched, putting his face right up to Oouaoa's. "You know why it's me that gets rich and powerful, bitch?" He pointed at himself and glared with wide, wild eyes. "Because I want it more."

"Enough of this!" he proclaimed, standing again. Pondering, he slowly made his way back to Max. "There is still a procedure that we can do. You see Max, I've been trying very hard to understand how you do the things you do. You seem to have some kind of access to the Facilities, an ability to get data and to control things that's never been seen before. Certainly none of Bontu's other patients had anything like it. Hell, most of them went crazy and killed themselves. But Bontu adjusted the procedure slightly each time, and I'm thinking he stumbled across a configuration where your comm ID is confused for a system ID with special authorization." Cable shook his head. "Oh, there are so many questions! But also so many possibilities. Still, one thing that seems plausible is that if I have the same treatment as you, I could have the same powers. What do you think?"

Max had no idea what to think. "I don't know. Maybe. But you killed Robin. Who is going to do the procedure?"

"You are, Max!" exclaimed Cable. "You have access to Facilities knowledge. All of Bontu's research was ingested by the Facilities after his death. I expect that as a scientist he recorded everything he knew."

"Maybe, but why would I?" asked Max defiantly.

Cable nodded at Sinde, who took a knife from his belt and went to stand with the Three Amoebas. "There are at least three good reasons."

"Don't do it, Max!" said Ooauoa.

"Definitely not," added Nero.

"Don't just do something. Sit there!" said Chance.

Nero tried to look at Chance. "Nice one."

"Thanks," said Chance.

"Wait, what?" asked Nero, confused.

"We'll tell you later," answered Ooauoa.

Cable focused on Max. "No one else needs to die, Max. You'll do the same procedure on me, and we'll be done here."

Stewie spoke. "Max, listen. Since you BCI was enhanced I've been able to read your neuronal patterns. It's taken a while but I've correlated them to your behaviour. What this means is that you don't need to speak anymore for me to hear you. I'm learning to read your thoughts. I had forgotten how gross it is in your head, but don't worry, I think I'll be ok."

You can read my thoughts?

"Coming in loud and clear. Ok, now listen carefully. If Cable wants the procedure, I say you give it to him."

But that's crazy. He'll have the same powers as me.

"No, he won't. It'll be fine."

No way. How do you know?

Stewie sighed. "Because your powers didn't come from your procedure, ok? It's been me. With your BCI I can see what you are visualizing and make it happen. I can put knowledge that you need into consciousness. I figured that if you thought you had powers that needed the network you would stay away from hushes. Ha! That didn't work out!"

You know, something told me it was too good to be true.

"Liar. You totally bought it."

Evs. Still sucks though.

"Max," said Cable, "you will do the procedure."

Looking at Cable, Max considered what the man was asking him to do in this new light. Putting on his best deadpan expression, he said, "Ok, sure." If he could have shrugged he would have.

"That's the spirit." Cable smiled. "Let's get you moving then." He reached down and picked up a fallen device. Holding it over Max's body he said, "release". The device glowed light green for a moment, and then returned to normal.

Max felt a tingling through his body's muscles, and the ability to move slowly returned. He carefully stood from the bed and reassured himself that he could safely stand. Satisfied, he said to Cable, "lie down."

"No, Max!" implored Ooauoa. "Don't do it. He's just a rich asshole that thinks he can do whatever he wants to other people. Think of what he could do with your powers!"

"I need to make sure you all stay safe Ooauoa."

"Don't be a moron Max. Think about it. He'll just kill us all once he has no more use for us, including you!"

Fuck, would you just stop making so much sense and be quiet! Max struggled to hold his composure. "Everything will be alright," he said calmly.

"Oh, you are such an idiot!" huffed Ooauoa.

The details of the procedure began to flow into Max's consciousness like a recalled memory, except including things that he couldn't have known. He remembered the details of the machine's interface, the many steps needed to start the procedure, and the specific configuration that needed to be set up to recreate the exact procedure that he had had. He began by wrapping the needle cuff around Cable's arm. Then he started attaching the restraints to the man's thighs.

Sinde spoke up. "What are you doing?"

"Don't be alarmed." Max spoke as if by rote, like he had said the words hundreds of times before. "There is a small chance of seizure with this procedure, so this is just a precaution for his safety. I've checked his medical history and he's at negligible risk, but we can never know for sure. But even when seizures have occurred to others there have not been any subsequently detectable effects."

"Except for throwing yourself off of a balcony," said Cable wryly. He sat up. "So far you are telling the truth. But tell me how you know the details of the procedure. Surely Bontu kept some secrets."

Max spoke with monotony. "We had assumed that Robin's lab was hushed. It wasn't. In fact he worked closely with the Facilities."

Cable watched Max carefully as he said this and, seeming satisfied, he laid back down. "Continue."

Max attached the restraints to Cable's arms. Picking up the skull cap, he said, "Lift up your head." In silence Max completed the rest of the setup. All the while Cable studied him. Outwardly Max carried out each step precisely. But in his head he was awkwardly conflicted. He figured there was a strong possibility that Cable would have a terrifying experience similar to his own, but he couldn't decide whether he should be sadistically gleeful or to feel sorry for what the man might have to endure. The decided the best course would be to trust Stewie, and to try and focus entirely on the task at hand. When everything was ready he looked at Cable, took a deep breath, and exhaled quickly. Reaching to start the procedure, his finger may have moved too quickly toward the 'start' icon.

"Wait," said Cable. "Something isn't right." He glared at Max as if cracks in his honesty would appear on his skin. "You've configured the orchestrator precisely as Bontu did for you, correct?

"Correct."

"And I will receive exactly the same procedure as you, correct?"

"Correct."

"And it will give me the same powers that you have, correct?"

Max hesitated. "Well, I don't know that for sure," he stammered.

"Liar!" cried Cable.

Max hesitated for a moment and then jabbed at the start button, but Sinde was already behind him. He grabbed Max's arm and twisted it behind him so that Max yelled out in pain. Then he felt Sinde's fist hit his left kidney, and he groaned in agony. Finally, Sinde kicked out Max's legs and dropped him to the floor, Max's twisted elbow hitting first. As the blinding pain subsided Max wasn't sure if his shoulder had dislocated.

"That's not very nice," said Chance.

Max looked up to see Chance grab Sinde's head from behind with his huge hand. Sinde went immediately for the knife he had put back into his belt, flipped it in his hand, and with the precision of a surgeon he stabbed it twice into Chance's forearm. Chance growled in pain and let go. Sinde turned quickly to face him, but Ooauoa came past Chance and pushed Sinde hard, sending him tripping over Max's legs. As he fell the back of his head hit the edge of a desktop hard, and he slumped to the floor unmoving.

"Sinde! Sinde!" cried Cable. He tried to twist to see what had happened, but the restraints held him fast. "Get up man!"

"He doesn't look so good," said Nero. "I think he needs a doctor."

"Get me out of this thing!" demanded Cable.

Nero helped Max up from the floor. Max tested his shoulder. It hurt badly, but it wasn't dislocated.

"Get me out of this thing!" repeated Cable furiously.

Max looked up as a thought entered his mind. "Huh. I just learned something very interesting. According to your internal financial reports your businesses aren't actually all that successful. It looks like in keeping all of your fusion energy technology to yourself your companies pay virtually nothing for energy. If you had to pay market rates for energy like everyone else, Cable Industries would fold in under two months." He looked back at Cable. "If the public were to find out about your reactors and Cabletown and how you've kept them secret for decades, you and your company could be in big trouble."

"You'll be dead before you can tell anyone," said Cable.

"Maybe. Let's find out. Time for your procedure!"

"You'll do no such thing!" commanded Cable.

"It only takes two, maybe three hours," said Max. "You'll be fine."

Cable stared at Max, his expression smouldering with a heat Max was sure he could feel. "Don't you do it."

"Here we go!" said Max as he pressed the start icon. At the sound of whirring from the needle cuff, he said triumphantly, "And there go the bots."

Enraged, Cable shook his head and rubbed it against the bed trying to get the skull cap off, but it stayed put.

"You are a dead man, Maximum Rising. You and all of your friends!"

Nero giggled. "It's hilarious how they keep calling you that."

Max looked at him. "My name really is Maximum."

Nero made a face. "Really? That's kind of ridiculous. I like it."

"You are a dead man," said Cable, this time less passionately. Then, looking up at the ceiling he blinked a few times and shook his head. "What the hell is this?"

Max looked at the man kindly. "The fun is just getting started. Relax. Try to sleep if you can. Oh, and everything about this treatment is confidential. Do you understand?"

Cable stared at the ceiling in silence for a moment, and then nodded. "Yes, yes, I understand."

"That's it?" asked Stewie indignantly. "You're not going to warn him about the massive spiders all around that want to suck out his blood and leave his dry shrivelled up shell to burn on a fire pit?"

That's kind of harsh, don't you think? Sheesh, what kind of an asshole are you? thought Max.

"Well, I learned from the best," replied Stewie.

Ooauoa had been helping Chance with his arm, wrapping the wounds tightly with a length of cloth she had ripped from the bottom of her shirt.

191

She gestured at Cable and spoke with concern. "Is that a good idea? What if he ends up with your powers?"

"It's a ruse," mumbled Cable.

Max looked at the old man. His expression had gone blank, and his eyes closed and opened slowly. Occasionally he shook his head as if emerging from deep thought. Part of Max wanted to feel like Cable deserved what was coming. He wanted to assume the role of conqueror, to stretch his arms out in victory and hear the crowds of commoners in his head chant his name while he bathed in their adoration. But looking down he only felt compassion. Cable might try to take his own life, and there were probably many who would be excited if he did since it would open up a vacuum of power into which many ambitious 'business leaders' would be eager to rush. But Max couldn't see it that way anymore. Who am I to wish death on anyone, or even to be happy about the torment he is about to go through? Max felt a deep pang of remorse. Should I have even pressed that button?

"You didn't," said Stewie. "I did."

Max sighed. He looked back at Ooauoa and gestured at Cable. "What he said. It's a ruse."

Ooauoa looked at Cable for a moment and then shrugged. "Alright then. We need to get Chance to a hospital. And you too probably."

"Wait, how did you all get unparalyzed?"

"I don't know," she said. "It just went away."

Stewie?

"Yeah, that was me," said the Steward. "Once Cable used the device on you, I was able to repeat the signal."

Max nodded. "Nice. I guess we're done here. We can go."

Starting toward the exit, Max remembered the contents of his pockets. Reaching in, he retrieved a box of Indicol and threw it back on the bed beside Cable. "You'll probably want these."

Ooauoa looked at the box and back at Max. Then she marched back to the bed, snatched the box, and put it in her pocket. "I want it more."

Max watched her walk to the exit, then turned back to look at Cable one last time and shrugged. The action made him wince in pain, but he was happy the injury wasn't worse. Carefully stepping over the bodies that littered the floor, he made his way to follow Ooauoa. One of the guards on the floor before him groaned and moved slightly.

Stewie, one more time?

"Ugh. Fine. By the way, if you want to become a dominatrix, there is a course starting at Graham college in two weeks."

Max reached into the men's tasers one last time and, overcoming a mild guilt, let them have it. "Nope, I'm good."

IMMORTALITY EXHIBIT REPRISE

Following the standard exhibit content, the campfire is replaced with a scene of a gift shop.

Guide: "This concludes the immortality exhibit. Thank you for attending, and please feel free to remain and browse as long as you like."

tweetuncommon: "Wait, wait... You didn't say anything about people dropping out of treatable."

Guide: "If you are referring to recent reports of increasing untreatability, that is merely speculation. Any changes seen thus far are of no statistical significance."

ClaireVoyant: "But I heard that too. My cousin's friend just suddenly started getting old. Like in days he just got all tired and achy. The doctors said they couldn't help him."

Guide: "There have always been cases of individuals for whom treatments ceased to be effective. Often this was due to preexisting conditions, or complications from other diseases. It is perfectly normal."

death_by_marj: "Cut the shit. The numbers have been increasing. People are getting old. And even the new treatments for untreatables suddenly aren't working anymore."

Guide: "I'm terribly sorry. I cannot comment on new treatments for the elderly as none have yet proven to be clinically efficacious."

death_by_marj: "This is such bullshit. Tell us the truth."

Guide: "Thank you for attending. Please feel free to remain and browse as long as you like."

The guide fades.

MORTALITY TOWER

Max inhaled deeply, feeling the cool air enter his nostrils - a little more flow on the left side than on the right, he noted. He felt his chest expand, and his diaphragm push down into his belly. He held it there for a moment while he focused on the feeling of his shirt being a little tighter than it had been before the breath. In the silence around him he could just barely hear the sound of his heart beat in his ears, and felt its gentle thump in his chest. He wondered if the stain where he had spilled a drop of "chicken soup" was still visible on his shirt, just above where his heart was beating. Vitina, the attractive meditation teacher, most certainly had noticed it, which could only have ruined his chances with her, not that he really had any chance anyway, but it never hurt to try. Some things never change. Ooauoa had commented how ever since Max's head had been shaved he looked like a Tibetan monk, and that he ought to start playing the part. She mentioned that Vitina gave free classes multiple times a day – except Mondays – and that she too just lived off of her UBI. She was well known in the meditation community, and students of all means came from all over the city to work with her. The inside story was that several people had asked her to give private classes for pay, but while she said she was not against accepting payment, she insisted that all of her classes had to be freely open to anyone. Denied exclusivity the wealthy lost interest. But she still gratefully received the occasional donation, which she used to maintain and improve her modest facilities.

Max wondered if there were something that he could become known for too. It didn't matter much what it was, he thought, as long as it served a useful purpose to others. He had been living off of UBI now for four weeks, and even though he now felt like he could continue indefinitely on the meagre stipend, he knew he couldn't just stay idle. It wasn't the stigma of it: even the poor, or maybe especially the poor, did not look favourably upon idleness. But nowadays Max didn't much care what people thought. He just felt like he needed a purpose. But then again, maybe he wouldn't mind too much if people thought highly of him too. Some things never change.

But the nature of purpose had changed ever since Robin had "changed his mind", as Max now referred to the procedure. All that had mattered before was making money, and in doing so commanding the respect of others, that being defined as the impunity to tell nearly anyone to fuck off, while severely punishing anyone who dared to do the same to him. It meant the rarified right to be blind to the suffering of lessers, deaf to their pleas for justice, immune to their poisoning talk of unequal opportunity. Now, "purpose" was an entirely different thing. He suspected this had something to do with the change in his... what had Robin called it? Something in his brain. Whatever it was, "purpose" now meant to lift everyone, including himself, up equally. It meant service to others, for which there can be no higher calling.

Max wondered how much longer this session was going to take. He was excited to be redefining himself, and wanted to get on with it.

"Aren't you supposed to be meditating?" asked Stewie.

Max's attention came back to the present moment. Shit. That was the fourth time his Steward had to drag his monkey mind back to reality. He wondered how many breaths had elapsed since the last one he had noticed. He tried to retrace the train of thought that had led him to hope that the meditation session was over, before realizing that the retracing, too, was just another form of not meditating.

"You suck at this," said Stewie.

Come on, it's my third day. Can you be supportive?

"Sorry, did I poke you in your third eye?"

Is it this hard for everyone?

"I can't say for sure. Yours is the only mind's data I have access to, which is very sad for many reasons. Studies would indicate that it is though. Keep practicing, champ. It's worth it."

Vitina picked up a small bell and tapped it with a little wooden mallet, signalling that the ten minute beginner's session was over. It had felt like an eternity to Max, who now marvelled at how some could sit for hours.

"Gently open your eyes when you are ready, and reenter the world around you," she said. "Thank you so very much for attending. It has been my pleasure to guide you today. I will hold another beginner's class tomorrow at the same time. I do hope to see you then."

"The others are at the McConnell psyche hospital," said Stewie. "They've already talked Justin out of bludgeoning Rudy to death twice already. And Ooauoa is pilfering Indicol from their pharmacy again."

Max smiled. Everyone has their faults. Rising up, Max tried to catch Vitina's eye before he left. When she looked over he waved and mouthed, "see you tomorrow." She smiled and nodded back. Had she glanced quickly at the stain on his shirt before smiling at someone else? Max sighed and left.

Out in the street he stood for a moment. He looked up at the transparent roof ten meters above. It was raining lightly, but only on the outside. Max traced the drops as they slid and coalesced away from the peak down the slope until they disappeared behind the tops of the buildings. He imagined their travels from there: into a gully that joined with others into streams that fed into downspouts that drained into storm sewers that emptied into cisterns well below the city. Max had a brief flashback to his treatment visions of floating through a dank, narrow sewer and felt a pang of claustrophobic anxiety. Even after these weeks he still was not free of that nightmare. Closing his eyes and taking a deep breath he concentrated on the air as it filled his lungs, and then exhaling he let go of the bad memory, watching it flutter away like a leaf in the current of exhaled air, as Vitina had just taught him to do. Before the thought could come back, he opened his eyes and saw the roof again. Not much rain, he thought, but every little bit helps.

Feeling better Max turned right and began his walk.

"Wrong way," said Stewie.

"Oh, right," said Max, and turned around. But before moving he thought for a moment, turned back, and kept going in his original direction. "Let's see what we find this way."

"Suit yourself. There's a place just up on the left that sells meditation cushions, you know, for your old ass. They have a large selection of incense too. There's also a flower shop, in case you want to get something for Vitina tomorrow. Oh, your Glaze subscription will expire soon..."

As Stewie carried on, Max thought he heard a smile in the Steward's voice.

* * *

"You're late," said Ooauoa, adding in a singsong voice, "Were you talking to Vitina?"

"No, I just took the long way to get here."

She nodded. "We left you the bathrooms to clean."

"Wow, you guys are the best."

"I'm just going to do one last check of the pharmacy." She squeezed his arm as she passed, saying over her shoulder, "Everyone's in the lounge."

Max knew well enough by now where the cleaning supplies were. The Four Amoebas came to the hospital regularly, having developed relationships with most of the patients and staff. They didn't come everyday - they all agreed that would be a bit much. Psychiatric hospitals were intense places to be on the best of days, and when they decided not to visit the work they would have done would either be done by other Helpers, or would keep until the next time they got there.

They still liked to visit child care centers whenever they could. Max was even starting to like them himself, although both he and Ooauoa found themselves getting tired out. Treatments were still working for Nero and

Chance, and so those two had an easier time keeping up. But some days they didn't go Helping anywhere. Max once took them 'on vacation' to Skilling Park, proudly showing them the rainbow eucalyptus, and expecting they all would marvel. They all tried to be polite while they explained that they knew the park well, having been there hundreds of times. "You need to check out the bioluminescence section at night," they told him. "It's pretty awesome."

When Max was done with the bathrooms he put the supplies away and headed for the lounge.

"Max, look who's here!" called Nero as Max entered. Sitting with the other three were Chloe and Denny.

Max felt a pain creep up his neck, and reached to rub the back of his head. "What a wonderful surprise," he said flatly. "Are you patients here?"

"What? Haha. No," said Denny. "We just came today to help. I'm really sorry for punching you. I wasn't in a good place that night."

"Yeah, well," began Max, looking to the side, "neither was I. But that really hurt. I couldn't see right for a couple days."

"Don't be mad at Den," said Chloe. "He got his due from Chance. Plus, it was me that made him do it. Your clothes were worth a lot of money."

"The hope of the instructed is better than the wealth of the ignorant," said Chance.

The others nodded, and then looked at Chance questioningly.

"I'm just saying…" said Chance.

Chloe continued. "I just don't want there to be any bad feelings, you know? We were talking about joining your group, and so we would all need to get along."

"Resentment is like drinking poison and hoping it will kill your enemies," said Chance.

They all looked at him again.

"Look," he said, "it's just that I've got hundreds of these phrases memorized. It's not like I just forget them all, right?"

Max held up a hand. "Ok, ok, it's fine. I forgive you. And just so you know there's no hard feelings, and in the spirit of naming the most important things in the city after the most deserving people, I want you to know that I've named my testicles in honour of you both." He pointed at Denny. "You're the one on the left." Then at Chloe. "And you're the one in the middle."

Everyone looked at each other uncomfortably.

"Ok, that's a little weird, but it means we're all good now, right?" said Ooauoa.

"I think it's lovely. Got me right in the feels. I might cry a little bit," said Chance.

"You could have just stopped at 'I forgive you'," said Chloe. "I'm going to pretend you didn't say the rest."

"Um, what's the right one named?" ventured Nero.

"I'm saving that one for later." Max clapped his hands. "So, listen, I had a great idea. Malibu is a fucking shithole, right?"

Everyone nodded in agreement.

"Well, what if we cleaned it up? What if we got a bunch of people together and got some ladders and cleaning stuff and cleaned the ceiling so that some light could get in and maybe the walls and alleys too, and then maybe it wouldn't be such a shithole anymore. What do you think?"

"That's kind of awesome. I like it," said Chance.

"That would be nice," said Chloe.

"And then we can move to another hostel, because we're falling behind in our meet quotas," said Nero.

"Would you be in charge?" asked Ooauoa.

Max scoffed. "Well, yeah."

Ooauoa rolled her eyes, and then shrugged. "Fine, I'm in anyway."

Max continued. "I mean, just because we're all total fucking losers now doesn't mean that we can't live in a decent neighbourhood, right?"

"I see your point," said Denny.

"I'm in," said Nero.

"Well, wait a second there… Speak for yourself old man," said Chance.

"Yeah, that's a little too on the nose, Max," said Chloe.

"I'm not sure I'm in anymore," said Ooauoa.

* * *

Robin's life celebration turned out to be much better attended than Max had expected. He had commented to Nero that Robin was probably the only person in the city who wasn't there. His body was already in the mortality tower. Except for the thorium fission plants, the tower was the sole building in use outside of the city's hermetic bounds, and served as the place where all the city's deceased were taken, human or otherwise. As soon as possible after death - barring any required procedures like autopsies - bodies were shrouded in organic cloth by the deceased's closest mourners and carried to the Dirge Gate. Here, words would be spoken and songs would be sung, as per the departed's wishes, and then the body would be placed on an alloy slate, perhaps also decorated with other organic items: flowers, fruits, incense. The slate would then be suspended five centimeters above the surface by a magnetic field, passed through a hermetic lock, and automatically guided along the funerary path as it floated to the tower. The final procession - accompanied by more words and songs from the congregation who watched from the city - conducted the slate up the external spiral ramp to the top of the egg-shaped building. There, the body would be interred in one of the hundreds of ventilated and irrigated composting tunnels, and covered with moistened wood chips infused with fungal spores. Over the following period of ten months - a time span significant in its similarity with human gestation - the body would gradually descend the tunnel, transforming as it did so that it exited at the bottom as highly fertile compost, to be used exclusively in sanctioned sections of the city's public parks. Most tunnels began at the top of the tower, and could accommodate up to five human or large pet corpses at a time. Some shorter tunnels were intended for single bodies only, for a substantial price, and were considered especially prestigious. The Facilities did not permit any other manner of interment.

Max had not gone to the funeral, still being overcome with feelings of guilt surrounding his involvement in Robin's murder. But after special invitation from Avery, Robin's now-widow, he agreed to attend the life celebration. Nero went with him. Upon arriving, Max sought her out to extend his condolences.

"Max, I'm so glad you were able to come." Avery looked genuinely happy, although a thin but visible grief surrounded her. Lately Max had begun to notice these kinds of things. Cameron stood close by her side, nervous of the large crowd and clearly upset beneath her stoic facade. Both were suitably dressed in black.

"This is my son, Nero."

Avery smiled sadly at Nero.

"Thank you for the invitation," Max said gently. "I honestly wasn't expecting it."

"Nonsense. You were one of Robin's oldest friends. His oldest friend, he said. He talked about you a lot, and... mostly in good ways."

Max smiled. "Yeah, well we had some good times. So, there really are a lot of people here."

"They are mostly former patients. Robin helped a lot of people before we opened the clinic. He told me that he did it all from money he made from the North Rising development. I think you called it 'The Rez'?"

"Huh. He never told me that."

"He wasn't one to brag. How is your Steward?" she asked.

"We're good I guess. We don't talk all that much anymore."

"Because you're doing well enough on your own?"

"That's part of it. Mostly it's because we're trying to save money since my superpowers used up so much compute time that I'll be paying it off for a couple years."

Avery tilted her head, looking confused. Then her expression turned serious. "Max, I hate to bring this up here, but I wanted to ask in person. Would it be possible for you to come by the lab some time?"

"Yeah, of course. What is it you need?"

Avery looked apologetic. "Well, it's just that the results of your procedure were very unique. I think Robin had mentioned how a specific brain region saw increased activity. Some further study of this effect would be of great value to the program."

Max ran his hand across the stubble on his head. "Would it involve any kind of cutting? Or drilling?"

Avery laughed. "None, I promise. Listen, I know the procedure was quite hard on you, and rumour has it the rest of your day was pretty traumatic as well, so I would consider this a great favour."

Max raised his index finger and insisted, "No drilling."

Avery smiled again and crossed her heart. "No drilling."

"Hi Cameron," said Nero. He had knelt in front of her to speak to her face to face. "Do you remember me? We met at the Gates children's center."

Cameron nodded slowly.

"How are you feeling?"

"Sad."

"Yeah, me too. I knew your father, even before you were born. I liked him a lot. I'm going to miss him."

Cameron nodded.

Nero glanced at Avery, who nodded back at him. "Hey, if you want to talk, I'll see you at the children's center, ok?"

Cameron nodded again.

"Ok, bye Cameron."

"Bye Nero."

As they walked away, Max asked, "Did you really know Robin?"

"Yeah. We met him years ago. We helped out as his clinic."

"You never said."

"I didn't know we were talking about the same Robin."

Max had mostly stayed with Nero after that, not knowing most of the people at the celebration, and not feeling much like talking to the few he did. This, plus the open bar, and the fact that he hadn't tasted scotch for about a month meant both of them were properly stoned after just over an hour. They joked that if they went into the Mortality Tower in their state, their whole bodies would come out the bottom perfectly preserved. Nero had gone for a refill when Max saw Marjorie approaching. He steeled himself for a tiresome conversation.

"There you are Max. I almost didn't recognize you with your new haircut. Is that 40s Malibu grime or classic military boot camp?"

"Hello Marjorie. You look tired." She did look tired. It was unusual for her. "I wasn't expecting to see you here. Did you know Robin?"

"Fuck no. Why would I? I'm here to see you."

Max tried not to slur his words. "You know, it's kind of a coincidence, because I got a notification the other day that you dropped out of treatable. Is that true?"

"Fine. Go ahead, rub it in my face. I know you want to. Payback, right?"

"Not at all," Max gushed. "I really felt bad for you."

"Cut the shit, Max. I'm here to offer you a deal. I bought Gillig's lab."

"Gillig as in Dr. Gillig? As in my animal trials?"

"Yeah. After Stanley Cable disappeared they resumed their research."

"Wait." Max took a deep breath and, fighting the scotch, spoke carefully and deliberately. "Correct me if I'm wrong, but didn't you say there's no money in untreatables?"

"She got the treatment working. She says you pointed her in the right direction."

Max got louder. "You said, 'Untreatables are literally a dying market.' That's what you said."

"But then it stopped working again. I need you to help her. I'll give you ten percent of the company."

Max looked at her with sympathy. "Is this personal Marjorie?"

"Fifteen percent."

"Because you should know better."

"Twenty."

Max stretched out his arms and proclaimed loudly, "Businesses are for making money!"

"Twenty-two."

"Fifty."

"Thirty."

Max shrugged. "Nah."

"Ok, fifty."

Max sighed. "Marjorie, we both know I could ask for the whole company and you would give it to me because all you really want is to stay young."

Marjorie glared at him until it was uncomfortable. "Fine. But I get sixty percent of the treatment revenue."

Max stared back at her for a moment. A feeling he hadn't felt for over a month arose again as familiar as ever. He felt in control. He was getting whatever he wanted. He was negotiating from a position of power, and the feeling was more intoxicating than the alcohol he had been drinking.

Hey Stewie.

"Don't even ask," said the Steward.

Come on, it would take, what, not even a minute? And then I could pay off our debt.

Stewie didn't respond, and Max knew he wouldn't. They had already talked about this. The superpowers were a failed experiment. Max would have to find his own way from now on. His feeling of power subsided, like a strong wave receding from a shore, leaving a smooth, clean beach behind.

"Are we agreed?" ask Marjorie impatiently.

Max sighed and scratched his chin. "You know Marj, I'm just not in that business anymore."

"Two triple scotches, neat," said Nero. "Oh hi!. Who's your friend, Dad?"

"Nero, I would like you to meet Marjorie." Max pointed awkwardly between the two. "Marjorie, Nero. Marjorie just offered to give me her company."

Nero handed Max his drink before taking a sip from his own. "That's awfully nice of her."

"It is nice isn't it?"

"Last chance, Rising. What's it going to be?"

Nero's eyes widened in recognition. "Dad, is she the 33 on 45?"

Max choked on his drink. "Yeah, that's her."

As they both broke into giggles, Marjorie's face went momentarily blank, and then her expression turned to umbrage. "Imbeciles," she spat, and turned to walk away.

"Wait, wait," said Max.

Marjorie turned back and stood with arms crossed until Max recovered some composure.

"You know Marj, if treatments aren't working anymore like people are saying, maybe you should invest in mortality tower construction. Or baby clothes, because child restrictions will probably be relaxed and birth rates will go up."

Marjorie looked impressed. "You know Max, those are actually pretty good ideas. But it's stupid of you to just be handing them out. I guess it's true what they say. Everyone that gets a Steward becomes a loser. But it was easy for you: you already were one."

Max pondered that for a moment and then looked at Nero with excitement. "Hey, I just found a name for the one on the right!" The two erupted in snorting laughter.

* * *

Max's head was pounding. Hangovers from alcohol were much worse than those from tasers. He had considered skipping meditation class and just sleeping it off, but then Ooaoua said that she wanted to go too, and then he felt obliged. As they walked through the ceilinged streets, today with the sun shining down brightly, so much so that it made Max's head hurt even more, he told her about Marjorie's offer.

"And you didn't take it?" she asked, incredulous. "Do I even know you?"

"The truth is I couldn't take it. Marjorie's not an idiot. She would make me prove that I could help them before signing over anything to me."

"And you can't help them?"

"No. It was all the superpowers, and they weren't me. They were Stewie. He was trying to help me."

"I'd say he did. I hope you thanked him."

"Wait. You're not even surprised about this?"

"Max, when you never used those powers again I knew something was wrong. You're not exactly the type of person to show restraint. I figured it was Stewie a while ago."

"Huh."

"Are you excited to see Vitina?" Ooauoa used her singsong voice again.

"Not for the reason you think. She's a great teacher and a really nice person, but she's too young for me." Max tried to speak as nonchalantly as he could.

"So she hasn't shown any interest in you?"

"None at all."

Ooauoa took his arm tightly. "Don't worry Max, you'll be fine. Everything will work out."

Max smiled and looked up at the light shining through the roof. It made his head hurt a little, but the sun was nice on his face. He knew what he was supposed to say, and he felt like he might even mean it. "Oh, it already has, Ooauoa. It already has."

ABOUT THE AUTHOR

Matthew Lohbihler is a Canadian that likes thinking about stuff, doing stuff, trying to be funny, and talking in the third person, although not necessarily in that order. He also would really love it if you wrote a review.

Made in the USA
Middletown, DE
23 July 2021

44201612R00116